THE SHADOW HUNTER

THE PHOENIX CHRONICLES
BOOK 1

R.J. PATTERSON

The Shadow Hunter

© Copyright 2021 R.J. Patterson

All rights reserved. No part of this book may be reproduced or transmitted in any form or by any means, electronic or mechanical, including photocopying, recording, or by any information storage and retrieval system, without the written permission of the Publisher, except where permitted by law.

This book is a work of fiction. Any references to historical events, real people, or real locales are used fictitiously. Other names, characters, places, and incidents are products of the author's imagination, and any resemblance to actual events or locales or persons, living or dead, is entirely coincidental.

First edition 2021

Second edition 2022

Cover Design by Dan Pitts Design

Published in the United States of America

Green E-Books

PO Box 140654

Boise, ID 83714

PRAISE FOR R.J. PATTERSON

"You can tell R.J. knows what it's like to live in the newspaper world, but with *Dead Shot*, he's proven that he also can write one heck of a murder mystery."

- *Josh Katzowitz,*
NFL writer for CBSSports.com
& *author of* Sid Gillman: Father of the Passing Game

"Small town life in southern Idaho might seem quaint and idyllic to some. But when local newspaper reporter Cal Murphy begins to uncover a series of strange deaths that are linked to a sticky spider web of deception, the lid on the peaceful town is blown wide open. Told with all the energy and bravado of an old pro, first-timer R.J. Patterson hits one out of the park his first time at bat with *Dead Shot*. It's that good."

-*Vincent Zandri*, bestselling author of THE REMAINS

"In *Dead in the Water*, R.J. Patterson accurately captures the action-packed saga of a what could be a real-life college football scandal. The sordid details will leave readers flipping through the pages as fast as a hurry-up offense."

- **Mark Schlabach,**
ESPN college sports columnist and
co-author of Called to Coach
Heisman: The Man Behind the Trophy

OTHER TITLES BY R.J. PATTERSON

TITUS BLACK SERIES

Behind Enemy Lines
Game of Shadows
Rogue Commander
Line of Fire
Blowback
Honorable Lies
Power Play
State of Conspiracy
The Patriot
The President's Man
The Haitian Assassin
Codename: Killshot
Chaos Theory

BRADY HAWK SERIES

First Strike
Deep Cover
Point of Impact
Full Blast
Target Zero
Fury
State of Play

Seige

Seek and Destroy

Into the Shadows

Hard Target

No Way Out

Two Minutes to Midnight

Against All Odds

Any Means Necessary

Vengeance

Code Red

A Deadly Force

Divide and Conquer

Extreme Measures

Final Strike

THE PHOENIX CHRONICLES

The Shadow Hunter

The Reaper

Covert Invasion

The Cobbler

The Widow maker

A Bridge Too Far

THE SHADOW HUNTER

*For Jesse Meyer, for his friendship
and mad guitar skills*

CHAPTER ONE

BELVEDERE ISLAND, CALIFORNIA

BRADY HAWK TOSSED A GRAPPLING hook onto the balcony overhanging the second floor. He eased the rope toward him until he felt it catch. With a gentle tug, he pulled the line taut before testing it with his whole weight. Satisfied that the rope was secure, he scrambled up it before flinging himself onto the third-floor balcony.

"I'm on the third floor," Hawk whispered into his coms.

"Roger that," said Alex, his wife who was monitoring the operation from the comfort of her office in the mountains of Montana. "From the schematics, you're about twenty meters to the left of a laser security system guarding the entrance. You're going to need to be very careful."

"Any guards?" he asked.

"None that I can see."

Hawk drew a deep breath and exhaled slowly. It'd been five years since his last mission with the Phoenix Foundation, a black ops organization that worked hand in hand with the CIA whenever it was best that there was no trace of American government involvement. Since that time, he'd settled down in Montana with

Alex and had enjoyed creating a new life, a slower-paced life, a private life. Hawk and Alex both decided they hated it.

While they both enjoyed bringing up their son John Daniel in a stable environment, they craved the thrill of secret missions and the satisfaction of knowing that they were keeping people safe. It was what led Hawk and Alex to put their skills to use again, which was why Hawk was atop the mansion of Silicon Valley magnate Warren Frost. Inside Frost's third-floor office, his computer held records of hundreds of proprietary software codes and patents. All Hawk had to do was retrieve the files without anyone knowing he'd been there.

The stillness from being perched high above the house overlooking Belvedere Cove was almost enough to lull Hawk to sleep. Aside from the faint sound of the water lapping against the rocks below or the breeze rustling the leaves of a nearby snakebark maple tree, the only other sound Hawk could hear was his own breathing. He steadied it before proceeding toward the labyrinth of laser beams.

Using a pair of special glasses, Hawk could see the gauntlet he needed to get through in order to open the door. The fatal flaw Alex had identified in the security system was easily exploited if someone was agile enough to enter the laser field from the edge of the balcony. And Hawk was more than capable.

With great care, he took his time maneuvering through the beams, ducking beneath some, leaping over others. At one point, he came within an inch of tripping the system before he froze on one leg and recollected himself. After a deep breath, he continued and succeeded in reaching the door. Using a print he'd lifted off one of Mr. Frost's wine glasses the previous night at dinner, Hawk accessed the door.

"I'm in," he whispered.

Hawk went to work, attaching a device to the computer that allowed Alex to hack into the system. In a matter of minutes, she had identified the folder, copied all the data, and erased her digital footprint.

"Nice to see you've still got it," Hawk said in a hushed tone over the coms as he crept toward the door.

"You, too," she said. "The last thing I want is to be widowed right now. If I have to read that book to John Daniel every night without relief in sight, I swear I might take a flying leap off the mountain."

Hawk suppressed a chuckle, permitting only a faint smile. He knew exactly the book Alex was referring to, the one about Corduroy, the stuffed bear who wanders around a department store in search of a button before getting taken home. Like most kids' books he'd read to John Daniel, it was cute the first fifty times Hawk read the story. Then, it just got old. And John Daniel had decided that he couldn't go to sleep ever again without hearing the tale of Corduroy. Hawk had tried an array of other books, all collecting dust on John Daniel's bookshelf. But none of them would satisfy him, except for Corduroy.

Hawk put his hand on the doorknob, whisking him away from the familiar bedtime routine of John Daniel. Still on Mr. Frost's property, Hawk required full concentration to finish the mission. In ten minutes when he was speeding away from the scene, he could think about how much he still loved Alex and how much John Daniel's stubborn book choice reminded Hawk of himself—and his wife. But Hawk wasn't there yet.

After he turned the doorknob, he eased back outside and proceeded to work his way back through the laser beams.

"How am I looking?" Hawk asked over the coms.

"So far, the area is still clear," Alex said. "There aren't any guards patrolling the verandas on any level."

"Roger that."

Hawk secured the grappling hook once more before preparing to rappel to the ground. But just as he was about to push off from the side of the balcony, he heard the click of a gun.

"If you move another muscle, I'll fill you full of lead," a man said.

Hawk froze. "Alex," he whispered, "are you seeing this man next to me?"

"Negative," she said. "You're the only heat signature on the balcony."

"Well, unless Mr. Frost's guards are ghosts, the infrared feature on the satellite must be broken."

"I still see you on there," she said.

"Well, I've been made," Hawk said.

"Just wait. Use the time to come up with an exit strategy. After all, that's what you do best."

Hawk agreed, but the problem persisted: There was a huge amount of risk involved no matter what move he made, even the kind where he stayed still. Following a brief pause, Hawk responded to the guard.

"I'd show you my hands, but they're clutching this rope," Hawk said. "I'm going to walk slowly up to you."

"Okay," the man said, moonlight glinting off the barrel of the gun trained on Hawk.

Hawk took two steps up the side of the balcony before pushing off and sliding toward the ground. When his feet hit the ground, he felt a pair of hands on his shoulders and a gun jammed into his head. The pale light danced on the faces of two men as patchy clouds swept past the moon.

"Don't shoot," Hawk said. "I know Mr. Frost wouldn't want to have a mess to clean up."

One of the guards grunted. "Based on what we've seen, this would be nothing to clean up."

Hawk raised both hands in the air.

The other guard held out his hand. "Give me the flash drive."

Hawk eased into his pocket and pulled out the device. He kept one hand in the air as he dropped the device into the guard's open palm.

Before the man even had a chance to inspect it, Hawk stomped on one guard's foot and punched the other one in the throat. Hawk followed up with a roundhouse kick to the first guard's head, sending him flailing until he hit the ground.

Hawk sprinted toward the wall. Designed to keep people out, Hawk wished it wasn't as good at keeping people in as it was. He took a flying leap and tried to get enough traction to propel him upward, but his first pass failed. Backing up, Hawk tried again, this time his hands latching hold of the iron bars protruding out of the top. He'd nearly scrambled halfway over when he heard the click of a gun.

"If you so much as flinch, you're dead," another man said.

"I'm done," Hawk said over his coms.

"No, there's got to be a way out," Alex said. "You're almost there. Think."

Hawk was done thinking. He unceremoniously rolled toward the outside of the wall. He'd almost cleared it when he felt a searing pain in his right shoulder.

"I'm hit," Hawk said over his coms, followed by a flurry of cursing from Alex, "but I'm over."

He staggered to his feet only to feel a leg sweep his feet out from underneath him as he tumbled back to the earth. That was followed by a boot on his neck.

"The flash drive," the man said. "And this time I want the real one."

Hawk considered smashing the man in the face before noticing two other guards stepping out of the shadows with their weapons trained on him. Out of options, Hawk placed the device in the man's hand.

A lanky man dressed in a gray suit stepped out of the SUV parked on the side of the street and strode toward Hawk.

"I warned you that you'd never get away with it," the man said.

The overhead street light illuminated the man's face. His tightly cropped goatee accentuated his square jaw. A pair of thick-rimmed glasses were pressed firmly on the top of his nose.

Hawk sighed and shook his head. "Mr. Frost, I had no idea you were here."

"Apparently, you didn't think any of my guards were here either, which was the point of this exercise."

Hawk reached out and shook Frost's hand. "I must say that kind of technology makes breaking into your house somewhat of a fortress."

"Based on your near success, I'm sure you're going to recommend that I beef up my security."

Hawk nodded. "It could use some work. I'd recommend switching to QuadTech's laser fence instead of the laser tripwire system. Or better yet, use a combination of the two. Even the most prepared thief will have a difficult time lugging the equipment necessary to disable both systems."

"Good advice," Frost said.

"That's why you pay me the big bucks," Hawk said. "But these heat suppression vests your security team was using are amazing. Alex couldn't tell anyone else was here."

Frost chuckled. "Now that's the kind of endorsement I wanted to hear. We've got a tentative contract to manufacture these with Colton Industries once the testing is complete."

"Tell him they're genius," Alex said over the coms.

Hawk tapped his ear and smiled. "Alex is particularly impressed."

Frost leaned toward Hawk and spoke loudly. "Thank you, Alex. That means even more coming from you."

"I'm glad we could be of assistance," Hawk said.

Frost nodded. "This was an incredible exercise. Having some of the best operatives in the business—"

"Former operatives," Hawk corrected.

"Yes, of course, *former* operatives attempt and fail to break into my home office makes me feel a little more safe, even though we have some work to do."

"We're glad we could be of service."

"Would you like to come up for a drink?" Frost asked. "I've got a shot of 1964 Black Bowmore with your name on it."

"I never refuse some of the world's best scotch," Hawk said with a grin. "Just let me tidy things up with Alex."

"Of course," Frost said. "Take your time. I'll have one of my men direct you to my study."

"I already know the way," Hawk said.

He stepped away and reconnected with Alex, this time using his cell phone.

"So, what did you think?" Alex asked. "Were you comfortable getting back in the saddle?"

"It's like I never left. And you?"

"Aside from the fact that I would've gotten you killed tonight, I felt fine."

Hawk took a deep breath. "It wasn't your fault. It's new technology. You couldn't have known."

"But we failed."

"The point of the exercise wasn't necessarily to succeed. Frost simply wanted us to test out his innovative technology. We're still getting paid, and I'm coming home in one piece."

There was a long pause before Alex interrupted the silence.

"You still miss it, don't you?" she asked.

"Don't you?" Hawk said.

"I do, but little John Daniel is my world now—and yours too. We can't take the risks we used to."

Hawk nodded. "I agree. And that's why we're testing private and corporate security instead of saving the world."

"But that's what we're really good at," she said. "This stuff just pays the bills. And I know if I'm this conflicted, you are too."

"John Daniel is our world right now. So, I'm not sure I would call how I feel conflicted."

"Hawwwk, don't you lie to me," Alex said. "You know I can tell when you're lying."

He huffed a soft laugh through his nose. "You can't see if my right eye is twitching or not. Besides, we've talked about this before. I'll lose my mind if I just tend to the ranch and don't do anything else."

"You know I feel the same way, but I just get the sense that even doing this is going to make you want to get back into the field."

Hawk stared up at the clear sky, nearly devoid of stars due to the bright moon and light pollution from San Francisco just across the water. It was practically a blank canvas as opposed to the work of art sprawled across the Montana sky nightly.

"Those days are over for me," he said, trying to convince himself.

"You're lying, Hawk. Your twitching eye isn't the only tell you have."

"Even if I wanted to go back, I couldn't," he said. "The only person I trusted in Washington is retired, not to mention that I could never return to the city, not after living in Montana."

"Agreed," she said. "This is the perfect place to live and raise John Daniel. I'm glad we both know that."

"You did great tonight. I'll see you tomorrow, honey," he said before hanging up.

Hawk took another deep breath and looked skyward.

He hated lying to his wife.

CHAPTER
TWO

YAKUTSK, RUSSIA

EDDIE TYSON WIPED blood from the corner of his mouth as he collected himself after absorbing a right hook from a hulking Russian nicknamed Boris the Great. The concrete floor was cold and slick due to the sweat splashing onto the ground from the two fighters. Turning around to face Boris, Tyson set his jaw and glared at the man.

The Russian had four inches and a hundred pounds on Tyson, the expatriate who was quickly getting used to life in central Siberia. That disparity alone would likely be enough to make the fight seem like a mismatch. But at 6-foot-4 and 220 pounds of rippling muscles, Tyson looked more like the bruiser than his less-toned opponent. Boris celebrated his victories by draining kegs and patting his ever-growing belly, also a stark contrast to Tyson, who preferred to slam a single shot of vodka before exiting a jubilant arena where the crowd drank early into the next morning to either celebrate their good fortune or forget their folly.

Tyson spun to face Boris, who gestured with his index finger for his opponent to come closer. If this brawl had taken place on the street, Tyson would've taken a different approach. He would've gone for the knees first followed by a wicked throat punch. But that wasn't what Peter Smirnov, the event organizer, wanted. "Maximize the pain on your opponent to earn an additional bonus," Peter had said to the two men before the fight. Peter didn't want a fight—he wanted a show. And if Tyson wanted that extra money, he knew he needed to comply.

Tyson backed up, resulting in a chorus of boos from the crowd. That's when a man in the crowd put both hands on Tyson's back and shoved him toward Boris. Tyson leveraged the momentum into an unexpected burst toward Boris, who'd taken his eyes off Tyson for just a moment to soak in the adulation from an adoring crowd. By the time Boris could recover, it was too late.

Tyson ducked at the last moment, sliding low and just to the right of the oversized Russian. When he reached down to swat at Tyson, Boris stumbled and fell face first onto the concrete. Tyson scrambled to his feet and delivered three kicks before the Russian could even push himself up. A furious flurry of kicks and punches ended the match prematurely for Peter's liking. But the crowd didn't seem to mind, chanting Eddie's name. They didn't waste any time before hoisting him onto their shoulders and parading him around the room. Even the people who'd bet on the loser seemed to enjoy watching the Russian seethe over suffering defeat.

Tyson winked at Boris as he staggered to his feet.

"You think this is funny?" Boris asked in English. "I know where you live."

Tyson signaled for the men to stop. A hush fell over the crowd.

"What did you say to me?" Tyson asked again, this time cupping his hand around his ear.

"I said, *I know where you live*," Boris repeated before spitting in Tyson's direction.

"Good," Tyson said. "I'd prefer to fight outside where I could take you down in a matter of seconds instead of putting on a show for the people."

Boris growled and then lunged at Tyson. The American didn't flinch.

"I'll buy you a drink," Tyson shouted over the crowd, which had begun singing about his victory.

After a few trips around the room, Tyson was eased onto the ground. He sauntered up to the bar and ordered his customary shot.

"Another fine fight," said Ivan, the bartender. His surprising command of the English language made Tyson wonder if the man had been a spy in the U.S. in the past.

"*Spasibo*," Tyson said before throwing back the glass.

The revelers crowding around Tyson all cheered before returning to their prior conversations. He went to the makeshift locker room in the back of the warehouse to collect his gym bag and coat. Just to the left of the door, a striking young woman adorned in a fur coat shot him a knowing glance.

"Annika, how many times do I have to tell you no?" Tyson said.

She opened her coat, revealing a sequined low-cut dress. "The real question," she began in her clipped English, "is how many times will you deny this?"

Tyson stopped and shrugged. "As many times as you ask."

He resumed his march into the locker room, which didn't stop her from running after him.

"I just don't understand," she continued. "Nobody's ever resisted me like you do."

"I already told you, Annika, I'm spoken for."

"You Americans and your fidelity."

Tyson chuckled and shook his head. "How did you say that with a straight face?"

"It's not true, no?"

"Hardly," Tyson said. "Americans are virtuous in many

ways, but when it comes to temptation such as this, we're not known for putting up much of a resistance."

Annika leaned against the wall, easing her coat open again. "So what makes me so undesirable to you?"

"I have a wife," Tyson said. "I love her very much."

Annika slowly surveyed the room. "But she's not here."

"Opportunity is never an excuse to break one's vows."

"And when will she be joining you in the middle of Siberia?"

"Never," Tyson said.

"And you never expect to leave?"

"No."

Annika's bottom lip protruded as her face fell. "Just tell me you think I'm ugly so I will leave you alone."

"If you want me to lie, I will," Tyson said as he slid on his coat.

"Just say it so I can go away in peace."

Tyson was more than ready for Annika to leave, but he held firm. "I don't say things that aren't true."

As she leaned against the wall, she slid to the floor before turning into a blubbering mess. "I wish you hated me."

"Good night, Annika," Tyson said as he left her in tears.

He made it halfway down the back corridor before three men stepped into Tyson's path.

Twisting his body so he could penetrate the shoulders of the two men, Tyson found neither of them were interested in moving.

"We need to talk, Mr. Tyson," one of the men said.

"I'm sorry, but I'm in a bit of a hurry to get home."

Tyson tried again to get through the barrier they'd formed. He took a step back and tried to skirt them on the outside. But they shifted their feet, maintaining their imposing presence. Most of the time, he'd punch his way through, but he realized that these men were going nowhere—and they knew where he lived.

"You're not going anywhere until we've had a word with you," one of the men said.

Another man pushed open a nearby door and led them into a room. The cramped office was littered with a couple of broken desks and chairs that were no longer salvageable. A wooden bookshelf against the far wall was almost bare, save a few copies of Joseph Stalin's *Foundations of Leninism*. One of the fluorescent lights in the back corner intermittently flickered.

"Have a seat," one of the men said, nodding at a bucket turned upside down on the floor.

He pulled back the corner of his coat and revealed a holstered gun. Tyson understood that this was the international signal for "don't even think about objecting unless you want to die." He sat down and looked up at the men now spread out with their backs against the wall.

"That was quite a performance you put on tonight," the mustached man said as he ran his fingers through his hair. "You fight pretty good for a dead man."

"Dead or alive, that's how I've always fought," Tyson said with a shrug. "Now, what's the meaning of this? I don't suppose this is some strange FSB ritual."

The bald man stepped forward. "We need you to do us a favor."

Tyson eyed the man closely. "Are you asking or telling?"

"Mr. Tyson, you are here merely as a guest of the Russian government," baldie said. "We don't ever ask for favors."

"I'll be sure to remember that next time," Tyson said. "So what do you want?"

Mustache, who was sandwiched between baldie and mute man, stepped forward and asserted his position as the trio's lead spokesman. "Mr. Tyson, we've been more than gracious hosts to you over the past three years, but we no longer see this as an equitable relationship."

"What do you mean?" Tyson asked.

"You seem to be benefiting from this situation more favorably than the Russian government," mustache said. "And that's not how we do things here. If it's not equal, Russia deserves to get the extra benefit, not you."

"Especially not an American," said the mute, who Tyson noted was now four eyes.

Tyson shook his head. "Don't get me wrong," he began. "I'm very grateful for the opportunity to find refuge here. But I've given you plenty of information."

Mustache groaned and wagged his finger. "Information that we could've found out ourselves with little digging. We need more."

Tyson cringed inside, doing everything he could to resist the urge to show how he truly felt. Deep down, he despised the Russians and what they'd done to one of his former colleagues a decade earlier in Finland. They killed him when they discovered he was working for the CIA and dragged his body into the woods. Three years passed before some hunters stumbled upon what was left of his bones, picked clean by nature and time. Tyson would never give the Russians anything actionable, even though their refuge was the only thing keeping him alive.

"What more do you need?" Tyson asked. "I've given you the names of all the agents I worked with."

"And they all work at Langley," baldie said. "They're untouchable for us. We need field agents."

Tyson shrugged. "My last partner is dead and everyone else I've worked with is either retired or left the agency."

"Perhaps you need to make another visit to the Yakutsk Prison to refresh your memory," mustache said.

Four eyes peered over the top of his glasses and leaned forward. "I believe you could use a little dental work."

"I wish I could help you more," Tyson said. "But I've given the FSB everything I knew. If there was more, you'd be the first to get it. Besides, you need to relax and do less, not more."

"What do you mean?" mustache asked.

"I mean, America is destroying itself from within," Tyson said. "It doesn't need your help."

Mustache clucked his tongue. "You Americans are always so arrogant, thinking you got here all by yourself, completely unaware of what's really going on."

"Arrogance has nothing to do with it," Tyson said. "Americans are completely capable of being manipulated and divided."

Baldie grinned. "We're quite aware of this. Your rugged individualism can be as much of a liability as an asset. Take you, for example, Mr. Tyson. You're here all by yourself. You have no friends. You have no life. You won't even entertain the thought of some company."

"But I'm alive," Tyson countered.

"And what kind of life is this, living in the middle of Siberia?" mustached man asked. "There could be a better life for you in exchange for better information."

Tyson pursed his lips before responding. "I'll tell you what. Give me a week to think about it, and I'll try to come up with something better for you. Can you live with that?"

Mustache smoothed his facial hair downward, pondering Tyson's offer. "That sounds acceptable. But we will return in one week, expectant of much better intel or else there will be consequences, the kind I promise you don't want. Are we clear?"

Tyson nodded. He watched the men exit the room. When they were all gone, he exhaled.

He'd bought himself another week. It wasn't much, but he didn't care. The FSB was going to extract its pound of flesh sooner or later. Tyson preferred that it be later.

And if a week was all he could buy, it was better than nothing.

CHAPTER
THREE

CIA HEADQUARTERS | LANGLEY, VIRGINIA

ROBERT BESSERMAN STUDIED the report in front of him and considered how to proceed. Since he'd taken over the agency two years earlier at the request of President Franklin Norris, Besserman had only initiated pre-emptive strikes. The period of peace had been a welcome one after a tumultuous time between the presidencies of Conrad Michaels and Noah Young. Both of those administrations seemed to invite terrorist attacks. But that had all but disappeared under Norris's watch, though Besserman wouldn't have minded getting a little credit.

However, in the preceding six months, something had shifted on the international terrorism scene. The organizations that had lain dormant during the majority of Norris's tenure seemed to be stumbling out of hibernation, searching for a target to strike and destroy. Never had Besserman remembered receiving so much intel from his strategically placed agents all over the globe. If he didn't know any better, he would've thought it was a global conspiracy. But he was smart enough to know that unifying terrorist groups was akin to herding cats hyped up on catnip into a bathtub. It would never happen. Yet *something* was happening.

Besserman checked his watch and gasped. The time was getting away from him and he was already five minutes late to a briefing he'd ordered. One of his best analysts, Craig McMurtry, had floated the idea that perhaps a coalition wasn't being built but that maybe someone had decided to coalesce scores of terrorist groups by supplying them with funding. Besserman wanted to know more. To him, the idea sounded like chaos theory on hard drugs. And the idea of fighting back had given Besserman a couple of sleepless nights.

Besserman hustled into his seat at the head of the table and set his briefcase in front of him. Everyone else was staring at the projector screen, trying to figure out how to adjust the color.

"We've got a building full of the brightest minds in the country, yet not a damn one of you knows how to work the projector," Besserman said.

Several people seated at the table chuckled before looking at Besserman. He wasn't laughing.

"Let's go," Besserman said, gesturing for McMurtry to start. "If this is as serious as you're making it out to be, we're losing ground as we speak."

McMurtry didn't need to be told twice. He started by giving a background report about the inactivity over the past few years and when the change was initiated. In one month, forty-five agents reported back that the cell where they were imbedded had come upon a windfall of financial help. It wasn't out of the ordinary for three to five agents to share similar stories in a given timeframe. But even with the economy booming, forty-five was an alarming number.

McMurtry explained that several of the terrorist cells with accounts they were monitoring through unofficial channels were all receiving the money from different banks all over the world. Not one infusion of cash could be tied to the same bank. And neither could a name or organization be put on any of the accounts that originated the transaction. At first glance, McMurtry believed that highly-skilled hackers were likely to be responsible. But a thorough investigation found his theory wanting.

"So what's your new theory?" Besserman asked.

"I think this might be the work of a shadow organization," McMurtry said.

Besserman's eyebrows shot upward. "One that has legacy accounts at all these banks? I find that scenario almost as unlikely as what we're already dealing with."

"I agree, but just stay with me here," McMurtry said. "I think it's not as far-fetched as you might think."

Besserman sat up and leaned forward in his chair. "I'm listening."

"A little over a year and a half ago, there was a data breach at a bank in Zurich," McMurtry said, flashing a graphic of a newspaper headline on the screen. "Two months after that, another breach at another bank in the Cayman Islands. Then every forty-five to sixty days for the next year, there were breaches, some of them so small that they didn't even make major news. But someone was targeting banks. What information was stolen? According to digital forensics experts, nothing. Not a name. Not an account number. Not an email address. Not a phone number. Zilch. These hackers went through a lot of trouble, but never retrieved a single shred of information, according to the investigating companies."

"Then what were they after?" Besserman asked.

"No, that's the wrong question," McMurtry said. "What did they really get? That's what I want to know. Because these hackers weren't just showing off, taking their skills on the equivalent of an internet joy ride. They found exactly what they were looking for."

"And how do you know that?" one of the women at the table asked.

"I decided to investigate the company that handles these investigations," McMurtry continued. "Trans Global Security—or TGS—was started by a Saudi prince, Prince Ahmed Salman, who'd gotten his hand slapped numerous times for hacking into various systems. About five years ago, he proclaimed himself cured and announced that he was putting his skills to good use. He quickly raised the capital to start a global company that hired some of the best digital forensics experts in the world. They opened offices in London, New York, Paris, Sydney, Johannesburg, and Frankfurt. Now, they are viewed as the experts, dwarfing their competition in both talent and capital."

"And TGS investigated all of these breaches?" Besserman asked.

"TGS *and* their partners," McMurtry affirmed. "What I found was that no matter who was called on to investigate the various breaches, ultimately TGS was the one handling the process. Many of the smaller firms didn't have the bandwidth to launch a massive investigation."

"But TGS did?" another man asked.

"Exactly," McMurtry said. "Part of their visionary plan was to form partnerships with other similar businesses, seeing them as mutually beneficial as opposed to a competitor. And in this case, the smaller firms landed what was essentially a finder's fee, while TGS did all the grunt work."

"Isn't it usually the other way around?" another agent in the room asked.

McMurtry nodded. "Yes, which is what made this business model so unique. But TGS has been doing this for a while, essentially building its reputation and hours inspecting hacks. They've become one of the most trusted names in their field."

"And it was all started by a Saudi prince," Besserman said, shaking his head. "How did people not see this?"

"The truth is, Prince Salman raised the capital necessary to launch the company but then stepped away. Unless you knew the origins of TSG, you wouldn't have any idea that he was a part of it. He's not even listed on the website anymore."

"P.T. Barnum nailed it when he said there was a sucker born every minute," one of the agents at the table quipped.

"So what do you think the hackers actually got?" Besserman asked.

"What I think they found were dormant accounts, accounts that didn't have any activity for a decade or more and would've gone largely ignored," McMurtry said. "The owners wouldn't be monitoring it since they had likely forgotten about it. And the bank wouldn't be on high alert when money exited the account since the hackers utilized accounts with enormous balances."

Besserman stroked his chin. "And what was TSG's role in all of this?"

"They covered the hacker's tracks," McMurtry said. "They made it seem like nothing was gleaned in the hack. But in reality they were merely mining for dormant accounts to siphon money from."

"I have to admit, I'm impressed," Besserman said. "So we know the *what* and the *how*, but it's the *who* that we don't know. Is that correct?"

McMurtry nodded. "I wish I could give you more, sir. But I—"

"This is a great start," Besserman said. "You should be proud of this, Mac. This is the kind of work that gets you a corner office."

McMurtry turned three shades of red as he sat down.

A knock at the door stole everyone's attention before a perky blonde poked her head inside.

"Director Besserman, you have a call," she said.

Besserman sighed. "Take a message. This is an important meeting we're in right now."

"I'm sorry, sir. But I can't. It's the White House. There's an emergency meeting and your presence is requested."

Besserman shook his head as he stood.

This can't be good.

CHAPTER FOUR

BRIDGER, MONTANA

BRADY HAWK YANKED a bale of hay off a stack and carried it out of the barn. He constantly looked down, checking for John Daniel darting back and forth around him. A thin layer of snow blanketed the ground, while the surrounding mountain peaks were coated with a fresh foot of powder.

"Watch out there, little buddy," Hawk said as John Daniel zipped by, lost in his own world of make-believe.

Hawk couldn't help but crack a smile, happy that his son could play in the mountains and grow up far away from the rat race that consumed Washington, D.C. There was a time when Hawk didn't mind living in the nation's epicenter, but it seemed like ages ago now. He and Alex never imagined they could find such peace and contentment living on a mountainside in Montana, deciding to move into such isolation for a year to decompress from the enduring stress of keeping the country safe in the shadows.

"Dad, watch me!" John Daniel shouted from atop a hay bale.

Hawk turned toward the direction of his son's voice. The four-year-old had a piece of straw hanging out of his mouth as he crouched low. Once Hawk locked eyes with him, the boy jumped upward, leaping into the snow. He rolled a few times before coming to a stop and then scrambling to his feet. Throwing his hands in the air, he looked up at his dad.

"Was that cool or what?" John Daniel asked.

Hawk chuckled and nodded. "That was pretty great, son. Where'd you learn to do that?"

"I saw Spiderman do it on TV," John Daniel said. "I'm going to be like him one day."

Hawk appreciated the fact that his son could have a stable childhood. Growing up with a single mother wasn't easy for Hawk. She was always looking for work and trying to figure out ways to keep food on the table. The fact that Thomas Colton, CEO of Colton Industries, was believed to be Hawk's father and helped lighten the financial burden for Hawk's mother helped as he grew older. But everything felt fragile to Hawk, as if anything he counted on could vanish without any warning. And Hawk determined that wasn't how things would be for John Daniel.

Hawk smiled as he trudged through the snow back to the barn for another bale, thinking about John Daniel's re-enactment of a superhero scene. However, Hawk stopped in his tracks when he looked up and saw a person leaning against the edge of the barn.

Alex was walking hurriedly toward Hawk. "I tried to tell her you won't be interested, but she wouldn't take no for an answer."

Hawk glanced up at the woman wearing a dark pant suit and clutching a leather portfolio. He put his head back down and kept walking toward the stack of hay bales.

"Alex is right, you know," Hawk said as he wrapped his arms around another bale.

Morgan May was tapping at the dirt floor when Hawk turned around. "Right about what?"

"About not being interested," Hawk said.

"How can you say that? You don't even know why I'm here," she said.

Hawk lumbered toward the feeding trough before filling it with hay. He spread it out so the horses could get to it more easily before whistling.

"Tucker! Dusty! Come and get it," Hawk said. He waited for the horses to come running before returning to the barn.

Morgan hadn't moved.

"I warned you," Alex said to Morgan. "I hate that you came all the way out here for nothing, but we're not interested in returning to your world."

"Alex," Morgan said, "you were always a terrible liar."

"This isn't a lie," Alex said. "We love it out here. Just look at this place."

Hawk nodded. "Alex speaks for the both of us, Morgan. This is our life now. And it's that little guy's life too."

Morgan cut her eyes toward John Daniel, who was constructing a horse out of snow.

"Look, Dad. This one is my size," he said. "I'm gonna call him Snowflake."

Hawk and Alex both laughed softly and then offered John Daniel encouragement.

"He's definitely a cute kid," Morgan said.

Hawk shrugged. "What can I say? He takes after his mother."

Morgan offered a thin smile before it quickly faded.

"What are you doing out here?" Hawk said.

Morgan sighed and stared off into the distance. "You won't return my calls. And it feels like you're avoiding me."

"Unless you're selling ranch equipment, I'm not interested in whatever mission you're trying to wrangle me into."

"Actually, I wanted to speak with both of you about this particular mission," Morgan said, a faint smile creeping across her lips as she glanced at Alex. "I don't plan on leaving until you've heard me out."

"Fine," Alex said. "If it'll make you go away, I'll listen."

"Should we go inside?" Morgan asked.

Alex led everyone back to the house. They sat down across from the large fireplace situated in the center of the room.

"Don't you worry about John Daniel climbing up on the hearth?" Morgan asked.

Alex shook her head and laughed. "It only took one time for him to get too close before he figured out on his own that it wasn't a good idea."

Morgan leaned forward in her chair. "I understand the two of you are helping with private security now. Are you enjoying the work?"

"It beats getting shot at with real bullets," Hawk said.

"And I get to stay home most of the time," Alex said, glancing at John Daniel, who'd moved on to riding around the house on his metal fire truck that was more suited for outdoors. "But if I have to travel, my aunt and uncle live in Billings, which isn't too far away. John Daniel seems to enjoy his visits with them as well."

Hawk stared at the mix of snow and mud still clinging to his boots. "How's J.D.?"

"Oh, my uncle, the infamous Senator Blunt," Morgan said, shaking her head. "He's still enjoying retirement."

"He's not the one who sent you here?" Hawk asked.

Morgan looked at the floor and shifted in his chair. "To be honest, he told me not to come. He said you'd be reluctant to do anything for Magnum."

"Magnum?" Alex asked. "Is this the name of your new secret task force?"

Morgan nodded. "It's not quite as secret as I'd like it to be. But keeping our base of operations in Los Angeles has at least kept the meddling politicians out of our business."

"Good move," Hawk said. "Blunt was always proud of you and told me on several occasions that he anticipated you'd do great things in the intelligence field."

"We're just getting started, but I hope to prove Uncle J.D. to be a prophet."

Hawk wanted the conversation to end. He didn't want to be lured into joining any of her missions. He also wasn't sure he could resist, which would devastate Alex. They'd both agreed that their life of harrowing adventure was over. No more globe-trotting. No more danger. No more risk taking. They'd entered a new phase of their relationship with the birth of John Daniel and decided they couldn't continue as they had. Someone else would have to save the country from imminent threats. They were done.

Morgan explained briefly that Magnum had been designed to replace the Phoenix Foundation, picking up where it had left off several years ago. She was working with CIA Director Robert Besserman for off-the-books operations, the kind where the U.S. government couldn't be involved no matter how badly it wanted to. Then she shared that she'd hired Mia, the infamous Helenos-9 black hat hacker, as well as Big Earv, a former Secret Service agent that Hawk and Alex knew well from their time in Washington.

"So you want to get the band back together?" Hawk asked.

"In a manner of speaking, yes," Morgan said. "I can tell you more later about what we do and how we operate, but I first want to tell you about this mission."

"I could save you the time," Hawk said. "We could just call this visit good, and you can drive back to the airport knowing that you tried."

"Or you could at least hear me out," Morgan said. "I've come this far. What would it hurt to listen for a few seconds more?"

Hawk sighed and looked out the window at John Daniel. "I really do appreciate you thinking about me, but Alex and I can't leave. We have John Daniel to think about now."

"Well, we have an operative who may never see his son again unless you help us," Morgan said.

Hawk squirmed in his chair, reluctant to ask the question

because he was afraid of what Morgan might tell him. But he also couldn't let her leave without at least knowing who was in trouble.

"Do I know this operative?" he asked.

"I think so," she said. "Do you recall serving with Eddie Tyson?" Morgan asked.

Hawk pursed his lips and nodded almost imperceptibly. "He was one of the Navy SEALs I met during training. We have quite a history."

"Go on," she said.

"On our final training mission, my oxygen tank started leaking when we were trying to investigate a shipwreck. We had to swim through an old destroyer that the Navy sank off the coast of our base at Coronado. On our way out of the wreckage, I got hung up on some rusted metal, and when I tried to get free, some of the structure collapsed, pinning me down. Tyson gave me his tank while he freed me from the debris. If he hadn't been able to get me loose so quickly, I don't like to think about what would've happened. But I have a feeling you know this already."

Morgan shook her head. "I knew you were close, but I didn't realize he'd saved your life."

"Yeah, we didn't exactly put that in the post-op report," Hawk said. "So what's going on with Tyson? Is he in trouble?"

"Yes, very much so," Morgan said. "And he needs your help."

CHAPTER
FIVE

YAKUTSK, RUSSIA

EDDIE TYSON LOOKED at his bloody knuckles as the Russian who'd once appeared invincible was lying prone on the concrete floor. The crowd shouted at the fallen fighter, urging him to continue with the match. Tyson took a deep breath as he shot a sideways glance at the event's organizer. Peter gave Tyson a knowing look, one that he was about to ignore.

The Russian staggered to his feet amidst the chants of "Ursa, Ursa, Ursa!" The Russian Bear was his nickname, and tonight's bare-fisted brawl was supposed to be staged. With a handful of Russian generals in town visiting the Yakutsk prison, the owner instructed Tyson to go three rounds before taking a dive in the fourth. But five rounds into the match, Tyson was getting the best of his opponent.

The Russian staggered to his feet and spit in Tyson's direction.

"You missed," Tyson said.

Bear growled through gritted teeth. He backed up a few steps before rushing toward Tyson. Diving to his left, he avoided all contact. Tyson scrambled to his feet and hit the unsuspecting

Russian in the back. Bear turned around and grabbed both of Tyson's arms, lifting his feet off the ground. As Tyson struggled to free himself, the crowd laughed and shouted, delighted by the power move.

"Finish him! Finish him!" they chanted in Russian.

He had seen the Bear's signature move before and wanted no part of it. Frantic to escape Bear's grip, Tyson drew his leg up and kicked backward, jamming his opponent in the stomach. The shock of the blow was just enough for Tyson to break away. He hustled across the room and spun around to find Bear charging toward him.

This time, Tyson didn't have a chance to evade the Russian. Instead, Tyson dropped to the ground and aimed a kick toward Bear's kneecaps. The Russian buckled and collapsed, falling on his side with a thunderous clap on the concrete.

The bloodthirsty crowd gasped as their hero lay motionless.

Tyson glanced over at Peter, who set his jaw and shook his head subtly. The warning wasn't heeded.

Tyson delivered several body blows before dishing out a half-dozen headshots. He would've happily continued, but the Russian tapped out, ending the match to a chorus of boos. In the corner of the room, Tyson noticed the generals tearing up their betting slips and throwing them onto the ground. A scantily clad woman presented a tray full of glasses of vodka that one of the men knocked out of her hand, sending the drinks crashing to the floor.

Tyson resisted the urge to smile as he shuffled toward the locker room. He only took one full stride inside it before Peter started berating the American.

"We agreed that you would take a dive in the fourth," Peter said. "But what was that? You knocked him out in the fifth."

"Maybe you should be talking to Bear for not being able to hold his own," Tyson said.

Moments later, Bear shuffled through the door, his face already starting to swell from the beating he'd taken. If he was upset about the way the fight had gone, he didn't show it, instead taking a seat near his locker and changing in silence.

Peter put his hands on his hips and paced, muttering to himself. Tyson ignored the man and started changing. After Tyson finished putting on a fresh pair of sweatpants, he heard the door whine as three familiar men entered the room. One of the men looked at Bear and Peter, who both understood that they needed to leave.

"So," Tyson said, "you came back for another show. And it hasn't even been a week."

"It's been five days, but this is no laughing matter," the mustached man said. "Were you aware that there were generals here to witness your fight tonight?"

Tyson nodded and refused to suppress a smile any longer. "They got one helluva show, didn't they?"

The bald man settled onto a bench across the room. "One of the generals wanted to put you in the Yakutsk Prison immediately."

"And who could blame him?" the bespectacled man chimed in. "He lost five thousand dollars on that fight."

"That explains why Peter wasn't as mad as I thought he was," Tyson said.

"Peter will be dealt with in due time, but you are the person who ruined the visiting generals' evening," mustache said. "And that doesn't reflect well on any of us."

"So, what are we gonna do about this, gentlemen?" Tyson asked. "Are you just going to keep threatening me?"

Mustache shook his head. "No more threats. Just promises. And there's only one way out of this for you."

"Sorry, but I don't have any more information for you," Tyson said.

"We already know," baldie said. "Instead, you'll be delivering a package for us."

Tyson smirked. "A package? Has Russia run out of couriers?"

Mustache shook his head. "We need you to make a special delivery to North Korea."

"Oh, no, no, no," Tyson said. "That's not happening in a million years. You might as well put a bullet in my head right now because I won't set foot in that country. They'll tear me from limb to limb if they catch me."

"We're aware of what you did there," mustache said. "But there are consequences for your actions, including your reckless ones tonight. You will atone for what you did."

"Like hell I will if it means going into that cesspool of a country," Tyson said, shaking his head. "Like I said, shoot me now or take me to the prison because those people are sick, and I have no doubt that you'll just be using me and then handing me over to them."

"You will do what we ask," baldie said.

Tyson sneered in disgust. "Unless you plan on physically forcing me to drive there, dream on, *Comrade*."

"When we come, you better be ready," mustache said. "There will be no grace extended to you again."

Tyson glared at the men as they filed out of the room. He finished gathering his things and stood to leave.

Peter returned and looked at Tyson. "You should've taken the dive in the fourth."

Tyson mouthed a few choice insults at Peter before exiting the locker room.

IVAN VOLKOV ignited a cigarette and took a long drag before releasing a lungful of smoke skyward. He smoothed his mustache and looked at General Nikolai Orlov. The other two FSB agents accompanying Volkov flanked him, their hands dug deep into their pockets.

"What did the American bastard say?" General Orlov asked.

"He said he would refuse," Volkov said.

"Who does he think he is?" Orlov asked, the veins in his neck protruding. "We have given him a sanctuary here from his own government, and this is the thanks we get? I should march in there and put a bullet in his head right now. It's what he deserves."

"But we need him," Volkov said. "There's unsavory business that would be far more beneficial to attach to an American traitor than to anyone in the Russian intelligence community or the military, for that matter. Why sacrifice one of our own when we don't have to?"

Orlov squinted as he stared off in the distance for a moment. "There are other ways we can coerce him, aren't there?"

Volkov nodded. "It's always about finding the right pressure points."

"I read his file," Orlov said.

"And?"

"He has children back home, does he not?"

"Three, to be precise," Volkov said.

"The youngest is a little boy," Orlov said. "We know where they live, and even if we threaten Tyson, he won't make any attempt to warn his family for fear that he will expose them all."

"Make the delivery or we kill his son?" Volkov asked. "Is that the right pressure to apply?"

"Maybe not kill. We don't want to turn him into a man with nothing to lose. Perhaps a kidnapping will suffice."

"I'll deliver the message," Volkov said. "I'm sure it will soften his stance on not going."

"It better," Orlov said. "He owes me five thousand U.S. dollars. Tell him it's nothing compared to what I normally do to people who steal my money."

Volkov shook Orlov's hand. "Consider it done, Comrade."

Volkov and the other two agents saluted Orlov before he spun on his heels and disappeared into the darkness.

CHAPTER SIX

LOS ANGELES, CALIFORNIA

HAWK AND ALEX piled into the SUV parked alongside the curb at Los Angeles International Airport. Hawk hated flying into LAX for the simple fact that it required venturing out into the city's gridlocked traffic. And that was saying something after living in the nation's capital.

Morgan May adjusted the rearview mirror and offered a polite smile. "How was your flight?"

"Not as comfortable as your uncle's jet," Hawk said. "But flying first class into LAX does have its privileges."

"Did you meet someone famous?" Morgan asked.

Alex smiled. "Jennifer Garner. If there's a better person in Hollywood, I wouldn't believe it."

"Did you give her your professional assessment of her portrayal of a spy?" Morgan asked with a wink.

"I doubt she'd believe me even if I told her," Alex said.

"Well, I'm looking forward to seeing the Magnum headquarters," Hawk said, redirecting the conversation back toward the business at hand. "I'm especially interested how you can hide such a facility in plain sight in this city."

"Sticking with our Hollywood theme so far today," Morgan began, "it's not exactly in plain sight."

Alex leaned forward in her seat. "Then where is it?"

"I guess you could say it's a little movie magic."

The short fourteen-mile journey from the airport to the gates of Paramount Studios took just over a half-hour, which was nearly a record time, Morgan noted aloud.

"What are we doing here?" Hawk asked. "We don't need to be entertained."

"We're at the Magnum headquarters," Morgan said.

She wheeled the SUV around a corner and down into an underground parking lot. After securing her vehicle, she led Hawk and Alex to a stairwell. They descended two flights of stairs before Morgan waved an access card in front of a black panel next to a door. A click released the lock and Morgan tugged on the handle. She gestured for Hawk and Alex to proceed.

They strode down a dim corridor that twisted left and then right and then left again before reaching a more well-lit section of the structure. Morgan approached a door and placed her face in front of a screen. A quick retinal scan granted them access.

"We're here," Morgan said.

"Underneath Paramount Studios?" Alex said before letting out a low whistle. "I never would've believed it."

"If half the actors in Hollywood knew they were working on top of a secret government site, they'd lose their minds," Morgan said with a wry grin.

Hawk's eyebrows shot upward. "Half?"

"You're right," Morgan said. "More like ninety-five percent."

"That's why we prefer Bollywood movies," Hawk said, flashing a quick smile at Alex. "We don't have to worry about our favorite actors getting political, one way or the other. Because sometimes I just want to watch a movie and not think about all that stuff. I mean, does anyone really care about the political opinion of an actor anyway?"

"I think you know the answer to that question already," Morgan said. "Or at least it'd be unanimous here."

Hawk chuckled. "You're more like your uncle than I first thought."

"I'm glad to see you're keeping an open mind," Morgan said. "Follow me."

They continued down a sterile hallway until they reached another set of doors that began to open as they approached. Inside, a handful of men and women sat at computer terminals busily typing or talking on the phone.

"Welcome to Magnum," Morgan said.

Morgan gave them a brief tour of the facility, which contained a research division dedicated to developing new technology to help with counterintelligence. She tapped on the window and a young man sporting a pair of goggles and a white lab coat hustled over to her.

"Zachary, I'd like for you to come meet someone," Morgan said.

Zachary nodded before striding over to the exit. His goggles sat cockeyed on his nose and his hair appeared as though he'd just been jolted by a substantial number of volts from a recent experiment.

"Ma'am," Zachary said as he nodded at her. "Sorry for my appearance. We were working on a device that could disable all electrical currents within a 25-foot radius by shorting them."

"Looks like that didn't turn out as well as you might've hoped," Alex quipped.

Zachary put his hands on his hips and shook his head. "Not in the least."

"This is Dr. Zachary Levinson, or, as we refer to him around here, Dr. Z," Morgan said. "We stole him straight out of Cal Tech. He was valedictorian and after only six months of working here had a dozen patents pending on new surveillance devices."

Dr. Z beamed like a child being bragged upon by his parents. He smiled and tilted his head back ever so slightly.

Before Morgan could continue, Dr. Z eyed Hawk. "I'm working on a prototype car that perhaps you'd like to road test for me sometime."

"I'd be down for that," Hawk said. "Just name the time and place."

"We still have a few kinks to work out, but in due time," Dr. Z said.

"I can wait," Hawk said. "I don't want my hair to ever look like that."

They all chuckled before Dr. Z excused himself and scurried back into his lab.

"He's quite a character," Alex said.

"Dr. Z is the breath of fresh air we need in the intelligence community," Morgan said. "One of the first things I wanted to establish at Magnum was a culture of trust. After that, I wanted everyone to enjoy working here. Spies take themselves too seriously. And while there's definitely a time for being serious, we still need to enjoy what we're doing or else we'll get burned out."

Morgan resumed their tour, leading them to the digital team, which was headed up by Mia Becker, a former colleague of Hawk and Alex's.

Mia gave Alex a lengthy hug before exchanging pleasantries.

"I'm so excited that you're going to join the team here," Mia said. "Morgan has plenty of her uncle's intelligence intuition in her, but also her own spunky style. And I hate to admit this, but as much as I loved working for Senator Blunt at the Phoenix Foundation, Magnum has so much more potential."

"Wait, wait, wait," Alex said. "We're just visiting. Don't get too excited yet. We haven't agreed to join the team."

Mia winked and nodded, her brown pony tail bobbing up and down. "But you will. I'm sure of it."

The trio caught up on the past few years before Morgan continued to show off the rest of the facility. They descended another level, which opened up into a massive workout facility. Malik Earvin, a former Navy SEAL who later worked for the Secret Service, was engaged in hand-to-hand combat training with three other men. When they took a break, Morgan motioned for Earvin to join them.

Earvin grabbed Hawk's hand, almost swallowing it, before pulling him in for a hug.

"Big Earv," Hawk said as he drew back and patted the hulking man on his bicep, "is it me or have you grown since the last time I saw you?"

"I've gotten a little stronger," Big Earv said with a grin, "and you look like you've shrunk. Probably just a combination of those two things."

"Get outta here," Hawk said.

Big Earv laughed, his baritone voice echoing off the gym walls.

"And of course you two are well acquainted with one another," Morgan said.

"What is this place?" Hawk asked.

"It's more or less a continuing education for combat," Big Earv said. "Close quarters combat here and then we have a range through that door for firearm training. We have a standard shooting range as well as a long-distance one."

"How long of a distance?"

"On the level below us, there's a specially designed one that's a thousand meters," Big Earv said. "It can even simulate various conditions such as wind and cold that will affect your shot."

"Incredible," Hawk said.

They caught up on a few personal matters before Morgan led Hawk and Alex back upstairs. She invited them into her office and shut the door.

"So what do you think?" Morgan asked as she settled into the chair behind her desk.

Hawk and Alex, seated side by side across from Morgan,

both looked at each other and shrugged, neither one of them anxious to speak. After a few moments of awkward silence, Hawk answered first.

"This is a state-of-the-art facility," Hawk said. "It's got everything an agent in a black ops program could dream of, plus a staff that's large enough to handle bigger threats than anything we could take on by ourselves at the Phoenix Foundation—"

"Not to mention the technology to make it happen," Alex added.

"I mean, what's not to love about it?" Hawk said.

Morgan leaned forward on her desk, resting her chin on her knuckles. "How come I get the feeling that there's a *but* coming?"

Hawk sighed. "We've talked about what this would mean for us, for John Daniel. And the truth was we don't want to raise him in Los Angeles. He's got an idyllic childhood in Montana."

"But is it your idyllic life?" Morgan asked. "Just mountains and horses and trees? You guys are good with that for the rest of your life?"

"You're selling us on Montana all over again," Alex said.

"Frankly, we've seen the world and what it has to offer," Hawk said. "And Montana feels like home in a way neither one of us can describe. It's like entering a simpler time when we weren't all worried about terrorists and plots to kill thousands of innocent people."

"But it's because of people like you that anyone can live in Montana and enjoy that kind of lifestyle," Morgan said.

"Exactly," Hawk said. "And it looks like you've assembled a formidable team here already. What's another duo like us going to add to your roster that you don't already have?"

Morgan didn't blink. "The best," she answered flatly. "You two are the stuff legends are made of. You took down corrupt politicians hell bent on destroying this country. You eliminated terrorists who were determined to murder massive amounts of

American citizens. You exposed shadow organizations that wanted to turn the world on its head. Not someone else. *You*."

Morgan leaned back in her chair. She appeared satisfied, as if she was a lawyer who'd just delivered the closing arguments to a case she knew she was going to win.

"Alex and I talked before we came," Hawk said. "And we almost didn't come at all. But we thought we owed it to ourselves to see what we were saying *no* to."

"Before you say anything else," Morgan interrupted, "let me just say that you don't have to work on site. We can set you up at home where you can operate in Montana. We'll even provide you with the money to afford a full-time nanny for John Daniel when you don't have time to drop him off at your aunt and uncle's house."

"That's very generous of you," Hawk said, "but we decided that we will help you for this mission. But only this mission."

"That's great," Morgan said. "I can work with that."

"Eddie Tyson meant too much to me to just leave him twisting in the wind in the middle of Siberia," Hawk said. "I will bring him home and give his son his father back."

Morgan pulled a cigar out of her top drawer and cut off the tip. She bit down on it before tossing it aside.

"I don't know how Uncle J.D. did that, but it's not for me," she said before standing up and sauntering over to the wet bar in one corner of the room. "But we must celebrate, even if it is for only one mission."

Hawk patted Alex on the leg as the two of them exchanged a knowing glance. He hoped this mission would end successfully as well as satisfy the itch he had to return to the field. Montana felt like home, but he couldn't suppress his urge to flirt with danger for the sake of his country. He'd have to tell Alex how he felt soon. But he could wait.

"Cheers, everyone," Morgan said as she offered a tray of tumblers to her two guests.

They clinked glasses before each downed a healthy serving of scotch. When they were finished, Morgan leaned on the wall behind her desk.

"Welcome aboard, you two," she said. "Now let's get to work."

CHAPTER SEVEN

WASHINGTON, D.C.

PRESIDENT FRANKLIN NORRIS worked the toothpick over in his mouth as he stood near a window in the Oval Office and peered out at the South Lawn. A few stray leaves tumbled along the faded grass, while the trees swayed with the wind. Overhead, the gray skies matched Norris's mood after he'd just received his daily security briefing.

For the past three years, his time in the White House had been relatively devoid of any drama. The country's economy had exploded while experiencing an unprecedented time of peace. For the most part, military troops had remained stateside and terrorists had been kept at bay. But in the past couple of weeks, Norris sensed the tremors of an impending seismic shift. The security briefing confirmed his intuition.

Emma Washburn, Norris's chief of staff, swiped through a tablet situated on her lap.

"I guess it's time to get to work," Norris said.

"Well, sir, you do have several important calls today," she said, tucking her curly brown locks behind her ears. "But I can postpone them if you want me to."

Norris turned around to face Emma and shook his head. "There's no need to push anything back. I'm sure I can manage this growing crisis with everything else I have."

"In that case, I suggest you schedule a meeting with the Joint Chiefs of Staff this afternoon," she said. "They may have a better sense of what North Korea is up to."

While North Korea had once been considered one of the biggest threats to the U.S., the isolated country's inability to obtain viable nuclear weapons relegated them to the status of a rebel rouser, and nothing more. Their current leader, Kim Yong-ju, found an audience on social media and liked to post incendiary messages. Years of threats that never yielded even a hint of danger grew to be dismissed, the fodder of late night TV show hosts looking for a cheap laugh. But for the past six months, Kim Yong-ju had gone silent, leading to plenty of speculation as to what he might be up to or if he'd just dropped the grift out of frustration.

But when Norris sat through the morning security briefing, he realized Kim Yong-ju was serious about striking the U.S. and shredding his international image of being all talk and no action. Norris had served in the Marines and had once considered military action as the most direct route to peace. But with an election looming, he wasn't sure that would sit well with the American people. Nobody wanted to be dragged into a protracted war. If he could swallow his pride and let Kim Yong-ju rattle his saber, Norris decided that a path of restraint could achieve a better resolution as well as keep his image pristine for voters.

That wasn't an easy proposition for Norris, who was bent toward conflict.

"I know your inclination is to fire a pre-emptive strike, sir, but I don't think that's going to play well," Emma said.

Norris looked up at his chief of staff, her eyebrows arched upward, giving him the impression that her statement was more of a question.

"Is that what you think, or are you just playing a hunch here?" he asked.

"Americans want peace, plain and simple."

Norris nodded. "But sometimes peace is only achieved through a more violent means."

"You could be right about that, but look at what's become of previous administrations that pursued peace in that manner," she said. "Their legacies are left in shambles, and those presidents are widely mocked and remembered with disdain."

"I can't govern, worried about what others might say," Norris said. "And I certainly won't let my decisions be dictated by what might get me elected. The American people put me here because they trusted me to lead them into peace and prosperity, something I've been quite adept at during my first term. And come hell or high water, I'm going to do what I feel like is best for this country."

"That's a noble sentiment, sir," Emma said. "But what happens if your great ideas are muted because of this one incident?"

"Then so be it," Norris said, twirling the toothpick around his mouth with his tongue. "I'm not a fortune teller. But I do know that letting Kim Yong-ju go unchecked isn't just bad for America. It's bad for the entire world. Someone like that needs to be taught a lesson."

"So you want to strike?" she asked.

He paused and took a deep breath, contemplating the situation. "Not necessarily. It all depends on the intel. For all we know at this point, Kim Yong-ju might be all hat and no cattle."

She furrowed her brow. "I'm not sure I get that analogy."

Norris sighed. "You've probably never seen a classic western in your life."

"Would that be one of those movies with Marion Michael Morrison?"

Norris grunted. "It's John Wayne. And, yes, he's a legend. However, I'm surprised you know his real name."

Emma shrugged. "My father tortured me by making me listen to Ray Stevens songs. He's got a tribute song to Marion Michael Morrison, who my father told me was the famous western actor."

"All hat and no cattle is a way of saying that he's got a big mouth but isn't willing to back it up."

"So you're going to make him back it up?"

Norris nodded. "If it comes to that. But I'm betting that he's just yapping his gums, desperately trying to get attention like he always does."

"And if he's not?"

"Then we'll strike," he said. "For me, we just need more intel. And it's not easy for us to get anything out of Pyongyang."

"So, just to be clear, you're taking a more passive approach?"

"More like wait-and-see," Norris corrected. "I'd be fine with obliterating Kim Yong-ju's ass and exposing him for the charlatan that he is. But he might do that on his own. And there's no need to get involved in a protracted conflict if we don't have to."

"On that point, we agree," Emma said. "Like I said before, the more we can maintain a posture of peace, the better off we'll be when it comes to polling."

Norris sighed. "Americans care about two things—money and safety. If you can give both of those things, you'll be a god in their eyes."

Emma stood and clutched her tablet close to her chest. "Sounds like you know what you want to do. And I won't advise you otherwise."

"Put it this way. I'm leaving the option open to striking North Korea if they keep this up. But it's not going to be my first move."

"Understood, sir. I'll make sure to pass that along to the communications team."

"Thank you," Norris said before dismissing her.

He checked his watch. With only five minutes to prepare for

his meeting with CIA director Robert Besserman, Norris needed to get moving.

"Is that all?" Norris asked.

"All for now. But let's catch up later this afternoon. I want to hear what Besserman has to say."

"Sounds like a plan," Norris said. "I'll call you later today, and we can discuss how to move forward."

Norris waited until Emma was gone before heading over to his desk and pulling out a secret stash of bourbon. The stress was starting to get to him.

A few minutes passed before there was a knock on the door. It opened and Besserman strode inside.

"Getting an early start, sir," he said.

Norris shrugged and chuckled as he stared at his glass. "Desperate times call for desperate measures."

"You're finally starting to feel the pressure of the office?" Besserman asked.

"Between North Korea's saber rattling and the upcoming election, I'm certainly feeling something."

Besserman settled into a chair across from Norris's desk. "Considering all that this country has been through in our lifetime, I'm not sure this even registers a blip on the radar of challenging situations."

Norris interlocked his fingers behind his head and leaned back in his chair. "You're probably right. But that doesn't change the situation we're in."

"You know that Kim Yong-ju is just trying to get under your skin, right?"

"He's doing a damn good job of it."

Besserman chuckled.

"What's so funny?" Norris asked.

"You remember that time at Timberlake Camp when Dick Larson threatened to tell everyone that you kissed Aubrey Chapman?"

Norris grunted. "How could I not? That's burned into my memory like an enduring nightmare."

Besserman grinned. "You haven't even told Priscilla about that, have you?"

"It was a long time ago, Bobby."

"But it still bugs you, doesn't it?"

"How couldn't it? I wanted to punch Dick Larson in the face."

"And if you did, you both would've gotten sent home. But you exercised restraint, and what happened?"

"Dick ran his mouth and got into a fight."

"And he was gone by Wednesday," Besserman said.

Both men laughed while reminiscing about the event.

"I think your dad said I should've knocked his front teeth out to teach him a lesson," Norris said.

"My dad never saw a fight that he didn't like."

Norris smiled. "The lone front tooth dangling from the top of his gums was proof of that point."

"He didn't take anything from anybody," Besserman said. "That's pretty much how he wound up with a purple heart."

"He received a purple heart from his time during the war?"

Besserman nodded. "Your father never told you that story?"

"Not that I recall."

"Well, it was a staple for my dad, telling it at every dinner party I think he ever attended. The version I remember is that they were in France after storming the beaches of Normandy, and a man made a rude comment about your dad. My dad approached the man, who looked like a German soldier. When he pulled out a grenade and yanked out the pin, my dad grabbed the explosive device off the floor and hurled it through a window. The grenade detonated in the street, sparing everyone inside. Several soldiers proceeded to beat the German before taking him prisoner. If my dad hadn't acted so quickly, who knows if either of us would even be alive?"

"Wow," Norris said, his eyes widening. "I've never heard that story."

"It's a good one," Besserman said. "And all true. My father was adamant about not embellishing war stories."

"So what you're trying to say is that I need to pounce on the grenade and throw it outside to avoid disaster?" Norris asked with a wry grin.

"If you can do that," Besserman said. "Otherwise, I'd bomb the shit out of Kim Yong-ju. It'd shut him up for good."

Norris worked over his toothpick before responding. "I'm not sure that's the most prudent move."

"Of course not, but it's the one that'd make you a hero to the world—if it came to that, of course," Besserman said. "I'd never recommend you doing that unless the situation called for it."

"I understand. I'd rather my tenure be one known for peace."

"But you don't always get that choice," Besserman said. "In the meantime, the agency is hunting down the truth. I'll keep you posted on what's happening and let you know if such an action is necessary."

"I'd appreciate that," Norris said.

Besserman stood and offered his hand to Norris. The two men shook.

"It's good catching up with you, Bobby," Norris said. "You know I trust you implicitly."

Besserman nodded. "It's a trust I take seriously."

The CIA director exited the room, leaving Norris alone with his thoughts. His presidency had suddenly become more difficult—and Norris wasn't about to back down from the challenge, whatever decision needed to be made.

CHAPTER
EIGHT

BRIDGER, MONTANA

HAWK SPREAD the hay out in the trough before calling for Tucker and Dusty. The two Appaloosas galloped toward him and went straight for their morning ration. He rubbed the manes of both animals before letting them eat in peace.

"You two better be good for Alex," Hawk said. "If not, I'm going to have some stern words for you when I get back."

Hawk felt a tug on his pants and looked down to see John Daniel clad in his pajamas and slippers and clutching a blanket.

"Do you really have to go, Daddy?" John Daniel asked.

Hawk knelt next to his son before tousling his blond curly locks. "I won't be gone that long, son. And mommy will be here for you."

John Daniel's lip protruded as he looked at the ground. "But I want you to tuck me in at night."

Hawk lifted John Daniel up and set him on top of the fence so they could see eye to eye. "I know you like having me around. And believe me, I like being around, too. Reading Curious George stories to you every night is sometimes the favorite part of my day. But there's another little boy like you whose daddy has been missing for quite some time."

John Daniel furrowed his brow. "And does that boy miss his daddy?"

"Oh, very much so. And if I don't go help his daddy, he can't come home. So if I promise to come back, will you let me go?"

John Daniel scowled as he thought in silence for a moment. "Sure," he finally said with a shrug.

When Hawk lowered him to the ground, John Daniel took off running. Hawk watched his son scamper back inside the house before the sound of a vehicle rumbling up the driveway stole his attention. A black SUV came to a stop near the house and Morgan May climbed out.

She put on a pair of sunglasses and surveyed the property before meeting Hawk halfway.

"Welcome back," Hawk said. "But I told you it wasn't necessary to come all the way out here again. If I didn't know any better, I'd start to think that you like it out here better than Los Angeles."

Morgan flashed a quick smile. "I'd join you out here in a heartbeat. We'd be neighbors if I could buy up some acres next to yours. But the action's in the city, and we need to have a presence in a large population center not named Washington."

"I'm not sure there's much difference between Washington and L.A."

"L.A.'s less political," she said. "There aren't a hundred bureaucrats running around, sticking their nose in all your business."

"Fair point," Hawk said.

She nodded. "You ready to go?"

"Let me grab my things."

Morgan followed Hawk into the house, making small talk along the way. Once they got inside, they found Alex presiding over breakfast, coaxing John Daniel to eat his cereal.

Morgan shook her head. "Unbelievable. Super Mom by day, saving the world by night."

Alex chuckled. "Sometimes I think it's easier to hunt down and eliminate terrorists than it is to get your kids to eat their breakfast."

They all laughed before Hawk darted upstairs to grab his bag. He returned to the kitchen and gave Alex a long hug.

"I'll be with you every step of the way," she said.

"And I'm going to make sure of that," Morgan said. "Expect a delivery of all the latest state-of-the-art technology. I'm having a Magnum tech deliver it in person so he can set everything up for you. It'll be like you're in the office with us whenever you're online."

"Thank you," Hawk said as he shook Morgan's hand.

"No, I'm the one who needs to be thanking you," she said. "If it weren't for you, we'd have no prayer at getting Eddie Tyson back."

Hawk gave John Daniel a hug. "You're the man of the house now, son. And I want you to be helpful to mommy while I'm gone. Can you do that for me?"

John Daniel's lips quivered as tears streamed down his face. "I love you, Daddy. Come back soon."

"I will, son."

Hawk kissed John Daniel on the top of his head before grabbing his gear and heading toward the door. Morgan led him back to the SUV.

Once they were inside, the driver wheeled around and headed off Hawk's property. He looked through the back window and saw Alex waving goodbye with John Daniel, who was wrapped up in his favorite blanket.

Morgan looked at Hawk. "I know this isn't easy for you, but I appreciate your willingness to help."

Hawk didn't say anything. He wasn't overly emotional, but he didn't want to talk about it. If he did, he was certain he'd start tearing up. He wanted to dwell on happier thoughts. Leaving his family was about the most difficult thing he'd done in a while. But there was also an anticipation for the mission, an excitement he hadn't felt in quite some time.

He took a deep breath and turned his gaze toward Morgan. "Tell me the truth now. How's J.D.? Is he all right?"

"He's still J.D.," Morgan said. "He's chomping on cigars and grousing about the state of politics in America today. Though there is one notable change."

"What's that?"

"His choice of drink now is scotch."

Hawk's eyes widened. "Are you serious?"

"You finally got to him," Morgan said. "He's abandoned bourbon from what he told me."

"Did you tell him your efforts to recruit me were successful?"

Morgan smiled. "I must say I enjoyed sharing that bit of news with him."

"I'm sure that rankled him."

"Actually, he said he was impressed. Didn't think I could persuade you to help out."

"As hard as it is for me to leave Alex and John Daniel, it would've been even harder for me to live with myself if I could've done something about Tyson but chose not to."

For the next few minutes, they enjoyed the scenery, staring at the early morning sun spotlighting the towering peaks.

Then Morgan shifted in her seat before speaking. "Hawk, there's something you need to know about this mission."

"And what's that?"

"We don't have a ton of intel on Tyson. Everything we have on him indicates that he's still in prison, but we received a message recently that he might be out."

"What does that mean? Out of prison and just living in Russia still?"

She sighed. "Maybe. We're not sure if he isn't doing this on his own volition right now, if he really isn't imprisoned anymore."

"That's crazy," Hawk said, waving at her dismissively. "I don't think I ever met a bigger patriot than Tyson, not to mention he'd never walk out on his family like that."

She looked out the window again, shaking her head subtly. "People can fool you sometimes."

Hawk scowled. "Not Tyson. He'd never betray his country."

She turned turn Hawk again. "All I'm saying is, don't let your friendship blind you. While it's been a motivating factor for you to volunteer for this mission, it's also been a reason why I was initially hesitant to ask you to go."

"And how could I possibly let that compromise this mission?"

"You need to be prepared for the possibility that Tyson may not want to come home."

Hawk stroked his chin. "Are you suggesting that instead of an extraction, this might be more of a fact-finding mission?"

She shrugged. "Maybe both. I don't know. But just beware that he might not be the same person you once knew. I felt it was important for me to tell you this myself before you left."

"You should've told me that up front," Hawk said.

"Does that change your mind now? I can still have this SUV turn around and take you back home."

"No, Tyson still needs my help. And I owe it to him after what he did for me. Just next time tell me everything. No more games. Your uncle would've never done that."

"If I had told you that initially, would you be sitting in this car right now?"

Hawk pursed his lips, pausing for a moment to consider her question. "Probably not—to be honest with you."

Morgan smiled. "Then I'm doing exactly what my uncle would've done. He always did everything he could to secure the best person for the job."

"Maybe, but I still don't like it," Hawk said. "Just promise me you won't do that to me in the future."

She arched her eyebrows. "The future? Are you suggesting that there might be more missions you'd be willing to go on?"

"Let's not get ahead of ourselves," Hawk said. "I need to survive this one first."

CHAPTER NINE

30,000 FEET OVER NORTHEAST MONGOLIA

HAWK CHECKED HIS COMS as he prepared to make a HALO jump. The pilot signaled that they were one minute out from the jump point. The back of the C-160 hummed as the ramp lowered, resulting in a blast of cold air. After one final equipment check, Hawk eased toward the back of the plane.

"Good luck, Agent Hawk," the pilot said over the coms.

"Thanks," Hawk said before he turned and leaped out of the plane.

Hawk zipped toward the ground, his face turning numb. Jumping from thirty thousand feet was never a pleasant experience for him no matter where he did it. But in the winter into frozen tundra? It was nothing short of sheer torture.

As Hawk neared the ground, he pulled his rip cord, opening his chute. In less than thirty seconds, his feet sank into the fresh coat of snow blanketing the hinterlands of Mongolia. He gathered his parachute and then dug a hole. Burying his chute was standard protocol, though he wondered if it was worth the trouble in such a remote area.

Once he was finished, he began a twenty-kilometer hike

across the border and into Russia. The sun rose over the mountains, taking away a little bit of the bite from the frigid temperature. On his journey, he didn't see a soul. The route had been meticulously plotted, providing him with unfettered access into Russia. But Hawk realized why it felt so desolate. The ground was undoubtedly too frozen to cultivate for most of the year, not to mention that in a vast region, no sane person would settle out here.

By 2:00 p.m., Hawk had reached his next destination—the banks of the Onon River. Despite the low temperatures, the Onon flowed as it did year round, winding a path through the snow-covered terrain. The river provided Hawk a faster and more direct route to his final stop, Yakutsk.

For the most part, his trek along the river was uneventful, save for spotting a pack of wolves eyeing him hungrily as they followed him along the banks. However, the animals eventually lost interest. But if they had stuck around, they possibly would've been rewarded for their patience.

Hawk went over a rocky segment of the river, but didn't escape unscathed. When he returned to peaceful waters, he noticed that the air in his inflatable was leaking. He tried to determine the source, but no hole was visible on the outside. Running his hand slowly along the sides, he didn't feel any air being forced out. But it was obvious something had gone awry.

Hawk steered his vessel to the shore for a closer inspection. However, when he did, he scraped against some more rocks and the deflation quickened. By the time Hawk was safely out of the water, his kayak had been reduced to little more than a small seat affixed to a sheet of rubber. He bit his lip and shook his head, irked at his new dilemma. According to his GPS, he had another ten kilometers to travel before he reached the nearest town with a highway that could get him to Yakutsk. The plan was to steal a car in the middle of the night and drive to Yakutsk. But Hawk was exhausted and knew if he had to walk to the nearest town, he'd be unable to continue without a good night's sleep.

Hawk stashed his blown out kayak beneath a tree and trudged through the snow toward the road. The Onon River would've taken him to a nearby city, where he could've beached his craft and slipped out of town in a stolen vehicle in a matter of minutes. But the journey had just become more difficult—unless Hawk changed his approach.

He tried to contact Alex and let her know what he was doing, but he was in such an isolated area that his coms couldn't even link up with a satellite.

I'll have to tell her later.

Hawk knew she'd worry, fearing the worst. It's what she did most of the time these days, more so than when they were both working for the Phoenix Foundation. He figured it had to do with the fact that John Daniel was in their lives now. Alex had grown up in a single-parent family and had expressed to Hawk on numerous occasions how she didn't want that for their kids. It was also part of why she hesitated to agree to let him go on this mission.

No matter what happened, when Hawk didn't check in at the appointed time, he knew she would start to panic, running endless scenarios through her mind about how he might have died. But Hawk wanted to put Alex's mind at ease and decided there was a way he could meet both of his original objectives. It'd require just a few adjustments.

If this had been normal circumstances, Hawk would've stayed out of sight as he navigated through the Siberian hinterlands. But there was nothing normal about this operation, at least for Hawk. He usually had some sort of satellite support from Alex or drone support overhead. But this was rugged and raw, man versus wild. Hawk's survival depended upon instinct and creativity in the midst of a fluid situation.

Hawk noticed on the map that the Onon River flowed beneath one rural highway several times before cutting through the heart of a small village. Instead of hiking all the way to the town, he decided to hike just one more kilometer before trying to find someone to give him a ride to the village. From there, he'd steal a car and continue his journey to Yakutsk.

It wasn't the ideal plan, but it was better than trying to navigate his way through central Siberia while running on fumes. In a country fraught with pitfalls, he needed to be mentally alert if the mission was going to be a success. And keeping Alex sane was equally important.

When Hawk reached the road, he started walking toward the nearest town, thumb out, ruck sack slung over his shoulder. He ambled along, straining to hear the sound of tires thrumming on the dilapidated Russian highway. While Hawk hadn't spent too much time in Russia, he never remembered the roads being so awful. Potholes the size of basketballs, both in depth and width, marred the smooth surface. Hawk could only imagine what kind of hell he was about to face while driving to Yakutsk. He didn't see a scenario where he wasn't changing at least one tire victimized by the pocked highway.

After ten minutes, Hawk had seen two vehicles, neither of which showed any interest in slowing down to pick him up. But that changed when an SUV rolled around the corner and eased past Hawk before slamming on its brakes.

The vehicle backed up and a man in the passenger seat rolled down his window.

"You need a lift?" he asked.

Hawk nodded and hustled over to the car. He got inside, and the driver didn't wait for Hawk to find his seatbelt before stepping on the gas. They started talking in hushed tones. And while Hawk was only catching bits and pieces of the conversation, he could tell the man driving wasn't happy with the decision to pick up Hawk.

"It's our best chance out," the passenger side man said. "We let him take the car and we go home."

Hawk scowled and leaned forward, speaking Russian. "This

car isn't stolen, is it? Because it wouldn't be good for me if you got pulled over."

"Did you make the FSB mad?" the driver asked, eyeing Hawk through the rearview mirror.

"Not yet," he answered with a wry grin.

The angst on the two men's faces melted into a hearty laugh.

According to Hawk's GPS, the town was about ten kilometers ahead.

"Where are you going?" the passenger asked.

"Wherever you take me," Hawk said. "My boat sprung a leak and I started walking for help. Once I get to a place where I can make a phone call, I will get someone to help me."

The two men looked at each other and smiled.

"Ask him," the driver said in a whisper to the other man.

"No, you ask him."

Their exchange continued for a few minutes, both reluctant to ask whatever it was that seemed so pressing.

Then Hawk interrupted them. "Do you need to ask me something?"

Before either man could answer, the driver muttered something and glanced in the rearview mirror. Hawk could tell something was troubling the man. The passenger then turned around and looked past Hawk and through the back window.

Both men started cursing as the driver pushed the accelerator to the floorboard. Hawk jerked backward, unable to deal with the initial inertia. He turned around to see another car speeding up behind them.

"Get ready!" the driver shouted. He reached into the console and produced a gun. Hawk reached inside his ruck sack and wrapped his hand around his gun. The SUV roared down the highway, each bump jarring Hawk. The larger the pothole, the more pain Hawk experienced when his head smacked up against the ceiling.

Hawk glanced out the back again and noticed the car was

gaining on them. Then two men poked their heads—and their weapons—out of the side of the backseat windows.

"Get down!" the driver shouted seconds before a hail of bullets battered their SUV.

Hawk stayed down as the vehicle swerved back and forth across the highway. The men in the approaching car continued assaulting the SUV.

When there was a lull in the shooting, Hawk peered just above the back seat and fired back. His first few shots stunned the two men in the front as they started screaming at him.

"What are you doing?" the driver said. "Those men will kill us."

"Aren't they already trying to do that?" Hawk asked.

"They're just trying to scare us," the passenger said. "They're not going to kill us, at least not yet."

Hawk ducked down and eyed the two men cautiously. "If we get them first, we won't have to worry about them doing anything to us later."

"You don't know who we're dealing with," the passenger said, all color gone from his cheeks. "Those men are ruthless. They won't just stop with killing us. They'll make our entire families vanish."

"What'd you do to make them so upset?" Hawk asked.

The two men shrugged and shook their heads subtly.

"That bad, huh?" Hawk said before turning around and firing a few more shots.

Seconds later, another burst of bullets sprayed their SUV. This time, one of them found its mark, piercing a tire and sending the SUV careening off the road. As it left the highway, it hit something on the shoulder, launching the vehicle into the air. When it came back down, it bounced and then tipped over onto its side before skidding what felt like an eternity to Hawk.

He winced in pain, disoriented from the accident. Outside the closest window, all he could see was a wall of snow. That was the last thing he remembered before he lost consciousness.

CHAPTER
TEN

YAKUTSK, RUSSIA

EDDIE TYSON SUCKED a short breath in through this teeth as he repositioned the bag of ice on his leg. It'd been three days since his last fight, but he still wasn't fully recovered. Peter had called him earlier, begging for him to come in for a match that evening. But Tyson knew his limits, which required far more recovery time now that Father Time was getting some punches in of his own.

He pulled out his phone and scrolled through the list of world times. Charlotte, North Carolina was fourteen hours behind Yakutsk. And no matter how well he knew the difference, it always confused him.

The clock on the wall read 10:21 P.M., meaning it was 8:21 A.M. in Charlotte.

Sheila would be getting the kids ready for school. He missed the frenetic pace of the morning and always enjoyed watching Sheila work her magic as she rounded up all the children and had them ready to leave the house looking like rock stars. When she had left him alone with the kids for infrequent trips out of town, they were lucky to make it to school fully dressed with their books and lunches.

He groaned as he hobbled over to his laptop and used his secure server to tap into the family computer located on a desk near the breakfast nook. After he connected, the image came across clear. It was almost as if he hadn't disappeared from their lives for the past year.

Sheila was already put together, wearing a white blouse and skirt. Her hair looked as if she'd just walked out of a salon. The only thing missing was her lipstick, which she saved for the time she'd spend sitting in Charlotte's congested morning rush.

Samantha was looking far too old for her age, wearing clothes that he wouldn't have approved of. Tyson had argued plenty of times about his teenage daughter's attire, which was a stand Sheila obviously didn't want to make with him gone.

Joey was busy playing a hand-held video game, complete with virtual reality goggles. That also was a pet peeve of Tyson's. He'd told Sheila a hundred times that she shouldn't let video games be a babysitter. And as much as it inconvenienced her to fight Joey about it and listen to him whine about how all the other mothers of tweens his age let their kids play video games, she went along with Tyson's request. Whenever Joey claimed to be bored, Sheila sent him outside or gave him a book to read. But that too seemed to be a battle she didn't want to fight alone.

Then there was Caleb. Their four-year-old son was sitting at the table like an angel, carefully guiding each spoonful of Cheerios into his mouth without spilling even a drop of milk.

Tyson smiled as he watched his son dutifully eat his breakfast.

"All right, gang," Sheila said, snagging her tumbler and filling it with coffee. "Two minutes and everyone needs to be in the car. Sam, help your little brother get buckled in. Joey, take the goggles off and join us back here in reality, ok, bud?"

Nobody bucked her, much to Tyson's surprise. Sam whisked Caleb out of his chair, tucking him beneath one arm while toting her backpack with the other. Joey nudged his goggles onto his forehead and grabbed the rest of the things. Tyson continued watching until Sheila glided across the kitchen and disappeared.

Tyson turned off the computer and sighed. The ache in his heart rivaled the pounding pain in his leg. He reminded himself that they wouldn't even have the life they were living if he dared to return home. He'd be dead within a week—and so would the rest of his family.

But for now, Tyson had to be satisfied with being a ghost and catching glimpses of their life without him. Every time he logged off, he wondered if he should continue to torture himself. He wished he could just forget about them, but they were the reason he was here—and the reason they were all still alive.

It was just one moment, a moment he wished he could erase from his life. But what he saw, what he knew—it scared him. He realized the immediate danger he put everyone around him in with just the simple knowledge of its existence. He'd even tried to forget it, cramming it into a memory hole. But every morning when he woke up, there it was, staring him in the face.

He hobbled back to the couch and adjusted the ice pack over his knee. He closed his eyes and drifted off to sleep. But the pounding on his front door startled him awake.

Bleary eyed, he tried to focus on the clock. An hour had passed since he stopped watching Sheila.

Who the hell is banging on my door at this time of night?

He peered through the peephole and growled. One by one, he released a series of deadbolt locks, all of which had come with the house. When he first moved in, Tyson ignored them. But after a few weeks, he found listening to the click of each one somewhat cathartic after returning from a day out in Yakutsk.

Tyson cracked open the door just wide enough to see a Russian general standing in front of him with a pair of aides.

"General," Tyson said with a nod of his head, "is there something I can help you with?"

"May I come in?" the general asked.

"I'd prefer to keep this conversation brief," Tyson said. "You woke me up and I'd rather get back to sleep."

The general ignored Tyson's plea, pushing past him. "Let's sit down and talk."

Tyson sighed and waited for all three men to enter his apartment bringing the bitter cold with them. He shut the door and followed them into the living room where they'd all made themselves comfortable.

"I'm going to get straight to the point," the general said.

"Okay," Tyson said. "What's this all about?"

"We know where your family is, Mr. Tyson," the general said.

Tyson's eyes widened. The whole purpose of finding refuge in Russia was to avoid this type of strong arming from powerful people. Tyson now realized he was the fool for thinking the Russians wouldn't play the same game. But he wasn't going to acquiesce to their threats without pushing back.

"I don't believe you," Tyson said.

"Perhaps you should be more careful about how you keep up with your family," the general said. "You use your computer to check on them quite often. And thanks to you, we know exactly where they live."

Tyson stood and clenched his fists. He set his jaw and glared at the general, who gave a disinterested glance.

"Don't you dare threaten my family," Tyson said with a growl. "I think you saw what I did to your precious Bear."

The general chuckled and waved dismissively at Tyson. "First of all, I could put a bullet in your head right now if I wanted to and you couldn't stop me. And nobody would care since you're already dead."

The general gestured for Tyson to sit down, but the American didn't move. With just a glance from the general, his two aides moved toward Tyson, who decided against fighting and took his seat.

"Now, I don't want to harm your family. I really don't. I have a family of my own. They're the most precious people in the world to me, and I'd do anything to keep them safe. And that's why I expect your full cooperation on the assignment we're giving you. Based on everything I know about you, keeping your family safe is your top priority, is it not?"

Tyson nodded reluctantly.

"So we have an understanding, right?" the general asked as he held his palms out. "You comply with our little request, and we keep your children safe."

Tyson sighed. "I understand."

"Good," the general said. "Someone will return with all the details later this week. Just be ready to leave whenever we tell you to. And I suggest you start packing now. It's going to be a long trip."

The general rose along with his aides, Tyson right behind them. For a moment he considered how he might take all three of them out. But then the idea was gone, buried for good. If the general knew where Tyson's family was, someone else in the Russian military did too.

I'll have my revenge.

He ushered them outside without another word and relocked the dozen or so deadbolts before going to bed.

Tyson climbed under the covers and turned the lights off, lying in the dark and staring at the ceiling.

What I'd give for just one more hug from Sheila ... and Caleb, too.

CHAPTER
ELEVEN

CENTRAL SIBERIA

HAWK AWOKE to the odor of gasoline and burnt rubber. His shoulder ached and he took a few seconds to orient himself. Shattered glass lay all around him and the SUV's engine hissed as it idled. After unbuckling his seatbelt, he grabbed his ruck sack and surveyed the damage.

In the front seats, the front windshield was gone, pieces of it covering the two Russians. Both men appeared unconscious with slight scrapes and cuts on their faces. Hawk checked for a pulse to make sure they were alive. Once confirming they were, Hawk went to work.

The vehicle had come to rest on its side against a snowbank, giving him only one option to exit. With the driver's side resting on the ground, he muscled open the back passenger side door. Then he dragged the driver out and moved him a safe distance away from the car.

When Hawk returned to get the second man, he noticed the car starting to smoke, increasing the urgency to get him out. As Hawk was climbing out, he noticed a fire lapping up the fuel, which was leaking from the tank. He growled as he climbed out and hustled the man away from the danger.

The first man started to regain consciousness, scowling as he watched Hawk pull the second man through the snow.

"What happened?" the man asked in Russian.

Before Hawk could respond, the vehicle exploded, sending debris in every direction. He dove on top of the two men to protect them from the shrapnel, which peppered the snow around them.

Hawk peered through the smoke and noticed the outline of another man walking toward them with purpose. He held a machine gun at his waist. Once he skirted the flaming vehicle, he started spraying bullets, apparently unable to identify where the occupants of the vehicle were.

Meanwhile, Hawk scrambled to get both men behind a berm of snow before setting up to return fire. He pulled out his pistol and eased his head just high enough over the snow to see the man still firing his weapon. Hawk took careful aim and waited for the man to stop shooting for a moment.

As he surveyed the carnage of the wreck, he smiled to himself. Satisfied that he'd completed his task, he turned back toward his car.

That's when Hawk used two shots to take the man down, one shot to the back of his head and another into his upper back. The man plunged face first into the snow.

A few seconds later, Hawk heard the voice of another man calling for his cohort. Hawk eased along the embankment a few meters to get a better position. The moment the next man stepped into view, Hawk put him down as well with a pair of shots.

While Hawk thought he'd only seen two men in the car tailing his, he waited to be sure. After a couple of minutes when he didn't see any movement, he eased over the snow and crept toward the men he'd shot. He pocketed their weapons before checking to see if they were dead. The fire from the SUV crackled behind him along with intermittent hissing and secondary explosions. Hawk hustled over to the other car, which was still running. He got inside and drove it over to the two Russians.

Hawk helped the two men into the vehicle. They were more coherent this time, though they were still foggy about all the details.

"You need to see a doctor," Hawk said in Russian. "Where's the nearest hospital?"

The man who'd been driving waved dismissively at Hawk. "We have our own doctor. Just take us back to our office."

"I don't know where your office is."

The man pointed down the road in the direction they'd been traveling before the attack. "Just drive that way."

Hawk put the car in gear and started down the highway. He glanced in the mirror at the fiery scene, dark plumes of smoke still rising from the crash.

"Thank you," the man from the back said.

Hawk nodded subtly. He wasn't certain he'd made the right call in saving the men. Whoever they were, they were into something dangerous. And by virtue of association, Hawk might have been at risk as well. But he needed an ally and saving the lives of the two men who'd so generously picked him up was the best way to ingratiate himself to them.

The driver of the SUV, who was now sitting in the passenger side up front with Hawk, turned back toward his comrade and starting talking in hushed tones. Hawk couldn't make out what they were saying but interrupted them to check for directions.

"Just keep driving," the man said. "It will be a while."

The Russians continued their conversation for a few minutes before the driver turned to Hawk.

"Who exactly are you?" the man asked.

Hawk had his cover ready. "Ivan Popova, former Russian military."

The driver shook his head. "No, I don't believe it."

"It's true," Hawk said. "Don't you believe me after what you just saw? I was a sniper in special forces."

Hawk kept his eyes fixed on the road in front of him, gripping the steering wheel tighter with each passing moment of silence.

Finally, the driver spoke. "Your accent—I can't quite place it."

Hawk didn't miss a beat. "When you travel the world as I have and speak multiple languages, you tend to lose what makes your original accent distinctive."

"Where have you served?" the other man asked.

"Where haven't I served is the better question," Hawk said. "I have been sent on covert missions all over the world and have even spent time undercover in the United States."

Hawk shot a quick glance over at the driver to see if he was buying the ruse, but Hawk was unable to read the man due to his blank expression.

He shrugged. "I'm not sure I believe you."

Hawk scowled. "I just saved your life. Do you think I'm some threat to you?"

"Maybe," he said before he pulled out a gun and trained it on Hawk. "But I know someone who's a little more discerning. You can speak to him."

HAWK FOLLOWED the man's instructions, turning off the road after several more miles and pulling onto a long asphalt driveway. The surface surprised Hawk after enduring a stretch of teeth-rattling potholes, courtesy of a communist highway department. The road was also clear of all snow, providing a smooth ride. However, Hawk didn't notice any structures in his line of sight, which extended all the way to the sugar-frosted mountains.

"Where does this lead?" Hawk asked.

"Just keep driving," the man said. "You'll see soon enough."

After a couple of minutes, the road banked to the left and down into a small valley. The drive snaked around the back of a rock and up into the mountains. Hawk glanced in the rearview mirror, watching the plain disappear as he entered the forest.

"If you're going to kill me," Hawk began, "there's no need to make me drive all this way. I'm sure no one will find my body."

The two men chuckled. "Who said we want to kill you?"

Hawk looked at the gun. "You are pointing a weapon at me."

"It's just to make sure you do what I tell you to do," the driver said. "I'll only kill you if he tells me to kill you."

"And *who* is that?" Hawk asked.

"You'll meet him soon enough."

Once Hawk thought he couldn't go any higher, he crested the mountain and found himself on the backside of a sprawling estate overlooking the valley on the opposite side. Ancient pine trees soared overhead, their limbs limp from the weight of the snow. They framed the picturesque three-story Tudor house, which was both grand in size and style.

I must be about to meet a famed Russian oligarch.

Hawk parked where the driver instructed before following the two men into the house. Armed guards stood near the door, nodding at the men as they entered.

"What happened to you two?" one of the guards asked, squinting as he studied their nicked faces.

"Nothing, but you should've seen the other guy," the driver quipped.

Inside, servants scurried around the room, offering to take the trio's coats and give them a drink.

However, the driver waved them off from assisting Hawk. "He's not a guest just yet."

Hawk felt naked without his gun walking into such danger. Despite his combat skills, he wouldn't have a prayer of surviving should he be inclined to attempt an escape.

The driver gestured for Hawk to enter a room that contained a sizable dining room table surrounded by chairs and a small serving table in the corner. A couple of oil paintings of Russian commanders adorned two of the walls, while a large mirror hung on the other.

Hawk hoped his good deed wasn't going to spell his doom. Left in the room by himself, all he had to keep himself company was his thoughts.

I should've just taken the other car and driven off after I killed those men.

Hawk was acting on instinct. The accident kicked in his fight-or-flight mechanism. And Hawk didn't know how to flee. He felt indebted to the two men for their kindness, though now he wondered if they hadn't picked him up for some other nefarious reason.

After sitting alone for ten minutes, the door swung open. Hawk turned around in his chair to see who was entering.

His eyes widened when he recognized the man. He felt his stomach drop.

It was Andrei Orlovsky.

"Well, well, well," a grinning Orlovsky said as he strode toward Hawk, "it looks like someone brought me a most unlikely gift."

CHAPTER
TWELVE

MONTANA

ALEX POSITIONED her cell phone between her ear and shoulder as she poured John Daniel's cereal. Two minutes into a meltdown, he was screaming because the first bowl she poured had too much milk. On the other end of the line, Morgan May tried to calm Alex about the fact that Hawk had spoken to her since his HALO jump and his tracking beacon had suddenly gone offline.

"I'm sure it's just because of the satellites over that part of the country," Morgan said. "The companies running those things don't want to waste money extending coverage into barren stretches of land."

Alex sniffled as she tried to hold back the tears.

"But I need to know he's okay," she said, emphasizing each word.

"I understand," Morgan said. "I'm as concerned as you are."

"I doubt that," Alex snapped. "I don't hear any screaming children in the background where you are."

"Just relax and give it some time. He'll show up sooner or later—and I'm sure he'll be just fine when he does."

Alex slammed the cereal box down on the table and sat down. John Daniel continued his whining, pointing at the milk jug in front of him.

Alex sighed and then poured the milk, careful not to fill it up too high and incur the wrath of an emotional preschooler who was clearly missing his father. When she was finished, she slumped into the chair before leaning forward. She rested her head on one of her hands and tried to focus on what Morgan was saying.

"Alex? Are you still there?" Morgan asked.

"Yeah, I'm still here."

"Are you all right?"

"Define all right," Alex said before bursting into tears again.

John Daniel shoveled two spoonfuls of cereal into his mouth before declaring that he was full and wanted to get out immediately.

"You sound like you have your hands full," Morgan said. "I can let you go if you—"

"No," Alex said. "Don't go. I need someone to talk to right now. And I can't very well tell anyone around here what I'm doing."

"If you need to vent, by all means, please vent."

Alex didn't wait for Morgan to ask twice. For the next couple of minutes, Alex covered a wide array of topics, ranging from her struggles as a single parent for a few days to fear of Hawk getting killed to her desire to return to work.

"You want to return to the team full-time?" Morgan asked.

"Maybe," Alex said, forcing a long breath through her nose. "I don't know. It's all so crazy right now."

"What is?"

"My life. I live in isolation on a ranch with my husband and a four-year-old son. And I was a good analyst at one point, able to identify openings by which to accomplish certain objectives both on the fly and with plenty of time to study. Now, my analyst skills are reduced to estimating when we should buy diapers next and how many."

"Don't underestimate the power of a woman who can manage a busy home."

"But that's the thing," Alex said, throwing her arms into the air. "I'm not even busy. Half the time, I just want to curl up in a chair on the front porch and read the latest Nora Roberts novels. And I've done it so much lately that I'm not sure I can function under all this stress. And what's bizarre is that I used to thrive off stress. Now, I can't even handle the slightest bit of it."

"If you'd like some busy work, I've got plenty of that too," Morgan said. "Maybe it'll help you take your mind off things."

"Nah," Alex said. "I don't find busy work interesting enough to take my mind off of it. I need real work, the kind that requires me to be on top of my game."

"That's in short supply around here," Morgan said. "But I'll see what I can do."

Alex hung up and despaired as she scanned the mess John Daniel had made.

How do you do that so quickly?

Alex felt if she could answer that question, she'd write a book about it and have enough money to retire to an island somewhere in the South Pacific. Parents the world over would be begging her for advice, asking her to speak at conferences and go on television programs. In short, how preschoolers could turn a room upside down so effortlessly in the blink of an eye was one of those mysteries of the universe. But she could ponder that later. At the moment, all Alex wanted to do was relax, something that was next to impossible due to the chaos John Daniel had created in just a matter of minutes.

Her phone buzzed again and Alex jumped.

Is it Hawk?

Her face fell as the phrase "unknown number" materialized on the screen. She hated that terminology because a more accurate message would say, "The person on the other end of this line thinks they're important but they don't want you to know their number." For a brief second, she considered sending the call to voicemail. But then again, Hawk was calling from a sat phone, which might conjure up the same message. She swiped the screen to answer the call.

"Hello?" she asked excitedly.

"Alex," said a woman in a smooth voice, "oh, thank goodness you answered. I know how much you hate those 'unknown number' messages, but that's just how it is over here at the NSA now."

"Hey, Mallory," Alex said, trying to hide the disappointment in her voice.

Mallory Kauffman was a longtime friend of Alex's who'd worked her way up the chain of command at the National Security Agency, ascending to the position of technology and systems directorate. She oversaw the development of new technology for intercepting messages by foreign and bad actors. And every once in a while, she leaned on her good friend for help.

"What's wrong, Alex?" Mallory asked.

"Nothing. Why?"

"Don't try to brush me off, Alex. I know we haven't seen each other in a while since you moved away, but don't act like we're not friends. I can tell when something is bothering you."

"I'm not really supposed to say."

Mallory sighed. "I have a higher security clearance than you, and I'm calling from a secure line. I doubt it's not something I don't know about."

"I can't really divulge any details, but Hawk is on a mission and I haven't heard from him in a while."

"Oh," Mallory said, sounding surprised. "I didn't realize he was operational again."

"He's going to help a—" Alex caught herself, pausing before continuing. "He's in a remote area and I'm supposed to help him when I can. But at the moment, I don't even know if he's alive."

"I know that can't be easy for you. I'm sure he'll get in touch soon. Isn't that how he always works?"

"I guess so, but that was before we had John Daniel. And I don't want to be raising this kid alone. He needs my full attention right now, but my nerves are shot as I'm worried sick."

"Okay, just relax. Are you sure I can't help you?"

"Yeah, there's nothing anybody can do right now, unless you want to re-task some satellites for me."

Mallory chuckled. "Just like the good ole days, eh?"

"Well, now that you mention it, I always hesitated to get you to help because I didn't want you to get in trouble. But now that you're in director's position—"

"I'll do it," Mallory said. "Just tell me where to point it."

"I can't," Alex said with a sigh.

"Unless you're working with Magnum, you can tell me anything."

Alex remained silent.

"Okay, that explains it," Mallory said. "I won't press any more, but I can't redirect any satellites unless you tell me where."

Alex hesitated, unsure if she should reveal the name. "He's in the center of a large cold country. Not sure if that gives you any idea, but that's where those satellites need to be aimed."

"Consider it done," Mallory said.

"Thank you," Alex said. "Now, what was it you wanted? I'm sure you didn't just call to see if you could help me out."

"Actually, I was calling to see if you could help me. But I can tell you've got a lot on your plate right now and I don't want to trouble you."

"No, no. It's fine. In fact, maybe it'll help me get my mind off of things."

"Are you sure?" Mallory asked.

"Yes, of course. I need something to distract me, and I'm sure whatever you're about to give me will do just that."

"Great," Mallory said. "We've got a mystery going on over here and we could use your analyst skills."

Alex glanced over at John Daniel, who was dragging a couple of blankets across the living room floor in an attempt to build his third fort of the day. She sighed and shook her head, yielding the battle for the time being.

"I'll be happy to dive in and help," Alex said. "It'll beat cleaning up five messes an hour while worrying about Hawk. Now, is there anything else I need to know before you send me the files?"

"Right now, we don't have a whole lot to go on. But it's quite obvious that someone has access to these cables and is sharing them openly with certain people in the international community. President Norris is—"

"Oh, the president knows about this?"

"Yeah, and he's irate about it. That's why there's so much pressure to figure this out. And so far, all of our analysts have struck out in determining the source of this leak. But you're the best, so I thought I'd at least ask you to help me. Well, beg really. I'm not above that. We need your help in the worst way."

"I said yes already," Alex said. "You don't have to grovel."

"But I will. This is a big deal and we need the best and brightest in the country working on it, even if those people don't happen to live in Washington anymore."

Alex laughed. "I do miss getting together for coffee."

"Me too. But if you figure this out, maybe I'll fly you back to the big city so we can grab a cup together and catch up on the past few years."

"I'd like that," Alex said. "But even if I don't figure this out, you can still invite me. I'd love to visit you in Washington again."

"I'm going to hold you to that," Mallory said. "And I'm sending the files as we speak."

The two women ended the call, and Alex turned to look at what mischief John Daniel was getting into. At first when she scanned the room, she didn't see him as she was searching along the floor. That's why she didn't notice him standing on top of the counter preparing to dive headlong into a pile of pillows he'd amassed. He wore a cape and goggles and held his hands out in front of him.

"John Daniel, what do you think you're doing?" she asked as soon as she noticed him.

She jumped out of her chair and ran toward him, but he'd already jumped. He looked at her with a devious smile before his soft landing gave way to a giggling fit. Alex stopped and joined him, laughing at his dangerous game. He was too much like his father, Alex thought, and she decided that letting John Daniel spread his wings—both figuratively and literally—was a better way to keep her sane than worrying over his every move.

She sat down at her computer and opened up the file Mallory had sent.

At first, Alex wasn't sure what she was looking at, but as the hours ticked by, she noticed something.

Her eyes widened as she made the connection.

They're never going to believe this.

CHAPTER
THIRTEEN

WASHINGTON, D.C.

PRESIDENT NORRIS ENTERED the situation room at the White House and took a deep breath. While he'd been inside this room a handful of times before, the stakes had never been this high. During his tenure, the world at large had been at peace. There had been a few clashes between tribes in Africa, a few separatist groups stirring up trouble with Russia, a terrorist bombing in Paris. But that was it. Given all that had transpired during the previous two administrations, none of those conflicts were hardly worth mentioning.

However, today was different. A sense of angst and uncertainty marked the mood in the room. Huddled in a nearby corner were the Joint Chiefs of Staff, while other cabinet members stood clustered against the far wall.

Once everyone recognized the president, their conversations stopped.

"Let's have a seat, everyone, and see if we can figure this thing out," Norris said, taking his seat at the head of the table.

He scanned everyone seated at the table. With a slew of advisors sitting alongside military personnel, he knew it wouldn't be easy to get them to reach a consensus about anything. Fortunately, he wasn't trying to get everyone to agree. He simply wanted to hear what was happening so he could make an informed decision. After all, he was the one with the most to gain or lose by the fallout of his ultimate order.

Barbara Wheeler, Norris's highly diplomatic Secretary of State, clasped her hands in front of her and cleared her throat before speaking. "Mr. President, I believe what's going on here is a lot of saber rattling. Kim Yong-ju would only know how to give the order to fire a nuclear weapon if it was on the video games he reportedly plays around the clock. I'm sure this is all just a big smoke screen."

Norris stroked his chin. "Smoke screen for what?"

"I don't know," she said. "Maybe they don't want us to pay attention to the nuclear reactor they're building in the northeastern part of the country."

"Is that really happening?" he asked.

"As we speak, though from everything I've read, they have no idea what they're doing."

James Miller, the vice-chairman of the Joint Chiefs of Staff, leaned forward in his chair and raised his hand to speak. Norris nodded at Miller.

"I believe what Madam Secretary Wheeler is trying to say is that Kim Yong-ju couldn't find his own ass with a map," Miller said. "But we don't have any intel that can confirm or deny that North Korea is in possession of nuclear warheads. Therefore, I'd recommend that we launch a pre-emptive strike."

"If they're bluffing, we'd just be starting another conflict that no American wants," Norris said.

Brent Gaston, the Naval Chief of Operations, templed his fingers and shifted in his seat. "None of us want another conflict, including General Miller," he said. "But this one might be necessary. We need to make sure the tail isn't wagging the dog here. A quick strike would remind Kim Yong-ju who's the real world power today and end these shenanigans. I think if we used a strong show of force, he'd back down and think twice about puffing his chest out, even if he never intended to throw a punch."

Wheeler shook her head. "I think that's a mistake. North Korea should be ignored until they decide to play with the rest of the world. Wasting our military's time on them only validates Kim Yong-ju's opinion of himself. He's not interested in war, but just being recognized as a member of the world's leadership might be enough for him."

Norris scowled. "But we can't let this become a precedent that every rogue leader will follow in the future."

"Of course not, sir," Wheeler said. "We can find a way to help Kim Yong-ju save face while not appearing to bow to his tantrums."

"And how do you propose we do that?" Norris asked.

"I have a few ideas, starting with an initiative we've launched with several countries in that part of the world to work together on innovative technology ideas," she said. "We could invite North Korea with the caveat that they back down from the war mongering rhetoric and stop threatening our ships in that region."

Miller tapped his pen on the table and exaggerated a sigh. "Sir, diplomacy doesn't work with the North Koreans, especially Kim Yong-ju. If you let this slide, he'll try to play you again. And every time he shares a message or a video that hints that he might have a nuclear weapon or a WMD, we'll be jumping. If you let this game begin, I can promise you that it'll be something that haunts you all the way to the ballot box next November."

Norris stood and paced behind his seat as he considered both sides.

"Anyone else have a different perspective they'd like to share?" he asked.

A few other cabinet members offered support of either Wheeler or Miller's ideas, but nothing fresh or innovative emerged.

"This situation can't be that black and white," Norris said. "There has to be a way we can keep the peace without instigating a protracted conflict."

Miller chuckled.

"Is something funny, General?" Norris asked.

"You act as if anything about a conflict with North Korea would last any length of time. We could send a wave of bombers into Pyongyang, and we'd never hear from Kim Yong-ju or any other North Korean leaders for a long time. I'd say we could send them back to the Stone Age, but I'm pretty sure they're still living in it."

Norris waved off Miller. "As the world's peacekeepers, we have a tremendous responsibility to respect every nation's sovereignty, not to mention make sure that our conflicts remain between military might and avoid civilian casualties at all costs."

"Sir, with all due respect, if North Korea has nuclear capabilities, your virtuous stance won't bring much comfort to the thousands of Americans that will die and the millions more that will be grieving such devastating loss."

"At the end of the day, everyone in this administration has to sleep with the choices we make," Norris shot back. "And defaulting toward war every single time we sense a threat would be a grave mistake."

Miller placed his hands palm down on the table and pursed his lips. "Sir, exactly how many times have I recommended we engage the enemy since I've been a part of your Joint Chiefs of Staff?"

Norris shrugged. "I guess I can't remember any specific occasion."

"That's because I never have," Miller said. "I didn't suggest taking action when the Russian carrier ships were cruising closer than they should have to Alaska. I didn't suggest action when China was caught selling weapons to militants in the Middle East. And I didn't even think it was worth a ten-minute discussion when Venezuela chose to announce it was developing nuclear capabilities to defend itself against the 'imperial aggressors to the north.' So, if I'm suggesting we take some action, it's because the situation warrants it."

Wheeler shook her head. "This is what I was talking about earlier, sir. The general has been searching for a reason to justify those huge military expenditures in the most recent budget."

Miller set his jaw and glared at Wheeler. "Our military is why Americans don't worry about getting bombed in the middle of the night and experiencing a nuclear winter. We're keeping this country safe, and I'm sorry if you think that's a waste of taxpayer dollars. But I happen to think it's the best money we spend."

Wheeler narrowed her eyes and leaned forward. "Now you listen to me, I—"

"Knock it off, you two," Norris said. "Do I need to remind everyone that the reason you're here is to advise me? You give me your ideas and suggestions, and then I decide. That's how it works. You've both made your position clear, and now I'm going to tell you what we're going to do."

A hush fell over the room, the tension was palpable. Norris took a deep breath and then sat down.

"Here's what we're going to do," he said. "General Miller, I want you to put together a plan for a pre-emptive strike, and I want it on my desk by four o'clock this afternoon. Understand?"

A faint smile crept across Miller's lips. "Yes, sir."

"Secretary Wheeler, you can work on a backup plan in case I change my mind," Norris said. "As much as I don't want to do this, I feel like it's the best course of action. Now, everyone, let's get to work."

General Miller nodded at the president and gave him a faint smile along with a fist pump. Wheeler, however, remained in her seat.

"Barbara, are you all right?" Norris asked her as he prepared to leave the room.

She bit her lip and stared at the wall in front of her. "You can't listen to Miller. He'll lead you astray."

"Come on, Barbara. You know what I'm facing here. I don't want the last thing people remember before they go to the polls later this year is that I'm weak on national security."

She sighed. "You can't use polling numbers to govern. The people put you in this office to make decisions, not bend whichever way the wind blows. Grow a backbone and be a leader. And that starts with you standing up to Miller. If you're worried about how people will perceive you now, just wait until you put us in another Vietnam—an unpopular, unwinnable, and unnecessary war."

"Like I said, Barbara, write up a plan and if I like it better than Miller's, I reserve the right to change my mind."

"I could give you a million ideas," she said. "And all of them will be better than trying to win a contest between two leaders trying to show who's more macho."

Norris interlocked his fingers behind his head and looked at the ceiling. "You really think North Korea is bluffing?"

"We don't have any actionable intel, which tells me that Kim Yong-ju is probably leaking that information just to get you all riled up. He's going to play you for the fool while gun-slinger Miller coaxes you on."

He paused for a moment before answering. Barbara's critique was hard to take, but he knew she was right. It's why he appointed her to the position. She'd never minced words before when she was serving in the Senate and becoming the Secretary of State hadn't changed her.

"Okay, I'll sleep on it," Norris said. "And just know that as of right now, I'm still undecided about what to do, but your way seems to make more sense."

"And I know that's what you'd rather do," she said. "You always lead better from a position of strength rather than one of fear."

With that statement, Wheeler got up and exited the situation room, leaving Norris by himself with his thoughts.

He sat with Wheeler's words for a few minutes before getting up. He knew she was right.

All he needed from her now was a good excuse to tell Miller to shove his dreams of a conflict with North Korea.

CHAPTER
FOURTEEN

CENTRAL SIBERIA, RUSSIA

HAWK STARED WIDE-EYED at Andrei Orlovsky, who templed his fingers as he surveyed his prisoner. Orlovsky wore a tailored gray suit and a pair of black Salvatore Ferragamo moccasins. As he paced around the room, the scent of too much Italian cologne wafted behind him. The once world-renowned illegal arms dealer was still portraying himself as a VIP from Venice, like a 45-year-old man still bragging about his days as the star quarterback while working at a car wash. If Orlovsky hadn't been responsible for thousands of deaths, Hawk would've felt sorry for him.

"The infamous Brady Hawk," Orlovsky said as a faint smile spread across his face, "delivered to me as if you fell out of the heavens. This is a most pleasant surprise to my day."

"It's only going to get worse from here."

Orlovsky chuckled as he walked over to the corner of the room where a liquor caddy rested on a serving table. He poured a pair of drinks and then handed one to Hawk.

"It's vodka," Orlovsky said as he sat down in a chair across from Hawk. "It's a custom for old friends to drink together in Russia."

"Who said anything about us being friends?"

The two men who'd brought Hawk to Orlovsky's compound stood against the wall near the door. They both tried to stifle laughs. Orlovsky turned slowly toward them and glared.

"Do you find his comment funny?" Orlovsky asked.

Their smiles disappeared as they turned silent.

Orlovsky threw back his drink and slammed it down on the table. He smacked his lips and shook his head while studying the glass.

"It's like nectar from the gods," Orlovsky said. "I hope you enjoy Russia's finest."

Hawk placed his glass on the table as well without having tasted a drop. "I'm more of a scotch guy."

Orlovsky shrugged. "We drink vodka in Russia."

Hawk glanced around the room, admiring the decor. What the house lacked in location, it made up for it in style and craftsmanship. The crown molding contained ornate carvings of soldiers engaged in battle. And from Hawk's first glance, the scenes depicted appeared unique.

"Quite a place you've got," Hawk said. "It's much nicer than your home in Venice, but it's in Siberia, so I'm not sure it's worth it. By the way, what *are* you doing out here in the middle of nowhere?"

Orlovsky pulled a cigarette case out of his coat pocket and ignited the tobacco. He took a long drag before exhaling the smoke through his nose.

"I have the same question for you," he said. "At least my excuse is that I'm Russian."

"A Russian with connections doesn't live in the middle of Siberia unless he's either disgraced or hiding."

Orlovsky grunted. "You know little about Russia and even less about me."

"Enlighten me."

"I'd love to, but I need to take care of a little business."

Orlovsky reached into his coat pocket and produced a gun. With a cigarette dangling from his lips, he trained his weapon on Hawk's head. Orlovsky moved closer as Hawk placed his hands in the air in a gesture of surrender.

"Settle down," Hawk said. "I'm not here for you. Your men brought me here, remember?"

Orlovsky jammed the barrel of the gun into Hawk's head. "Do you have any idea what I had to endure while being held prisoner by the CIA?"

Hawk steadied his breathing, trying to remain calm. For a moment, he wondered if he'd be able to move fast enough to snatch the gun from Orlovsky, kill him, and shoot the other two men at the back of the room. But they were both armed, clutching their weapons. Then there were the armed men patrolling the perimeter of the house to consider. The odds were terrible, though they would give him a better chance of survival if Orlovsky's trigger finger twitched.

Orlovsky backed away, but his gun was still pointed at Hawk's head.

"It was horrible," Orlovsky said. "Inhumane even. I didn't even get three meals each day. My bed felt like it was made out of rocks. And I was awakened at odd hours of the night and interrogated by angry men who beat me over and over."

Hawk sighed and shook his head, remaining quiet.

"Don't give me that look," Orlovsky said. "This is just the kind of arrogant thing I would expect from an American."

"I feel sorry for you, Andrei," Hawk said. "You blame others, completely unaware that you are at fault."

"Me? At fault? I am innocent."

Hawk huffed a short laugh through his nose. "Selling weapons of mass destruction to terrorists who use them to kill thousands of innocent people hardly qualifies as innocent."

"How do you Americans say it? 'A man has to make a living'?"

"There are other ways to earn a decent wage that don't include finding buyers for stolen weapons."

"Someone has to do it."

"Based on finding you out here, I'm sure someone else is doing it these days," Hawk said as he scanned the room again. "You're not interacting with many terrorists out here."

Orlovsky took another long drag before removing the cigarette from his mouth and slowly releasing the smoke. "I've diversified my interests, which leads me to the reason we're having this conversation. I need a new driver."

Hawk furrowed his brow. "A driver? For what? You've got one standing behind you."

Orlovsky wheeled around and fired a bullet in the head of each of the men standing against the wall. They slid down to the ground and collapsed.

"They were useless," Orlovsky said. "They picked you up because they wanted to frame you for what they did to Maxim Popov and his men."

Hawk tried not to react to Orlovsky's brutal actions.

Orlovsky leaned down, getting eye level with Hawk. "Did that bother you?"

Hawk shook his head. "If they wanted to frame me, I can't say that I care what you did to them."

"They acted carelessly in picking you up and then in bringing you here," Orlovsky said. "They felt indebted to you because you saved their lives."

Hawk glanced at their bodies, blood still pooling around them. "And apparently it was all for naught."

"That's where you're wrong," Orlovsky said, wagging his index finger. "They shouldn't have brought you here, but I'm glad they did because I'm in need of someone with your skill set."

Hawk's familiarity with Orlovsky centered around his dealings with Middle Eastern terrorists in search of weapons and retrieving information about the clients. However, Hawk's interest in Orlovsky hadn't extended much beyond that. But Orlovsky seemed deeply interested in the man he'd been swapped for in a prisoner exchange five years ago.

"What if I told you that you being here wasn't just fate?" Orlovsky asked.

"I wouldn't believe you because I'm here on my own."

Orlovsky arched his eyebrows. "All on your own? You sure about that?"

Hawk nodded.

"So you just got up one morning and thought that you'd come visit Siberia. I hardly believe that's true."

Hawk grew impatient with Orlovsky's attempt at mind games. "Just tell me what you want or I'm going to walk out of here."

Orlovksy laughed. "I love a man with a great sense of confidence, even if it's misplaced. Because you'd be dead before you made it to the door."

Hawk sighed and drummed his fingers on the table.

"Perhaps this wasn't what you expected when you came here, but I have an opening—and you need a way out of here," Orlovsky said. "It's a perfect situation for both of us. I mean, we were once traded as prisoners, why can't we help each other out again?"

"And how are you going to help me out if I help you?" Hawk asked.

"Aside from letting you live?" Orlovsky asked with a smirk. "According to my men, you claimed to be needing a ride. I'm willing to give you one of my cars if you make one delivery for me."

"Whenever something is too good to be true, it probably is," Hawk said. "I have no reason to believe you."

"We must trust each other," Orlovsky said as he placed his weapon on the table in front of Hawk. "Surely you must know that Russians don't share their vodka with their enemies."

Hawk eyed the gun. Even if bullets remained inside it,

escaping a sprawling estate with as much firepower as Orlovsky had would be a fool's errand. The trust was as phony as the idea that if he wanted to pick up the gun and go, he could make it out alive. Hawk had no other option but to go along with Orlovsky's plan.

"Okay," Hawk said. "I'll do it."

"Excellent," Orlovsky said as he stepped over one of the bodies near the door. "I believe this might be the beginning of an unlikely partnership."

Hawk seethed as the Russian left the room.

CHAPTER FIFTEEN

BRIDGER, MONTANA

ALEX PEEKED through the cracked door of John Daniel's room. He was lying on his back, clutching the corner of his blanket in one hand and a Star Wars x-wing fighter he'd built with Hawk out of Legos in the other. John Daniel had crashed just after lunch, blissfully unaware that his father was missing halfway around the world. Alex was certain she detected a slight smile on her son's face.

During the peace that fell over the house when John Daniel was napping, Alex wanted to join him. She resisted the urge to curl up on the couch and sleep by a roaring fire. But without Hawk around, she didn't have time to waste. Dusty and Tucker needed to be fed, and Alex had work to do. Besides, she knew if she laid down, she'd probably never fall asleep despite her exhaustion. Not knowing where Hawk was created an underlying level of angst that wouldn't dissipate until she'd heard from him.

She put on her boots and traipsed out to the barn. Pulling a hay bale into a wheelbarrow, she delivered the afternoon feeding to the horses. Dusty and Tucker galloped over the snow and went after their food as if they hadn't been fed in a week. Alex had noticed that the colder it was, the more ravenous the horses acted.

"Good boy," she said, stroking Dusty's mane. The horse gave a quick snort as he snatched the hay with his teeth. She gave Tucker some attention before retreating into the house.

With Mallory Kauffman's assignment waiting, Alex turned on her computer and began analyzing the material. While working with Firestorm and the Phoenix Foundation, she had come across moles buried deep within the government's labyrinth of bureaucracy several times. As clever as they always thought they were, they couldn't hide from the fine tooth comb of a skilled analyst. Everyone left a trail. Whether it be a paper trail or a digital one, even the most careful spies would take a risk at some point. The more challenging cases weren't solved by someone acting carelessly, but by someone acting too carefully. Even a government employee who was above board on everything would make a mistake at some point, sending an email to the wrong person or purchasing an item using the wrong budget code. Those were natural mistakes, errors that didn't suggest anything further was wrong. But those who were worried about someone digging through their every move would move with such caution and precision that the perfect picture they painted would cast them as a larger suspect.

As Alex perused the files, she cross-referenced them with the intel that was supposedly leaked. Her search focused on who knew what information and when they knew it. Once she established that, she was able to sift through the emails to determine who was sharing the information. The problem the NSA analysts ran into was that the intel stolen never seemed to be passed along using digital means. Someone had been very careful to ensure that whatever they learned wouldn't be disseminated in an easy manner. Alex concluded the mole had to be sharing whatever they had gleaned through old fashioned spy craft. Perhaps it was through a brush contact or a handwritten note planted at a drop site. Due to the limitation of her research in Montana, she couldn't determine the how. All Mallory wanted was the who—and Alex was certain that she'd figured it out after a few hours.

The NSA team had pinpointed what information was being stolen, which made it easy for Alex to narrow down who the mole was. However, she still couldn't say definitively, but she'd done this long enough to know that there were rarely coincidences. And the person who appeared to fit the profile with access to the information was a U.S. State Department employee named Victor Edgefield.

At 37 years old, Edgefield had plateaued in his career at the State Department. Working in public affairs as an information officer, he was involved in policy meetings and worked on a team responsible for crafting the messaging the Secretary of State desired. Edgefield had been hired after an injury cut short his CIA career. But he'd been passed over for promotions several times over the past few years.

Around that same time, Edgefield inexplicably started gambling. Based on the sums of cash Alex noticed he started pulling out of his account, the gambling had started a little over six years ago. However, he was detained during a raid on an illegal gambling ring where he'd been playing poker. While he avoided charges, he didn't avoid his name getting put into a report. Alex also noted on Edgefield's phone records that he'd contacted a local prosecutor at this time, who promptly dropped the charges against a man named Manuel Diaz, the alleged owner of the operation.

Apparently, Edgefield's debts were large enough that his favor didn't result in forgiveness of the money he owed. Alex found more large sums of cash withdrawn until they suddenly stopped. Within a week after he stopped withdrawing cash from his bank account, the NSA team identified the first instance of sensitive information being leaked. Even more puzzling was who Edgefield was giving the intel too.

The leaks appeared to be random, sometimes showing up in newspapers and on major television news programs. At other times, the intel would appear in chat rooms on the internet or gossip columns on random blogs. There didn't appear to be any rhyme or reason to the leaks other than to make the White House nervous. But that changed when an embarrassing cable between the U.S. ambassador to the Philippines and Secretary Wheeler was shared on several websites. While the intel inside it wasn't all harmful, the frank assessments of other countries' public officials was at the least embarrassing, at the most diplomatic suicide. The result was a new determination from the White House to expose the source and shut it down permanently.

Alex finished compiling a brief report before she sent it to Mallory, who immediately called Alex back to thank her.

"This is excellent work, Alex," Mallory said. "I don't know how we missed it. Using the cash withdrawals with the arrest report to affirm the suspicion that Edgefield was gambling proved to be a great piece of detective work."

"Anything to keep my mind off Hawk being gone," Alex said.

"Glad I could help," Mallory said. "And whenever you can talk about that thing you can't talk about, give me a call."

"Sure thing," Alex said as she hung up the phone.

———

WITHIN FIFTEEN MINUTES, Mallory was holding for President Norris on her cell. When he came on the line, he dispensed with pleasantries and jumped right to business.

"Sir," Mallory started, "we believe we've identified the man responsible for the leak. Would you like for me to have him arrested?"

"I guess we could," Norris said. "But what if we waited? Would that be a problem?"

"What did you have in mind, Mr. President?"

"If he doesn't know that we know, why don't we use him to our advantage?"

"What do you mean?"

Norris sighed. "I think I know who's ultimately behind all this, but there's only one way to find out."

CHAPTER SIXTEEN

CENTRAL SIBERIA, RUSSIA

FROM THE PASSENGER SIDE, Hawk looked up at the Verkhoyansk mountains, their jagged peaks casting a dark shadow on the valley. As he continued to survey the area, he squinted at the small dirt road he noticed winding up the hillside and disappearing around a bend.

"This is where you take over," the Russian man driving said as he pulled the truck over onto the shoulder. "I will expect you to return within two hours. If you don't, I will assume you are dead. Are you clear on the instructions?"

Hawk nodded as he opened the door. He walked around to the driver side, where the man stood.

"Good luck, Mr. Hawk," the man said. "I will be right here waiting for you. Just follow the road and you'll be fine."

"See you in two hours," Hawk said as he slid into the seat and gripped the wheel.

The man shoved the door shut and gave Hawk a military salute before hustling over to a vehicle that had been trailing them. Hawk wasn't sure if the gesture was meant for good luck or condolences.

Hawk eased the truck onto the snow-covered road. The studs on the tires dug into the frozen terrain and didn't seem to have any problems with traction. And Hawk found that to be a big relief since his task required him to drive up a steep mountainside.

The task was somewhat simple in nature. Orlovsky wanted Hawk to deliver a shipment to another man, Igor Kalinsky. While Orlovsky didn't divulge the contents of the large package, Hawk could only assume it consisted of some sort of drugs. In preparation for the journey at Orlovsky's estate, Hawk gathered that Orlovsky's illegal arms trade business had dried up and so he'd moved on to other lucrative opportunities, though ones that required more work.

Hawk discovered that the estate was also the manufacturing facility for Orlovsky's operations and contained a handful of meth labs in the basement. The aging mansion had been updated with new ventilation systems that kept the labs' noxious gasses from catching fire. And while no one had told Hawk exactly what he was delivering to Kalinsky, Hawk figured it out.

Hawk fiddled with the dials on the radio, which could only tune into one station. It consisted of a mix of static and an upbeat style of polka he wasn't familiar with that included auto-tuned voices and synthesizers.

Listening to this is a special kind of hell.

He turned off the radio and focused on the rugged terrain. After he had driven for about fifteen minutes, the road narrowed. There wasn't enough room for two vehicles to pass for large portions of the drive, making the conditions even more dangerous. With no guardrail to protect him from dropping down into a rugged canyon, Hawk turned his entire attention to navigating the road to Kalinsky's estate.

Hawk rounded a corner and eased into a stretch of road that appeared to be enveloped by the trees. The already-waning afternoon sun was all but gone in the dark forest. Hawk rubbed his eyes and continued rumbling over the snow and ice.

After another half-hour of oscillating between flat segments and steep inclines, he started to descend. When he eventually emerged from the trees, he found himself in a valley on the opposite site of the mountain. At the base of the area, he noticed Kalinsky's estate, just as it had been described to Hawk.

He approached the gate and slowed down as an armed guard lumbered in front of his vehicle and held out his hand. Hawk stopped the vehicle and waited for the man to walk around to Hawk's window.

"What brings you here?" the man asked in Russian.

Hawk explained the purpose of his visit. Satisfied with the response, the man signaled to proceed, waving him through with the barrel of his weapon.

As instructed, Hawk drove around to the side of a large shed located about two hundred meters away from the house. Once he got out, two men approached him with guns and shouted at him in Russian.

"I was just told to make this delivery to your boss," Hawk said. "Don't shoot the messenger."

The men nodded and then worked together to retrieve the package, which was about the size of pallet and no more than a half-meter thick. They hoisted the large item out of the truck bed and retreated inside. Hawk remained inside the truck, awaiting further directions. After a couple of minutes had elapsed, a large bare-chested man with nothing on but a ushanka cap and denim overalls stormed out of a side door and headed straight toward Hawk. He caught a glint of light off an object in the man's hand and realized trouble was afoot.

Hawk threw the truck in reverse and gunned the engine. The slick surface made Hawk's truck slip for a second before catching the ice. When the tires caught hold, he flew backward across the open space leading to the exit. Hawk saw the man pull out his weapon and start firing.

With only one escape route, Hawk ducked low enough that only his forehead and eyes peered above the dashboard. He made a straight line for the gate. Guards scrambled to stop Hawk, but they were too late.

When Hawk struck the metal gate, it flew open in a flurry of sparks. Men peppered the back window with bullets but didn't do any damage that compromised the integrity of the vehicle. Through the new openings in the glass, Hawk heard more clearly the hum of the two-stroke snowmobile engines whining as they pursued him.

Driving a more stable vehicle, Hawk plowed through the snow. Over the next half-hour, he managed to increase the distance between them to about two hundred meters. As he veered around a corner, the road narrowed again, wide enough for just one vehicle to pass.

Hawk saw this as his opportunity to rid himself of Kalinsky's men. Once he rounded the corner and was out of sight, he scrambled out of the truck and up an embankment. Upon taking up his perch there, he eased into a prone position and waited for the snowmobiles to round the corner.

When the first man roared up on the truck, Hawk squeezed off two shots. The first one pinged off the windshield visor on the snowmobile. The second one hit the engine. However, the man kept going. When he realized that he was going to hit the back of the truck, he applied the brakes and braced as the vehicle skidded toward the truck's tailgate.

That slowdown was just enough for Hawk to hit the man in the chest and knock him into the snow. He tumbled off the edge and disappeared. Seconds later, the other snowmobiler suffered a similar fate, only this time Hawk didn't miss with any bullets. Instead, his only two shots were true. As soon as the man was hit, he fell limp. The snowmobile's momentum carried it into the other one before a slight redirect from the collision sent both vehicles careening off the side.

Hawk scrambled down the embankment and drove away, hoping that he wouldn't hear or see any more of Kalinsky's men.

However, when Hawk reached the highway, he'd almost

forgotten about his looming problem. To Hawk, there was little doubt that Orlovsky had told Kalinsky to have his men kill the new carrier. But Hawk wasn't interested in receiving confirmation. All he knew was that the giant standing in the road had a weapon in his hand. It was drawn and trained on Hawk.

This ought to be interesting.

Hawk needed a moment to think. He stopped the truck about fifty meters away from the main road. He revved the engine and weighed all his options.

After throwing the truck into gear, he shifted into drive and stared at the man, who was waving his arms and pleading with Hawk to stop.

That was the last thing Hawk wanted to do.

CHAPTER
SEVENTEEN

WASHINGTON, D.C.

THE SITUATION ROOM was buzzing when President Norris strode into it. He nodded in the direction of his Joint Chiefs of Staff before turning his attention to his cabinet. After he gestured for everyone to take a seat, he rubbed his hands together and opened up a portfolio on the table in front of him.

"As you all know, we've been dealing with a precarious situation with North Korea," Norris began. "For the first three years of my administration, we've experienced unprecedented peace in the modern era. And I fully intend for things to remain that way. The level of prosperity this country has risen to during that time is something every American can get excited about, no matter what party you belong to. And I must admit that it's a credit to each person in this room doing your job the right way to make sure we don't wander into a conflict. But with that said, we need to do something about North Korea."

"We're standing by, ready to strike, sir," General Miller said.

"I appreciate your enthusiasm," Norris said. "But I need to address how we're going to proceed. After the opportunity to review both a plan considering military action as well as one utilizing diplomacy authored by the State Department, I've decided that we should take a less confrontational route."

Miller raised his hand but didn't wait to be acknowledged. "But, sir, if I may—"

"No, you may not," Norris said. "I didn't bring you here to debate the merits of my decision, simply to inform you about why I'm doing what I'm doing. Now, Kim Yong-ju started out his tenure as North Korea's leader by rattling a lot of cages. But for the past five years, he's been relatively quiet. So it led me to question why he changed his tactic all of a sudden. If he was a democratically-elected official, I would assume that he realized what he was doing wasn't working and decided to take a different approach. After all, that's what I would do, especially if I felt like my plan wasn't working. I'd be more concerned about accomplishing what I felt was best for the people than I would about my pride."

Norris paused to take a sip of water.

"But as Secretary Wheeler pointed out in her report, North Korea is crumbling beneath the weight of our sanctions. If we can get Kim Yong-ju to the negotiating table, I think we can create a win-win situation for us all. We will lift some of the sanctions in exchange for tamping down all the saber rattling in the Pacific Ocean. He's got to realize that if he pushes us, we can obliterate the country. Mind you, that's not what I want to do, but it is an option if he wants to engage us in a conflict."

Norris saw General Miller crack a smile.

Norris continued. "So, while we need to be prepared for the possibility that he might get his hands on some nuclear warheads someday, that day isn't today. We should resist entering into a military conflict with North Korea and see what kind of results some targeted diplomacy will yield."

"Sir, with all due respect, Kim Yong-ju doesn't understand diplomacy," Miller said. "Like most terrorists, what he understands is force and might. If we demonstrate to him that we aren't going to tolerate his tantrums, he'll stop."

Wheeler shook her head and sighed. "Come on, General. Dealing with Kim Yong-ju is Psychology 101. He's feeling abandoned or neglected, so he acts out to get attention. We can do things to alleviate the suffering for the innocent people of North Korea without yielding our position of strength. He can sell it as a win to the people, but the rest of the world will know the truth —and be safer for it. We're not the only country that can get spooked by Kim Yong-ju's actions, so keeping him at bay should alleviate that potential pitfall as well."

Miller huffed. "So, we're going to treat him like a two-year-old who gets rewarded for throwing a tantrum? What gets rewarded gets repeated."

"Perhaps that's true," Norris said. "But I'm more concerned with the long-term picture. And if he's not firing anything at us and just threatening, we know he has no nukes, which is the most important thing to remember here."

Miller crossed his arms and leaned back in his chair. "I think it's wrong to assume that Kim Yong-ju's just throwing a tantrum. One of these days, he's actually going to get a warhead and hurl it at San Francisco or L.A. By the time we realize it, it'll be too late and we'll all wish we'd shown him that we mean business instead of kowtowing to his demands."

As the conversation started to get more tense, an aide entered the room and asked to speak with Norris. He walked over to the man.

"What is it?" Norris asked.

"Sir, you need to turn on the monitor," he said. "We have visuals on the missile."

Norris's eyebrows shot upward. "This missile?"

"Yeah, the North Koreans just fired one over one of our carriers patrolling the Pacific."

Norris nodded the remote. "Someone turn that monitor on."

When the screen flickered to life, they all watched grainy images of a missile soaring over the U.S.S. Roosevelt.

"What are we looking at?" Miller asked.

"This is footage from just moments ago when the North Koreans fired over the U.S.S. Roosevelt," Norris said.

Miller shook his head. "Sir, I think this changes things."

Wheeler glanced at Norris, her eyes pleading for him to disagree. But he didn't. He couldn't. Miller was right. It was one thing for Kim Yong-ju to beat his chest and and *talk* about engaging the U.S. in a conflict. But it was an entirely different matter to actually do it. Letting him off the hook would make Norris look weak and make the U.S. vulnerable to a more deadly attack, maybe even one that struck U.S. soil.

"Sir, remember what I said," Wheeler said.

"Sorry, Madam Secretary," Norris said. "This is an egregious error, one that can't be mended by making a few concessions through our sanctions. We need a show of force."

"The Navy is ready, sir," said General Adams, the Naval representative to the Joint Chiefs of Staff. "I just received confirmation that we can scramble our fighters and have them respond within the next fifteen minutes."

Norris drew in a deep breath and exhaled slowly before answering. "Do it."

CHAPTER
EIGHTEEN

CENTRAL SIBERIA

HAWK SKIDDED to a halt in front of the man, who opened the passenger side door and started swearing. He held his gun trained on Hawk and ordered him to get out of the vehicle. With his hands held high, Hawk obliged. He walked slowly in front of his captor, who didn't move, eyeing Hawk closely.

The highway was bumpy, undoubtedly littered with potholes underneath the ice. There wasn't a guardrail either to protect cars from dropping straight down into a steep canyon. Acting as recklessly on an icy surface as Hawk did was borderline suicidal, enough to unnerve anyone interested in living.

As soon as both men were in the vehicle, Hawk didn't waste any time in gaining an advantage. He grabbed the man's hand and yanked it through the opening in the steering wheel. Pulling back on the man's arm, Hawk applied pressure until it snapped. The man screamed in anguish as he squirmed in an attempt to break free from Hawk's grip. As the man tried to put the vehicle in gear, Hawk swatted the man's hand before slamming his head against the side window. After a series of hits, the man fell unconscious.

Meanwhile, the driver in the other vehicle noticed the fracas and attempted to help. He wheeled his vehicle around to face Hawk.

Hawk shoved the other man out of the driver's seat and took his place. By the time he'd got his bearings, he noticed the other car was headed straight toward him. Hawk threw his vehicle in reverse and waited for the right moment to accelerate.

With the approaching vehicle about fifteen meters away, Hawk stomped on the gas and drove backward up the road he'd just come from. The other vehicle didn't have a tight enough turning radius and found himself spinning his wheels on the ice after he'd stopped. Hawk seized the opportunity, accelerating straight toward the stalled vehicle. Metal crunched as the grill from Hawk's vehicle smashed into the passenger side of the other car.

The momentum from Hawk's SUV drove the car sideways until it stopped a couple of feet from the edge. The other driver rushed toward the passenger side to get out but then stopped when he opened the door and looked out.

"Adios, comrade," Hawk said before revving the accelerator and then nudging the car farther toward the edge. Seconds later, the man returned to the driver side window, pressing his hands against the glass and pleading for Hawk to stop. But Hawk ignored him before shoving the vehicle into the craggy canyon.

Hawk got out to inspect his work, certain that he'd succeeded. He peered over the edge and saw the car already on fire. As he turned around, he heard footsteps fast approaching. He didn't wait to assess the situation, instead darting toward his vehicle. The other man had regained consciousness and was sprinting toward him with his weapon.

Hawk ducked as bullets peppered the windshield. Keeping his head down, Hawk navigated back onto the road. Noticing the man pulling out his phone to make a call, Hawk drove toward the man before whipping the back side of his SUV into him. He hit the ground hard and slid on the ice, dropping both his phone and his weapon.

Hawk scrambled for the gun and snagged it first. The man climbed over Hawk and went for the phone. But he didn't make it more than a couple of steps before Hawk put a bullet in his back. The man groaned as he tried to get to his feet, but Hawk shot again, this time dropping the man for good.

Hawk pocketed the cell phone before dragging the man's body over to the edge and rolling it into the canyon with the rest of the carnage. He took a deep breath and surveyed the area. He couldn't see anyone in the vicinity. After one final sweep for any clues that a major struggle occurred, Hawk eased behind the wheel and headed north on the highway toward Yakutsk.

He glanced at the cell phone to make sure it had a strong signal. Being dark for so long, he didn't want to call Alex only to have the call drop within a few seconds. Once he was satisfied that he could hold a call, he dialed her number and waited for her to pick up.

On the fourth ring, she answered.

"Hello?"

"Alex," he said, unable to get out another word before she expressed her relief.

"Thank God, Hawk," she said. "Are you all right?"

"I am now," he said.

"What happened? I was really getting worried about you."

"Pretty much nothing has gone right so far. From my kayak getting a large hole in it to getting kidnapped by some Russian mafia to Andrei Orlovsky forcing me to do some dirty work for him to—"

"Wait, you just saw Orlovsky?"

Hawk sighed. "Yeah. He made me drop off some drugs for him and then had his goons try to kill me."

"Obviously they didn't succeed."

"Yeah, they're in the bottom of a canyon right now along with one of their vehicles."

"Did you get hurt?"

"Nah, just a few scrapes and bruises. I'll be all right in the morning."

"What are you doing now?"

"I'm driving to Yakutsk to finally find out what the hell is going on with Tyson. What about you? How's life on the farm? John Daniel?"

"I'm much better now that I know you're okay," she said. "I was really hoping we could do this together."

"Me too. Things always seem to run a little bit smoother when I've got you in my ear, walking me through everything."

She laughed. "I'm not sure that wasn't a pipe dream anyway with John Daniel running around."

"That bad, huh?"

"The little guy misses you," she said. "But he's living on the edge, just like his daddy. He's leaping off beds, climbing to the top of bookcases, and pushing the limits. There's no doubt he's your son."

"Well, give the little man a hug for me. I'll give you an update when I can. The problem is I need to ditch this phone before Orlovsky uses it to track me. I'll get a burner when I get to Yakutsk and call you again. Sound good?"

"Yes, but please make that a priority," she said. "Hawk, if something happened to you, I just don't—"

"I know, Alex. Just remember that we're doing this so another kid can be reunited with his dad."

"I haven't forgotten," she said. "But that doesn't make it any easier."

"Anything else?" he asked.

"Yeah, get out of there as soon as you can," she said. "There's some trouble brewing in the Pacific, major trouble."

"North Korea?"

"Yeah—and they're talking about nuclear war now."

Hawk grunted. "That's not what I wanted to hear."

"You and the rest of the world."

"I miss you," he said. "I love you. See you soon."

"Love you too. Be careful."

Hawk disconnected the call and then tossed the phone out of the window and into the canyon below. If Orlovsky could track the phone's location, perhaps he'd think that Hawk drove off a cliff.

As Hawk turned on the radio, breaking news bumper music interrupted the anchor. Then he proceeded to read a report about the tension between North Korea and the U.S. Hawk detected a hint of joy in his voice as he explained the scant details available to the public.

After letting out a string of expletives, Hawk returned his full attention to the winding roads. He needed to be in Yakutsk yesterday.

He just hoped Tyson would be there upon arriving in the central Siberian outpost.

CHAPTER
NINETEEN

WASHINGTON, D.C.

VICTOR EDGEFIELD RUBBED his knee and grimaced in pain. Since suffering a severe injury jumping from a bridge eight years ago, all the hours of physical therapy hadn't helped him recover. He sucked a breath through his teeth as he eased back from his desk at the U.S. State Department.

When he was forced out of the field, he lost his passion for the agency. Working as a desk analyst was torture, serving as a daily reminder that he couldn't be assisting on operations. Frustrated with his plight, he put in his early retirement papers. His supervisor used connections to get Edgefield a job at the State Department, working as an information officer. But instead of the job being what he needed for his mental health, he resorted to other means to get his adrenaline pumping.

At first, betting on sporting events was a passing fancy, but it grew into an obsession. And before Edgefield could stop, his debt had grown into a mountain. The hours he spent poring over statistics analyzing each game created a chasm between him and his wife Rebecca. She was five months pregnant when she learned how deep he was into gambling. He didn't tell her until three months later that he was a quarter of a million in the hole with an illegal bookie who promised to exact as much pain as possible.

The aluminum bat a man nicknamed The Hatchet put to Edgefield's knee exacerbated his injury. It also strained his marriage to the point that within a few months after Corey's birth, Rebecca left Edgefield. He didn't really blame her on the nights when he sat at home alone drinking a fifth of scotch. Given his state of mind, he wouldn't want to be married to himself either. Instead of marrying a spy, she woke up one morning to learn that she was married to a degenerate gambler.

As the debt piled higher, he never thought he could recover. But that was before the man with the scar on his face approached him. Scar Face went by the moniker The Hustler, and he asked Edgefield if he'd be interested in getting out of debt.

"Of course," Edgefield had said. "What do I need to do?"

"Sell your soul to the devil," The Hatchet had replied.

Edgefield had remained stoic. "Where do I sign?"

The two men broke into laughter, but The Hatchet was only partially joking. Edgefield didn't owe his soul, but he did owe his allegiance to someone other than his country. When he began scouring diplomatic cables for information that The Hatchet's superiors might find useful, Edgefield felt dirty, used, traitorous. But the guilt lessened each time he received a large deposit in his offshore account, which he quickly rerouted to Manuel Diaz, who stopped sending over any enforcers when he began receiving regular payments from Edgefield.

After the latest cable landed on his desk, he made a copy and tucked it into his coat pocket. He opened up his desk drawer and stared at the bottle of whisky peeking from behind the yellow legal pad. Instead of succumbing to the desire to take a little nip before he left the office for the day, Edgefield took a deep breath as he looked at the ledger. His debt was down to fifteen thousand. He was in disbelief, wondering how the number had dropped to such a manageable level.

One more and I'm out.

Edgefield sifted through a few more cables before he found one that would earn him the extra funds to end his makeshift indentured servitude. He pulled out his burner phone and took a screenshot of the cable, one that would be sure to get his contact's attention. Within seconds, a text buzzed on his burner phone.

Perfect. A deposit has just made to your account.

Edgefield smiled, reveling in a moment he feared would never come. He checked his banking app and then forwarded the final payment to Diaz. Once he was notified, Edgefield wrote back his contact.

I'm out. That's the last one

Edgefield interlocked his fingers behind his head and leaned back in his chair. He'd finally done it. The eight-hundred-pound gorilla on his back had finally been shed.

As he closed down his computer, Edgefield started whistling. He used to do it all the time, but he hadn't in years—until now.

"Got a date tonight?" his colleague, Eric, asked as Edgefield headed toward the elevators.

"Why do you ask?"

"I don't think I've ever seen you this happy."

"Sue me," Edgefield said, hitting the button to take him down to the parking garage. "I'm in a good mood."

"But you're never in a good mood."

"Sue me," Edgefield said with a sneer.

"And now you're back to the grinch."

Edgefield scowled. "The grinch?"

"Yeah, it's what we call you behind your back, or, in this case, to your face. Work's a lot more fun when you aren't acting like a grumpy old man all the time."

Edgefield flashed a quick hand gesture that wouldn't endear himself to Eric. But Edgefield didn't care. Nobody knew the kind of pain he'd been laboring under for the past few years. He put on as good a face as he felt was humanly possible. And if it made him seem like an old codger, so be it. Edgefield didn't have time, nor did he care, to worry about what people thought about him.

The elevator doors closed and then he began to descend to the parking deck. Before he reached the bottom, his cell phone buzzed with a message. He whipped out his phone and read it before his mouth went dry. His stomach began to churn.

The message was from his contact who'd been receiving copies of all the cables Edgefield considered relevant.

No you're not

Beneath the message was a picture of Edgefield's son. The implication was clear.

Edgefield wasn't done until they told him he was done.

CHAPTER
TWENTY

YAKUTSK, RUSSIA

WHEN HAWK ARRIVED IN YAKUTSK, he went straight to a store and purchased a prepaid cell phone. He next withdrew a thousand dollars in cash from an ATM so he could move more freely without getting tracked. It wasn't much, but it would have to suffice under the circumstances. After he secured a room at a dilapidated motel near downtown, he called Alex.

"Did you make it?" she asked.

"Finally," he said. "Driving through the middle of Siberia makes driving across Texas seem like a trip to the local grocery store."

"That's because you didn't have me to keep you company," she said with a laugh.

"I needed something other than that godawful electro polka music to keep me awake. I swear I'd tell the Russians anything if they made me listen to that garbage for hours on end."

"Do you at least have Bollywood movies on pay-per-view in your hotel room?" she asked.

"*Motel* room," he corrected. "And I'm pretty sure that's far too high of a production bar for this part of the world."

"That bad, huh?"

"Most of the programming looks like it was recorded on VHS."

"I'm glad to hear you took time out of this mission to watch television."

Hawk grunted. "I only turned on the TV while I was settling in, mostly out of morbid curiosity. It's a decision I already regret."

"So what's your next move?"

"Based on the operational briefing, the last known location for Tyson was in the Yakutsk prison."

"And how do you intend on getting into there? Because you better make damn sure you don't get arrested."

Hawk smiled. "Me? Get arrested? Whatever would I do that would land me in prison?"

"Hawk, stop kidding around. It wouldn't be a joke if they detained you for any reason."

"Don't worry. I've already hidden my backup passport just in case they try to play that game. And it wouldn't be the first time some bureaucrat took away my passport and used that as justification for keeping me in prison."

"Until the bribe was paid, no doubt."

"He never got a dime from me," Hawk said. "That happened to be once in Romania. I told the guard that if he didn't, when I got out I would hunt him down and he'd never get to use the money anyway. I guess I spooked him because he let me go in the morning."

"So what's your plan this time?"

"I need to talk with Mia," Hawk said. "Can you patch me through to her?"

"Give me a second."

Hawk heard a series of clicks before Mia's smooth voice came through on the other end.

"Agent Hawk, I'm glad to hear you're still alive after all your misadventures in Siberia," she said.

"Whatever you're hearing, it's all a bunch of lies," Hawk said.

"Even the part about you single-handedly dismantling an entire drug operation run by a Russian oligarch?"

"No, that part was mostly true," he said.

"Mostly?"

"All right, that might be a small embellishment."

"Small embellishment?"

"Okay, okay," Hawk said, conceding. "That's an outright lie, but I doubt my wife is making up stories about my exploits here."

"She thinks rather highly of your skills, though those of us who've been in the field with you know the truth."

Hawk chuckled. "And on cue, I have a question about some tech because I lost all my gear, and I have no idea how I'm going to create a makeshift device that will help us learn where Tyson is at the Yakutsk prison."

His voice continued rising, the tension clear to anyone listening.

"Calm down, Hawk. I'm going to get you taken care of. It's not that difficult."

"Not that difficult?" he asked as he stared at the water stains in the corner of the ceiling. "If it doesn't require me shooting someone from a kilometer away or punching them in the face, I'm not your guy."

"False humility is so unbecoming," Mia said. "You're more than capable of making this little device, especially if you still have that watch Morgan gave you before you left."

Hawk looked at his wrist. "Believe it or not, I still have it on—and even more shocking is the fact that it still works."

"Excellent," she said. "That's going to make this simple for you."

Mia proceeded to rattle off a list of supplies Hawk needed to purchase before he could put together a small device on the fly. She explained that if he did it right, he'd be able to connect his watch to the device that would enable her to gain access to the prison computer system. Once inside, she could help Hawk determine where Tyson was being held and scheme a way to get him out. That is, if Tyson was still alive.

Two hours later, Hawk had assembled the device and tested it on the motel's computer system. In a matter of minutes, Mia discovered that Ivan Antonov was staying two doors down from Hawk and had the room rented for just an hour.

"That ought to let you know what kind of place I'm staying in," Hawk said.

"Swanky," Mia said. "I can only imagine how tasty that gourmet breakfast is every morning."

Hawk eyed a rat darting across the hallway near the closet containing the meager computer system.

"This little gadget works fine on this piece of junk, but do you think it'll work on a more complex system?" he asked.

"As long as the information is getting relayed to your watch, this is all I need. I'll be able to hack in and tell you what size underwear the warden wears."

Hawk sighed. "You people scare me."

Mia giggled. "You should be very afraid, especially when you set 'I hate Tech nerds 45%' as your password."

"Now, why would you take offense at that?" Hawk asked as he disconnected the device. "I can see you getting upset if it's like eight-five or ninety percent. But forty-five? That's less than half. Nobody is going to get mad about that."

"I know one hacker who drained a ninety-two-year-old woman's bank account for the password 'HackersStink2'. You gotta remember, these were the kids who got made fun of and bullied years ago. Now, they can use their skills to capture any little piece of information about you that they want. You really should be mortified—and never use a computer again."

"Case in point—what we're about to do at the Yakutsk prison," Hawk said as he unlocked the door to his room.

"Exactly," Mia said.

"So now the fun part," Hawk said. "How am I going to get inside without having to get arrested?"

"I thought you'd never ask," she said.

THE NEXT MORNING, Hawk crouched behind a dumpster in a back alley, waiting for the Federated Uniform van driver to emerge from the building before sunrise. After about ten minutes, just as Mia had promised, a young man shuffled to the door. Hawk grabbed him from behind, placing him in a sleeper hold. Once he was out, Hawk shoved the man into the van. When they arrived to their motel room, Hawk fastened the man to a chair, blindfolding and gagging him.

Hawk proceeded to drive to the prison, taking over the man's route. His first scheduled stop was at a bakery on the outskirts of town. After he'd gathered all the dirty linens from there, Hawk drove to the famed Yakutsk prison. It was known for its remote location, making escaping an exercise in futility. Even if someone managed to break out, there wasn't anywhere to go. And Yakutsk wasn't big enough to hide forever. Eventually, someone would report the escapee to the authorities and earn a large bonus in the process.

When Hawk arrived at the prison, he flashed the man's badge and was waved through without even a second glance. His hat was pulled down low across his face, his profile darkened by the shadow cast by the cap's bill.

Once he pulled up to the loading dock, he was greeted by one of the prison staff, who rolled a large basket teeming with uniforms. Hawk was prepared to enter but not to handle an interloper that could spoil his operation. With the window of opportunity closing, Hawk realized he had to act fast.

"Excuse me," Hawk said in Russian. "The warden said he had a special garment he wanted us to pick up for him. Can you fetch that for me?"

The man nodded before turning around and lumbering down the hallway.

Once he'd disappeared around the corner, Hawk entered the prison and hustled down a long corridor until he reached the server room. The area was packed with wires connecting various servers to each other, while a large bundle of wires ascended into a small hole cut out of the ceiling.

Hawk whipped out the device and attached it to the wire. After activating his watch to initiate the connection, he called Mia.

"Are you in yet?" Hawk asked.

"Almost," she said. "Give me three more seconds and … done."

Hawk peered into the hallway to see if anyone was heading toward him. He eased the door shut and waited for Mia to perform her magic. He leaned against the wall and strained to listen to the approaching footsteps outside. By the pace and heavy footfalls, Hawk determined it was the staff member who'd just helped him, likely returning with the news that the warden didn't have anything to collect.

"Come on, come on," Hawk said.

"Still looking for it," she said.

"Just hurry it up, will ya? If you don't, I'm going to be the one in here on a more permanent basis."

Hawk heard the man in the hall calling for him. The footsteps became more harried and frantic. Instead of lumbering, he was sprinting up and down the corridor.

"I'm not seeing it," she said.

"He may be under a different name," Hawk suggested. "Try matching a picture to Tyson."

Hawk heard the man start checking every door and calling for him. "And make it snappy. I'm about to get caught."

Based on how loudly the doors were shutting, Hawk guessed that the man was three doors away.

"Okay, I got it," she said. "His new name is Dimitri Sokolova, and he's not imprisoned anymore."

"Then how the hell am I gonna find him?" Hawk asked.

"This file just so happens to have an address for him," Mia said. "He's in a special group called 'Fight Night'."

Two doors down now.

"Text it to me," Hawk said, his heart in his throat. "I have to go."

He ended the call and then disconnected the device from the computer. Then he waited until he heard the next door open. When it did, Hawk sprinted down the corridor near the entrance and shouted for the man when he re-emerged from the other room.

"There you are," Hawk said, calming his nerves as quickly as he could. "I went to the restroom. Did you place the warden's items in the van?"

The man scowled. "I was looking everywhere for you, but you weren't anywhere to be found."

"I'm sorry. My mistake."

He spun on his heels and returned to his van. In less than a minute, he was off the premises. He dialed Mia again.

"I take it you made it out," she said.

"And in one piece, too."

"Good," she said. "I just sent you the address. Good luck."

Hawk returned to his motel room to transport the delivery man a half-mile away before strapping him behind the steering wheel and removing his bindings. When he exited the vehicle, demanding to know why this had been done to him, Hawk was walking briskly along the sidewalk and never looked back.

He had an old friend to visit.

CHAPTER
TWENTY-ONE

WASHINGTON, D.C.

PRESIDENT NORRIS'S response to North Korea's literal shot across the bow of the U.S.S. Roosevelt had been swift and harsh. At General Miller's urging, Norris-ordered Navy jets scrambled into the air to attack a small North Korean destroyer. In a matter of minutes, the vessel sank, and the tension had been escalating ever since.

As Norris convened a cabinet meeting along with the Joint Chiefs of Staff in the situation room, he pondered if he should go through with his plan. In such a grave moment, engaging in spy craft seemed like a foolish move. But he couldn't have someone leaking all of the inner workings of his administration, especially with the election looming. Someone was not only trying to take him out politically, but they were also trying to undermine what authority he held for the rest of the term. The former struck at his pride, but the latter would hurt the American people, which was not something Norris would ignore.

Since the sinking of the North Korean destroyer, a standoff developed in the Pacific Ocean between the U.S. and Kim Yong-ju's troops. No more shots had been fired, but naval vessels from both countries had grown. This development had General Miller frothing to initiate more action.

"Sir, I'd like to begin by saying that I think you're doing an excellent job of directing our military in these uncertain times," Miller said. "I believe striking back was the right thing to do and apparently called Kim Yong-ju's bluff."

Norris wagged his finger at Miller. "Let's not be so quick to declare anything definitively at this point. It's only been a little over twenty-four hours since this all began. And I suspect our friends in North Korea aren't inclined to let this be the end of it."

"Their military is a house of cards," Miller said. "We could obliterate them right now."

"Of course we could, but just because we can, does that make it right?" The president turned toward Barbara Wheeler. "What do you think, Madam Secretary?"

"I think we need to tread lightly here, Mr. President," she said. "Looking at this through the lens of diplomacy, I see two heavyweight fighters who've—"

"There's only one heavyweight in this fight," Miller interrupted. "North Korea is more like a fly weight fighter trying to step into the ring with a behemoth."

Wheeler glared at Miller. "Are you finished?"

An awkward silence filled the room before she continued.

"I see two heavyweight fighters who've both landed the punches they hoped to in the opening seconds of the round. But for various reasons, neither wants to go on the offensive. For North Korea, it'd be great shame for Kim Yong-ju to lose to the U.S. military, which is exactly what will happen should he engage us. For the U.S., the world would view us as a bully. With nothing to gain through a military victory, I propose we consider another route."

"I'm all ears," Norris said.

"I think we can leverage this situation into a big win for us diplomatically as well as militarily," she said. "First, we invite Japan in to broker peace between us and North Korea. That will score us points as far as letting another country with a vested interest in peace in that region lead the talks. Second, we make great concessions to Kim Yong-ju as well, enabling him to save face with his people and appear to drive a hard bargain. He'll be able to boast about his negotiating skills to North Korean citizens and we'll get the benefit of having avoided an unpopular military conflict."

Norris placed a toothpick into his mouth, acting as if he was pondering her suggestion. The truth is he'd already made up his mind long before he entered the room. Deep down, he felt a little guilty for calling a big meeting in the situation room for a charade. But he had to make sure there wasn't any way the cable his office was about to send could be construed as fraudulent.

"Sir, with all due respect," Miller began, "this seems like a giant step backward to me. We have North Korea where we want them. They're shaking in their boots, fully aware that picking a fight with us is a losing proposition. There's no need to concede any ground to them."

Several other generals echoed Miller's comments, affirming his position.

Norris nodded at one of his aides, who passed out a report about a survey conducted by White House strategists.

"While you're studying these numbers, keep in mind that our goal is to serve the interests of the American people," Norris said. "And while I believe that keeping citizens safe is important, there are multiple ways to accomplish this that don't include bombing the hell out of North Korea."

One of the other generals shrugged. "Invading them would be a boondoggle, not to mention there's little of value there. We wouldn't get anything out of it."

"We don't make decisions to engage in conflict just to get something out of it," Norris said, his eyes narrowing. "At least, that's not how this administration is going to act. But just look at the numbers on that page, do you think the American people want to go to war with North Korea? Almost everyone seems to regard him as a narcissist who has a high level of self-importance."

"And he also has the capability of causing great harm to the American people," Miller said.

"Where's the proof?" Norris fired back. "We supposedly have the greatest intelligence agency in the world, yet not a single one of them can provide us with any actionable intel that Kim Yong-ju has what he claims to have. When he gets nuclear weapons, this conversation will be entirely different. Until then, I'm not about to drag us into another conflict like Vietnam with nothing to win and everything to lose, primarily starting with the lives of American soldiers."

Norris perused the handout indicating that more than eighty-five percent of Americans were against another conflict. He held up the paper.

"This shows that people like peace and prosperity—and they want to keep it. I'm not willing to jeopardize that on the hunch that North Korea might have nukes."

"So what are you going to do?" Miller asked.

"I like the Secretary's plan," Norris said. "And that's how we're going to proceed. Engage North Korea with peace talks in Tokyo."

Miller scowled. "This is a horrible idea, sir."

"You've made your position known," Norris said. "That'll be the end of that. Are we clear?"

Miller nodded without saying another word.

Norris dismissed the meeting. The trap had been set.

CHAPTER
TWENTY-TWO

YAKUTSK, RUSSIA

EDDIE TYSON UNLOCKED the series of deadbolts to his apartment and then slid his gym bag across the floor. He relocked the front door and collapsed onto the couch in the living room, closing his eyes and relaxing for a moment. When he got up, he stumbled over to the light switch and turned on the overhead fixtures.

Tyson shrieked as he noticed the man sitting in a lounge chair on the other side of the room.

"Holy hell, man," Tyson said. "You almost gave me a heart attack."

Brady Hawk grinned. "How are you, T-Bone?"

Tyson shook his head before returning to the living room. "You know how long it's been since someone called me that?"

"Based off your question, I'm guessing it's been a minute."

"Ten or twelve years, at least," Tyson said. "So, yeah, a lot of minutes."

"T-Bone is still a far better nickname than Dmitri."

Tyson cocked his head to one side. "How do you know that's my name? There's nothing linking my identity to that name."

"I wouldn't consider a picture *nothing*," Hawk said.

"How did you—"

"T-Bone, you think I just walked away from the SEALs with all that training and got a desk job in a place like Topeka processing mortgages?"

"No, but I—"

"I've worked for the government in one capacity or another for about a decade until recently."

"So you're here on your own?"

Hawk squinted. "In a manner of speaking. I was contacted about your situation and asked if I'd like to help."

Tyson withdrew and scowled. "My situation? What's my situation?"

"Well, up until last night, we all thought you were in the Yakutsk prison."

"Bastards," Tyson said with a growl. "You can't trust the Russians as far as you can throw them."

"Are you surprised that we thought that?"

"My death was faked, reported in the news and everything," Tyson said.

"We got a tip that you were in prison here," Hawk said.

"You came to break me out?"

Hawk nodded.

"You came all the way here just for me?"

"Do you remember that time we were diving in that wreckage off the coast during training?"

"Sure," Tyson said. "As I recall, you got stuck and needed some help getting free. So I helped you."

A faint smile spread across Hawk's lips.

"What?" Tyson asked.

"*I got stuck and needed some help*? That's quite the tame retelling."

"That's not how it happened?"

"Perhaps if you're just sharing a factual account, but it certainly didn't feel like that in the moment. I thought I was going to die. And if you didn't save me that day, I'm not sure I'd be alive to sit here and talk to you right now."

"Perspective, I guess," Tyson said. "I don't remember it being such a dire situation."

"You were born with ice water in your veins," Hawk said. "I've had to cultivate that trait."

Tyson crossed his arms and leaned back in his seat. "Well, I'm sorry you felt like you needed to come halfway across the world to save me, especially to this godforsaken place."

"What are you trying to say?"

"I feel bad that you've risked your life to come here to get me, but I'm not leaving."

Hawk leaned forward and knit his brow. "You *want* to stay here?"

"Hmmm," Tyson said, tapping his chin with his index finger. "The word *want* makes that such a loaded question. It's more like I *need* to stay here."

"Are you here on assignment?" Hawk asked.

"Oh, no," Tyson said, waving dismissively at Hawk. "I'm here because I want to be. In fact, I sought out the Russians and the FSB."

"But why? You're a patriot. This doesn't make any sense."

"It doesn't make any sense to someone who doesn't know what's going on. But if you knew what's really happening, you'd understand."

"Care to enlighten me?"

Tyson hesitated, unsure how much he should divulge, even if Hawk seemed like a trustworthy ally. "It's not really that simple."

"Are you worried about talking freely?" Hawk asked.

Tyson glanced around the room. "I regularly scan for bugs here, but up until a few minutes ago, I didn't think anyone could get in my apartment and re-lock the door without me knowing."

"I'm a well-trained agent," Hawk said.

"During my time here, I've learned that FSB agents go

through an extensive training process as well. But they've never penetrated my analog defense system here."

Hawk chuckled. "Deadbolts and bug sweeps? You're high tech and you know it."

"Look, the truth is, it's more dangerous for me to go home than to stay here."

Hawk's eyes locked with Tyson's. "What exactly are you running from?"

"I appreciate you coming here, Hawk. I really do. For you to leave your family and trek across the world to put your own life on the line, it's an incredible sacrifice. But that doesn't mean it was the right one."

"Why not?" Hawk asked. "Help me understand what I'm missing here."

"I'm not going back. Not now. Not ever."

"That's not an answer."

Tyson drew in a deep breath and then exhaled slowly. "If I tell you, you'd be at risk, too."

Hawk nodded. "It's a risk I'm willing to take."

"But I'm not gonna put that burden on you."

"Come on, T-Bone. I came this whole way and left my family to save you, to bring you back to your son," Hawk said, flashing a photo of Tyson's son. "I have a son about the same age, and let me just say that he needs you, if he's anything like my kid. Pretending like you're dead while building a new life here isn't what's best for him."

"He's still alive, isn't he?" Tyson asked.

"Yeah, but at what cost? He needs you."

"He needs me to be dead. And that's where I'm going to stay."

"Come on, T-Bone," Hawk said, handing a recent photo of Tyson's son to him. "Does that look like a little boy who can just go through life thinking his father is dead?"

"You need to respect my decision," Tyson said.

"Fine," Hawk said. "Can I at least get a drink with you before

I leave?"

"Why not?" Tyson said. "You came this far, so it's the least I can do."

Tyson emptied his pockets on the end table before getting up and ambling to the kitchen. He pulled a couple of glasses out of the cupboard and opened a pair of beers.

"Russian beer isn't any good, but it's all I've got to offer at the moment," Tyson said.

"Well, I'm sick of vodka already," Hawk said.

"You wouldn't last a week here," Tyson said as he poured their drinks.

Moments later, he ventured into the living room and handed one glass to Hawk.

"Cheers, my friend," Tyson said. "And best of luck on your journey home."

HAWK LEFT TYSON'S APARTMENT in bewilderment. The cryptic excuse, the conspiratorial tone, the willingness to shrug off his son—it all bothered Hawk. Despite his best to avoid striking an adversarial tone, Hawk hadn't succeeded. But maybe Tyson was justified in behaving this way, and there really was something else bigger going on. However, Hawk felt uneasy.

He picked up his burner phone and dialed Mia's number.

"Well, if it isn't Agent Hawk," she said. "We had a bet going that you'd been eaten by a bear in the wild."

"Did you lose any money?" he asked.

"Not a dime."

"That a way," Hawk said. "But that's not why I called today."

"Got any good news for me?"

"It's a mix of good and bad. The good being that I found Tyson. The bad being that he refused to come with me."

"Did he say why?"

"Nope. But I slipped that device Dr. Z gave me to the bottom of the end table in his living room. That ought to at least get you access to his phone and computer. I'm hoping you can then clear things up for us."

"I'll see what I can do," she said.

Hawk hung up, unsure if he'd just risked his life for a Russian defector.

CHAPTER
TWENTY-THREE

WASHINGTON, D.C.

VICTOR EDGEFIELD TOOK a picture of the email before sending it to his contact. Even as he watched the image vanish from his device, Edgefield cringed. He wanted to be done. After he'd racked up a large gambling debt, he wanted to do what he could to eliminate it. And while that meant betraying his country, he didn't want to be a traitor forever.

Later that evening, Edgefield almost couldn't believe the message when it came across his computer screen. It was exactly the kind of material his contact had stressed that he wanted, loaded with the insider information that had been prioritized.

President Norris was willing to negotiate with what amounted to a terrorist threat, disguised as a nation.

Edgefield re-read the message a second time and then a third. In the midst of a brewing crisis in the Pacific, Norris was willing to cede his position of strength in an effort to avoid any type of conflict. And while Edgefield wasn't an expert in international peacekeeping policy, even he could see it as a loser, no matter what the polls suggested.

But the poll attached to the email said otherwise as it

pertained to the voters. And if there was anything that Edgefield had learned during his time at the U.S. State Department, it was that the only thing that mattered to presidents was public sentiment. When the people wanted something, the president was more than willing to give it to them to retain a high approval rating.

Edgefield turned on the television and flipped to a news channel to see what else had happened in the world during the day. If he didn't know any better, he would've assumed the email he'd received was at the epicenter of the globe.

The newscaster set the scene for the situation in the Pacific between the U.S. and North Korea, explaining how the tensions had escalated. Then he turned his attention to an announcement from presidential candidate, Joseph Parker. The former senator from Ohio detailed how he would handle the potential conflict.

"I know President Norris is more inclined to get aggressive in a situation like the one with North Korea, but not me," Parker said. "I think it'd be best if we pursued a peace treaty. Japan is best situated to broker a deal between the U.S. and North Korea. I think our allies there could help create a situation that was beneficial to everyone involved."

Edgefield laughed aloud. The idea was preposterous. Kim Yong-ju wouldn't listen to anyone, especially the Japanese. He was so prideful and narcissistic that if he didn't come up with the idea himself, he wouldn't even consider it.

But the newscaster pushed the idea as if it was incubated in nothing less than a genius mind.

Within seconds, the station's social media page was awash with people dismissing the idea as sheer lunacy.

Edgefield chuckled, realizing that his contact had been duped, fed a complete lie. Whoever had been responsible for the email had almost surely wanted Parker to see it. And Edgefield had made sure that happened. While the concept made him smile, it almost made him nervous. Someone had figured out his role in feeding administration intel to Parker's team and used him to do so. At the end of the day, that meant that Edgefield had been compromised, which wasn't a good thing.

When Edgefield first started, he wasn't sure who he was ultimately working for, nor did he care. The opportunity to rid himself of the crushing debt made him reluctant to ask questions. He justified agreeing to help: *What would it hurt anyway? It's not like I'm giving away state secrets.*

And they weren't state secrets that could compromise national security. Edgefield's contact had wanted specific information related to policy moves. As time passed, Edgefield's hunch about who was receiving all the information grew stronger that it was someone connected closely with Joseph Parker, the man poised to challenge President Norris for the White House and possibly unseat him. That put Edgefield at ease, making him even slightly eager to assist in passing along what he learned from his position at the state department. If truth be told, Edgefield wasn't exactly a fan of Norris or his policies. The president seemed spineless, easily swayed by the prevailing opinions of the day. But from what Edgefield knew about Joseph Parker, he was far more principled.

Nevertheless, Edgefield knew he could lose his job if he got caught. A probe would undoubtedly lead back to him and that'd be the end of his career in Washington. Not that he was too concerned about it. He tolerated his job, but he wouldn't shed a tear if he was fired. He'd already lost almost everything he cared about—everything but little Olly, his six-year-old son.

Olly was the only reason Edgefield hadn't moved halfway across the country and started over again. His wife Rebecca was ambitious, something he didn't think much of when he first met her. They'd never intended to have any kids, both so focused on their own careers that they didn't have time for raising a child. As Rebecca's goals intensified, she also started to believe she could have it all and had begged him for a son. With Edgefield out of the agency, the idea of having a child didn't seem so farfetched. He went along with it just as his gambling debts started to catch up with him. And everything else in his life spiraled out of control along with it.

But not Olly. He kept Edgefield grounded and determined to stick around for every birthday party, school play, and t-ball game, even if Rebecca didn't hide her resentment toward him. And while he could've spent more time with his son, Edgefield wondered if cutting ties with The Hatchet would bring more freedom, creating more father-son moments.

Edgefield was jarred back to reality when his burner phone buzzed. He glanced at the name on the screen. It was The Hatchet.

"I take it you got the information I sent you," Edgefield said after he answered.

"You screwed over my employer," The Hatchet said. "In fact, you made him look like a fool."

"I don't tell you what to do with the intel I give you. That's up to you. You just asked me to pass it along."

"You played us and now you're going to pay a price."

The Hatchet ended the call abruptly, leaving Edgefield alone with his thoughts.

Pay a price?

It was an ominous threat, one that Edgefield was inclined to take seriously given what he knew about The Hatchet. But there wasn't anything Edgefield could do about it, other than arm himself. He couldn't report his complicity in scurrilous activities to law enforcement. And he certainly couldn't take the matter to his boss.

Edgefield convinced himself that it was all bluster and nothing to worry about. Then he got up and fixed himself a cup of tea before getting ready for bed.

―――

AS EDGEFIELD CLIMBED under the covers, he revisited The Hatchet's conversation again, replaying it in his mind.

Pay a price? What does that even mean?

He pondered how he might handle any future confrontations. He checked the drawer in his nightstand for his pistol before turning off the light. If anyone tried anything on him, he could handle himself. After all, he'd worked for the agency and was trained in how to deal with any attackers.

But all the training he'd endured didn't prepare him for the rude awakening he received an hour later.

A large hand clamped down over his mouth mere seconds before a needle pierced his neck.

Edgefield fought off the man, breaking free. Then he went on the offensive, rushing toward the man. But Edgefield took three steps before he collapsed, crashing face first onto the floor.

CHAPTER
TWENTY-FOUR

YAKUTSK, RUSSIA

HAWK SITUATED himself on the floorboard behind the passenger seat and covered himself with a blanket. He was counting on Tyson not noticing him hidden in the shadows of the dark parking garage when he got into the car. By Hawk's estimation, Tyson would need to be in the vehicle in the next ten minutes if he was going to make the checkpoint on time.

Before the mission, Morgan had given Hawk a vague warning about Tyson perhaps being resistant to return home. And while he had offered a plausible explanation, Hawk figured there had to be more to the story. He couldn't conceive how a patriot like Tyson could go from wanting to protect his family to outright betraying his country. And Hawk was intent on getting some answers—and stopping Tyson.

Hawk's muscles burned as he remained still, crammed into the car. It had been a few years since such dedication to his craft was required. Breaking into corporate headquarters and the private homes of CEOs was relatively easy work. His life was never in jeopardy and long stakeouts weren't necessary. But on this mission, Hawk had found himself tested at every turn, forced to survive and improvise. Now, he faced a more arduous task that wasn't something he was accustomed to doing, even when he was the best asset at the Phoenix Foundation: Hawk needed to turn someone. And just hours earlier, Hawk hadn't imagined it'd be something he would have to do.

When he broke into Tyson's home, Hawk bugged the apartment. He also attached a small fiber optics device to Tyson's phone that allowed the Magnum team to intercept phone calls and texts. Dr. Z had invented it, tucking it in a small compartment in Hawk's watch. The intel gathered from the device was why Hawk knew to hide in Tyson's car.

Mia snagged a text message to Tyson that gave him coordinates to deliver "the code." She wasn't sure what that meant when she initially read the note, but when she plugged in the coordinates and saw that it was located in North Korea, warning bells went off for her. Based on all the tension between the U.S. and North Korea, she figured it couldn't just be a mere coincidence that the Russians were having an American deliver a secret code to North Korea. When she'd told Hawk, he recognized the masterstroke the Russians were attempting to make—a proxy war.

For all their pride and bluster, Russia knew it couldn't defeat the U.S. in a war. But letting someone else without such awareness engage the Americans in a conflict? That was a job a delusional leader like Kim Yong-ju would embrace unwittingly. By the time he realized he was a pawn for the Russians, it'd be too late. His impulsiveness would take North Korea into the throes of conflict without a second thought. Meanwhile, Russia would take pleasure in seeing the U.S. military weakened and the superpower pilloried by other nations for bullying such a poor country.

While this was the theory Hawk had cobbled together based on his knowledge of geopolitics plus everything he'd gathered from Tyson's place, it was a plausible one. After thinking through everything, Hawk floated his theory by Morgan, who struggled to poke holes in it. And although it was possible that North Korea was instigating a showdown with the U.S. all on its own, Russia would undeniably benefit no matter if they were involved or not. If the Russians happened to catch wind about North Korea, Hawk was convinced that the two nations would partner together in some fashion. And what better way to stoke the fires of war by using an American operative to help make it happen.

However, the theory hinged on what "the code" meant.

Hawk crouched lower when he heard approaching footsteps. He waited until he heard Tyson buckle his seatbelt before revealing his presence.

"Well, well, well," Hawk said.

Tyson gasped and turned to glare at Hawk. "What the hell, man?"

"You're slipping, T-Bone. I could've killed you a number of different ways if I was an enemy spy."

"Stay down," Tyson said. "They could be watching me right now."

"And by *they*, are you referring to the FSB or the Russian military?"

"Does it matter? Either one of them would put a bullet in my head if they thought I had an American in the car with me."

"I'll stay hidden," Hawk said. "But I'm going with you."

"If you want to pretend like we're SEALs again while I drive to the store to get a gallon of milk and some eggs, be my guest. But I have a feeling that you're thinking this is something more."

Hawk glanced at the travel coffee mug resting in the cup holder, the steam wafting into the air. "You mean to tell me you're bringing your large coffee mug for a short trip to the market?"

"Yeah, it's o-six-hundred," Tyson said. "I'm barely awake."

"That's bullshit and you know it. Hell, T-Bone, I can smell the body wash you lathered all over yourself during your shower this morning."

Tyson sighed and leaned against his seat's headrest. "You can't come with me, Hawk."

"I know where you're going," Hawk said, "but you know you can't give that code to the North Koreans."

"I don't even know what it's for, and I don't think you should make any judgments on that either. Besides, you came here to take me home, but I'm not going. So your mission is over."

"Rule number forty-seven of espionage states: 'Be opportunistic. When your intended mission breaks down, take advantage of the situation if there's more intel to be gained.'"

Tyson huffed a laugh through his nose. "What are you doing? Writing a spy manual now?"

"Maybe I am. What difference does it make? I was sent here to bring you back, but I was also told to learn whatever I could. And what I learned is pretty damn frightening given what's going on in the world right now. Are you even aware that Kim Yong-ju is itching to start something with the U.S.?"

"Yeah. I still watch the news."

"And you don't think it's odd that you've been tapped to deliver 'a code' to a naval harbor on the coast of North Korea?"

Tyson remained stoic, keeping his gaze fixed directly ahead. He barely moved his mouth when he spoke. "I've considered the possibility of what they're asking me to do."

"They're *asking* you to do this? And you're doing it willingly?"

"Well, that's not exactly how it went."

"Then how did it go?"

Tyson sighed. "Either get out or shut up because I have to a job to do."

"You can't do this, T-Bone. I really don't want to have to hurt you."

Tyson chuckled and threw the car into reverse and backed out of the space. He idled for a moment. "You have no clue about what's going on. But if you don't want to get dragged out and shot or worse—imprisoned here in Yakutsk—I suggest you stay down."

The car lurched forward, the tires barking on the parking garage's slick pavement. Hawk, who'd dropped back down into his hiding spot, banged his shoulder against the car door as Tyson whipped the car out onto the main road.

"You really want to come all this way with me?" Tyson asked.

"I didn't get out, did I?"

"Nor did you shut up."

"No SEAL left behind, remember?" Hawk said.

"Well, I can guarantee if you make it out of Russia alive, you won't be bringing me with you."

"Please help me understand," Hawk said. "And I don't care if it puts me in danger. If there's someone with that much power, I want to know about it so they can be addressed properly."

"Hold on," Tyson said before going silent for the next few minutes. Eventually, he pulled onto the side of the road and told Hawk to get into the passenger seat.

Hawk sat up and furrowed his brow. "Are you sure this is safe?"

"We're literally in the middle of Siberia, and there aren't any cameras for hundreds of miles. Not to mention, this drive is going to take us two days. If I'm going to tell you everything, you should at least be up here to keep me company."

"Fair enough," Hawk said before he hustled out of the back and into the front.

Once Hawk was buckled in, Tyson returned to the road. He took a deep breath before he began.

"Have you ever heard of The Alliance?" Tyson asked.

Hawk pursed his lips and stared out at the snow-covered landscape. "I can't say that I have."

"Neither had I until I was working on a little reconnaissance project for my commander," Hawk asked.

"Which one?"

Tyson sighed. "I'd rather not say at this point. But I don't think you know him. Anyway, when I found out some information about The Alliance, I went to him with it. He told me to forget that I ever saw it."

"And that didn't fly for you, did it?" Hawk asked.

Tyson resolutely shook his head. "That only fueled my curiosity. Why wouldn't he want me looking further into The Alliance? And who comprised this organization? That's where I started."

"So how'd you end up here?" Hawk asked. "And by *here*, I mean exiled from your family."

"Eventually, I discovered there's a bureaucratic cabal running things. The president is just a figurehead. No matter how much Norris thinks he's in charge, he's little more than a puppet, his strings pulled by far more powerful men—and he's not even aware of it. And that put my entire family in danger."

"But why hide out here? Why fake your death?"

"Because of what I know," Tyson explained. "They tried to kill me twice, and I made their assassins disappear. After the second attempt, I realized there wouldn't be a third and my whole family was at risk. So, I asked for an assignment in Russia deep behind enemy lines, but I had no intention of ever fulfilling it. I just needed to get out of there and die so my family could be safe. Now that I'm dead, they're safe. There's no reason to mess with them."

"Who are you talking about?"

"Look, I know this might be frustrating for you right now, but I know you. And you'll end up in the same place I am in six months if you do what I think you'll do with all this information. It's just best that you don't know, especially since you can't do anything about it."

Hawk shrugged. "I'm more than capable of doing something about it. If it's someone who needs to be eliminated for the sake of the country, I won't hesitate to do it."

"I appreciate your patriotism, but this isn't just about one man. It'd be an endless game of whack-a-mole against well-connected people with deep pockets. It'd be like charging alone into an army of a thousand men like the Vikings of old with nothing but your sword. They'd surround you and gut you before you had a chance to even nick one of them with your blade."

"This sounds like a challenge," Hawk said with a grin.

"Don't even think about it," Tyson said, his tone measured and direct. "This isn't a joke."

For the next hour, they discussed their wives and kids as well as reminisced about their time serving together as Navy SEALs.

Tyson drove his car down into a desolate valley, surrounded by barren rock faces on both sides. As they did, an SUV roared up behind them.

"What the hell?" Tyson asked, his eyes widening.

Hawk turned around to see the vehicle closing fast. Tyson stomped on the accelerator, but the engine couldn't catch fast enough to avoid a collision. The trailing SUV bumped Tyson's car, nudging it forward.

"What is this all about?" Tyson asked. "Did you see me cut someone off a ways back?"

Hawk shook his head and glanced again at the vehicle. One of the men looked familiar to him.

"I've hardly seen a dozen cars since we started," Hawk said. "But I think I know what this is about."

"Hawwwk," Tyson said, glaring at his passenger, "what are you not telling me?"

CHAPTER
TWENTY-FIVE

LOS ANGELES

MORGAN MAY TAPPED a pen on her desk as she read Mia's report on Hawk's progress with Tyson. He'd sent her a text earlier reporting that he'd connected with Tyson and was joining him on a mission to North Korea for the Russians. Having Hawk team up with Tyson to help out the Russians wasn't exactly what she had in mind when she asked him to lead the operation. Her instinct was to pull the plug and order him back, but she'd been warned by her uncle that Hawk would often go off script—and that she wouldn't be able to argue with the results. Letting him roam wild in Siberia made her nervous, but she'd learned long ago that her uncle J.D. was a wise voice worth listening to.

She turned her attention to a few news sites she scanned every day, hunting for critical information that's in plain view, but the public doesn't understand the implications of it. Sometimes it'd be a CEO abruptly retiring or a company selling off to a competitor. But today it was a suicide, one committed by Victor Edgefield. She hadn't been deeply involved with the case, only getting briefed when Mallory Kauffman requested Alex's help and permitted it. But the leak had stirred Morgan's curiosity, prompting her to dive headlong into the developing situation.

Morgan cursed her breath, realizing what Edgefield's death meant. In all likelihood, they'd lost their opportunity to find out who he was working for. If someone had broken into his home and murdered him, staging the scene to appear as a suicide, there wouldn't be a shred of electronics left. Someone that professional would wipe all the electronics and local law enforcement wouldn't be the wiser. Not that Morgan wanted them digging any deeper into the case. Having to fight jurisdiction battles would only create a mess.

The short article in *The Washington Post* recounted that Edgefield had been a civil servant his whole life, working with the CIA before spending the latter part of his career with the U.S. State Department. It was short and sweet, sure not to attract any unwarranted attention. But it definitely sent a message to those who knew what was going on. The president's attempt to use Edgefield to identify who was gleaning all this intel from him had failed miserably. Instead of questioning Edgefield and trying to at least get him to talk, they had nothing to go on.

Morgan dialed Mallory at the NSA to find out anything else regarding Edgefield's death.

"I just saw," Morgan said.

"Yeah, it's a devastating blow to the investigation," Mallory said. "The president used a cabinet meeting to ensure that the information in the cable that came across Edgefield's desk would be verified by everyone present. But none of that matters now because it's quite evident that whoever was running Edgefield figured out he was either a pawn or playing them. Either way, they wanted to put an end to it."

"Have you seen photos from the scene?"

"We got a few this morning," Mallory said. "Common courtesy since Edgefield had worked in the intelligence community for a while before moving to the State Department."

"And?"

"Very professional job. It's just how I would've staged the house if I wanted to sell the idea that someone committed suicide instead of being murdered."

"So where do you go from here?"

"I'm not sure right now. We're going to search his office and home and see if there's anything we can find to link him to his contact, but I'm not hopeful."

"Understandably so," Morgan said. "I think it's pretty clear that somebody didn't want Edgefield talking."

"Or us to be able to trace anything back to them, which makes me that much more curious."

"I always start by asking who would've benefitted the most from the information going public. And I can't help but think it's someone with ties to Joseph Parker's campaign."

"You and I think a lot alike," Mallory said.

"Well, let us know if we can be of any assistance," Morgan said before ending the call.

Morgan stared out the window, deep in thought about any other way they could make the connection between Edgefield and his handlers. But while the mystery perplexed her, she had more pressing matters, starting with what Hawk was thinking by helping out Tyson on a Russian operation.

No matter what reason Hawk had, she didn't like it one bit.

CHAPTER
TWENTY-SIX

CENTRAL SIBERIA

THE SECOND BUMP from behind nearly knocked Hawk and Tyson off the road completely. Hawk held tightly to the handle over his window as Tyson handled the wheel as best as he possibly could under the circumstances. The patches of ice across the road created challenging conditions, causing the car to fishtail. But despite the vehicle absorbing a pair of jarring hits on the bumper, Tyson maintained control.

However, the third hit sent them into a spin.

Hawk tried to focus his vision on objects outside the car so he wouldn't get dizzy. In the moment, he wondered if they would ever stop. Mountains, road, barren plains, road, mountains, barren plains. The cycle felt like it repeatedly endlessly.

In actuality, the spinning probably lasted no more than fifteen seconds, but that was far more time than Hawk liked to surrender command of anything in his life.

Tyson let out what amounted to a drawn out expletive during the entire episode. When the car finally came to a stop, both men exhaled before scanning the horizon. The other car wasn't anywhere in front of them.

Hawk glanced over his shoulder to see the car roaring toward them.

"You've gotta move," he said.

Tyson stepped on the accelerator, but the wheels struggled to catch on the slick surface. And by the time they did, it was too late.

The other car clipped their tail end, resulting in a violent rollover. Hawk counted four flips before the car landed upright but about twenty meters off the road. Hawk unbuckled when he heard the other engine revving up.

"They're coming to finish us off," Hawk said. "We've gotta get out of here."

Tyson grabbed the small package from the backseat before scrambling outside. Just as both men got clear of the car, the SUV drilled Tyson's vehicle, the thick grill rendering the car inoperable.

Hawk and Tyson darted across the roadway, taking cover behind a snow bank that ran parallel to the highway. The SUV backed up slowly before pulling onto the side. Two men got out, both wielding weapons. One rushed over to inspect the damage, while the other scanned the horizon for Hawk and Tyson.

"I don't think he sees us," Hawk said, ducking down behind the snow.

"If he does, he's doing an incredible job of bluffing," Tyson said. "So you got a plan?"

"I like to keep it simple," Hawk said.

"Let's hear it."

"We kill those two goons, take their vehicle, and finish the mission."

"That's my kind of plan," Tyson said.

"Let's do it."

Hawk peeked back up over the bank. His sudden movement must've caught the eye of one of the men, who squeezed off a pair of shots before Hawk retreated to cover.

"So much for the element of surprise," Tyson said.

"I won't concede that just yet," Hawk said.

"You got a way to make us invisible?"

Hawk grinned. "Not quite, but what I've got in mind is a close second."

Then Hawk suggested they move in opposite directions while hiding behind the snowbank, splitting up to make it more difficult for the men.

"I like it," Tyson said. "And when we get back together, you swear to tell me who these guys are?"

"Of course," Hawk said. "And it's not a secret I want to keep from you."

"Well, I guess we'd both better survive, hadn't we?"

"I wouldn't have it any other way," Hawk said.

The two darted along the snowbank, Hawk moving south and Tyson going north. After they were separated by at least sixty meters, Hawk settled into a spot and decided to search for the men. Upon his first scan of the area, he didn't see anyone.

Where'd they go?

Without any of his gear, Hawk was flying blind. No Alex to talk him through the situation. No coms to even discuss with Tyson the best plan of action. Winning this gunfight came down to instincts.

The wind whipped across the valley, pelting Hawk with icy granules. The snow that had fallen at the beginning of the season had long since frozen, Mother Nature converting each flake into a hard object. Together they felt like a thousand tiny knives on Hawk's face.

Ducking back below the snowbank for a respite, Hawk considered where Orlovsky's men could be. And the locations were limited—in the car, behind the car, hiding behind the other snowbank, or face down in the snow bleeding out.

The last option was little more than wishful thinking for Hawk. He didn't have any sense that he'd struck either of the men. And though it wasn't entirely out of the possibility, he usually knew when he'd killed or wounded an attacker.

However, Hawk wasn't interested in letting the fight come to him. He heard a car humming along the highway in his direction and decided to use the car as a cover to move over to the other snowbank. The possibility existed that they could box in Orlovsky's men with Tyson on one side and Hawk on the other. As long as Tyson stayed put, it was an option. But Hawk had to find the men and get them out onto the roadway first. And at the moment, that was proving to be a challenging task.

Hawk crouched low before falling onto his arms and knees, crawling along the ground. After just a few seconds, the coldness from the snow numbed Hawk's forearms and elbows. That's when he noticed some movement in front of him.

One of the other men growled something in Russian and then darted around the back of a rotten tree that had tipped over, its fallen branches serving as a blind for the two men. Hawk froze and moved backward, fully aware that if he continued moving, he would be dead in a matter of seconds once they spotted him. He would've been helpless, completely exposed.

Hawk took shelter behind some brush and tried to get a better look. One of the men was on his cell phone, shouting at the person on the line.

If you hold still for a minute ...

Hawk steadied his weapon and took aim. He squeezed off two quick shots, cutting the phone conversation short. The man disappeared from Hawk's view. The yelling stopped too, replaced instead by groans of anguish.

As the minutes ticked by, Hawk grew more restless. He hadn't heard Tyson shoot but neither had Hawk seen another one of Orlovsky's men. The wind continued to beat Hawk, making him desperate to get out of the cold and find shelter. No matter how much danger lurked down the snowbank, he'd still freeze to death without a place to shield him from the cold and wind. His toes had become numb, his arms never warming after crawling through the snow.

With one man undoubtedly hit, Hawk realized his best odds

of survival were reuniting with Tyson. Moments later, another gust of wind slapped Hawk in the face. And he took that as his cue to bolt. He darted across the road and hurdled the snowbank on the other side. Without wasting any time, he rushed toward the spot where he'd parted with Tyson.

"T-Bone," Hawk called, "what's your twenty?"

Nothing.

The wind howled, mitigating any attempts he made to connect with Tyson.

Hawk was resigned to the reality of his situation. He needed to make visual contact with Tyson, which was also growing more difficult by the second. The wind was carrying along loose snow, adding to the drift on each side of the road. To make matters worse, the dark skies overhead opened up and were dumping more powder, swirling as it made its way to earth. Visibility shrank to no more than thirty yards.

Amidst all of the changing conditions and the unknown variables, Hawk was puzzled by the fact that Orlovsky's men hadn't driven away. Hawk and Tyson were as good as dead without a working vehicle in the middle of a Siberian winter storm. But the car just sat there, emergency lights blinking.

He stumbled toward where he'd left Tyson, continuing to call for him.

A minute or so passed before he found him, lips blue and eyes glazed over.

"T-Bone," Hawk said, shaking his friend, "can you hear me?"

Tyson nodded almost imperceptibly. "I got him."

"You killed one of the men?"

"I think so," Tyson muttered. "I shot him in the chest and watched him stagger across the road."

"Okay, I think I had a direct hit on the other guy," Hawk said, taking Tyson by his shoulders. "We need to get out of here now."

Tyson agreed and gestured for Hawk to lead the way. He kept his weapon trained in front of him as they moved across the roadway toward the car.

However, both men dropped to the ground as a gunshot pierced the air during a lull in the storm. Hawk scanned the highway shoulder and noticed a dark figure running toward them. Without any time to alert Tyson to what was happening, Hawk rolled over and fired three shots. Two of them found their mark, hitting the man in the chest. He crumpled to the ground.

Hawk rushed over to him and kicked his weapon away. The man gasped for air for a few seconds before he fell limp. Tyson came over to help Hawk drag the body behind the snowbank. There was no time or any need to bury the body. It'd be covered in ice and snow for another six to eight weeks before anyone would find him.

Hawk snagged the keys to the SUV from the man's coat pocket before turning toward the vehicle.

"It's time to get outta here," Hawk said.

"Roger that," Tyson mumbled.

Upon reaching the SUV, they found a man lying in the back trying to apply pressure to a wound to his midsection. Hawk trained his weapon on the man, who begged Hawk to shoot him.

"Please, have mercy," the man said. "I don't want to die like this in agony. Put me out of my misery."

"I'll oblige your last request," Hawk said, helping the man out of the car. "You were going to get it whether you asked for it or not."

"But before you do," the man said, holding up one hand, "I need to tell you something."

Hawk eyed the man closely. "Make it quick."

"Mr. Orlovsky just wanted me to deliver a message," he said, his lips quivering.

"And what was that?"

"He knows where you live. And he said you have a very cute son and that it's a shame what's going to happen to him."

The man grinned, his blood-stained teeth exposed.

Hawk hesitated. "You look like you took too much pleasure

in telling me that. Maybe I shouldn't even waste a bullet on you."

"No, please—"

Hawk fired a shot, hitting the man between the eyes. He fell face forward into the snow. "I wasn't even about to go back on my word."

Hawk and Tyson hustled over to the car. Tyson pushed the ignition button, and the engine easily came to life despite the temperature that had dipped well below freezing since the storm started.

"You got everything?" Hawk asked.

Tyson tapped his chest, the package crinkling as he did. "All right here."

As Tyson eased onto the road in the direction of the coordinates, Hawk reached for his friend's phone.

"What are you doing?" Tyson asked.

"I need to warn Alex. You heard what that man said."

"No, no, no. You can't use that phone. The Russians are listening. If they hear you talking to your wife on my phone, they'll know we're together—and there's no reason for me to believe that they'd just trust you."

"Come on, T-Bone. Alex doesn't stand a chance if she doesn't know they're coming."

Tyson shook his head and sighed, waiting a beat before responding. "I warned you about getting involved. And we passed the point of no return about five hundred kilometers ago."

"Go back. Maybe we can get one of the phones off Orlovsky's men."

"We don't have time," Tyson said "We've had enough delays already. If I'm a no-show, they're going to suspect that something happened. And when I finally show up, they won't trust me."

"Who? The Russians or the North Koreans?"

Tyson shrugged, straining to see the road in front of him. "Does it even matter?"

Hawk bit his lip and said a little prayer under his breath. Alex needed divine intervention if she and John Daniel were going to survive an attack by one of Orlovsky's hired goons.

CHAPTER
TWENTY-SEVEN

WASHINGTON, D.C.

PRESIDENT NORRIS POPPED an antacid pill into his mouth and then took a large gulp of water. The cabinet has assembled in the situation room to deal with a growing concern coming out of North Korea. And he knew it was bound to be a contentious discussion where the hawks and doves would be drawing lines and digging in. Ultimately, he'd have to make the final decision, one with great implications for both the future of the country and his own political aspirations.

Norris scanned a document one of his aides had slid to him regarding the current conflict. It replaced the one he'd been reading from his campaign manager that showed Norris headed for an easy re-election. His popularity had risen to Ronald Reagan levels, almost assuring him a similar reverential position in American history. But the preliminary polling showed that entering into a conflict with North Korea would put that smooth route to re-election in jeopardy.

Once the meeting began, the defense secretary explained that the Navy jets scrambled to show North Korea the U.S. military was taking their threats seriously had served their purpose. For the twenty-four hours following the initial altercation, Kim Yong-ju had gone silent. He hadn't pumped out any propaganda videos or thumped his chest on social media. But in the past two hours, things had changed quickly.

Several North Korean nuclear subs were being moved around to the port in Sonbong, which worried the Pentagon—and Norris, too.

"Why are we even here, sir?" General Miller asked. "I think it's evident to all of us at the table that we need to send another message, this time making it even clearer that we will not tolerate this foolishness from Kim Yong-ju."

Secretary Wheeler cocked her head to one side and scowled. "Not evident to *everyone* at the table."

Norris closed his eyes, wishing he was anywhere but the situation room, mediating a disagreement between his chief diplomat and the war-thirsty vice chairman of the Joint Chiefs of Staff.

"Can we please not do this today?" Norris said, smacking his hands on the table. "I think we should all act like the adults that we are. If we can't have an intelligent discussion about the pros and cons of launching an attack on North Korea to stop this nonsense, I wonder what we're doing here too."

"Sir, did you read my proposal?" Wheeler asked. "I think it outlines some important ideas that we can act upon to squelch this threat."

"I read it," Miller began, "and I don't think—"

Norris held up his hand. "That's enough, General. We all know how you feel. And we all know how Secretary Wheeler feels. What I want to know is how the rest of you feel—and if you think those feelings match up with the gravity of the situation we're facing. We're talking about the possibility of a conflict that will require great sacrifice from the American people, including the loss of life. Is this something people are willing to get behind to snuff out Kim Yong-ju and his regime? Will it be worth it to assist getting someone in power who can actually do something to lift that nation out of abject poverty and totalitarian rule?"

"That's not our job, sir," Admiral Brent Gaston said. "We spread democracy by modeling it, not by forcing it upon other nations."

"Agreed," Norris said. "But that ultimately doesn't change the situation we're facing here. We don't engage North Korea to help install a democratic government, but we certainly shouldn't ignore an opportunity to do so through a conflict."

"Is this what you want your legacy to be, sir?" Miller asked. "Because I think that'd be a great one."

"An even better one would be to bring peace through negotiations," Wheeler chimed in.

"Okay, enough," Norris said. "I can see this isn't headed anywhere. Let me mull this over before announcing my decision to this cabinet. And if you have any Hail Marys, say them now because we need all the help we can get."

Norris didn't move as the room emptied out. He spread out the documents in front of them, his eyes bouncing from one to the other as he considered his next move. A peaceful resolution was ideal, but it was also unlikely given Kim Yong-ju's penchant for abruptly leaving summits after everyone believed significant progress was being made.

The more Norris looked at the poll numbers, the more he was inclined not to engage the North Koreans. But would that decision be based off his desire to achieve peace by other means or his White House ambitions? He couldn't be sure—and his inability to discern the difference ate at him.

―――

TWO HOURS AFTER the meeting, no one on the Joint Chiefs of Staff had heard from the president. And waiting longer put the U.S. in a defensive position instead an offensive one.

And Admiral Brent Gaston wasn't interested in waiting.

He picked up a phone and called the captain in charge of the U.S.S. Ronald Reagan patrolling in the Pacific along with the U.S.S. Roosevelt.

"It's time," Gaston said. "Move to Phase One."

CHAPTER
TWENTY-EIGHT

KHASAN, RUSSIA

HAWK EYED TYSON AS he pulled off the road less than two kilometers from the border of North Korea. Just ahead of them, a sign notified them that they were approaching the *Most Druzhby*, or the Friendship Bridge, which spanned the Tumen River separating North Korea and Russia.

"I need to make sure I have all my papers in order," Tyson said.

"Are you sure you have to do this?" Hawk asked.

"If I don't, they'll just send someone else who will."

"But think about it, T-Bone. You don't really know what's inside there, but I can tell you that the drumbeats of war are creating quite the rhythm these days. And if the Russians are trying to start a war by proxy, giving the North Koreans nuclear weapons, you can't guarantee that you're keeping your family safe by doing what you're doing."

"What am I supposed to do? I'm out of options."

"Work with me here. Maybe we can get in there and sabotage this mission for both the North Koreans and the Russians."

"That's a suicide mission, and you know it. And I have a

feeling that those urges you had to rush into danger have subsided since you got married and had a kid, right?"

Hawk sighed. "I have more people to think about these days than just myself. But my ultimate goal in doing this job is to help others, not assuage my insatiable desire to get another adrenaline fix. As long as I keep things in perspective, I'll always do the right thing."

"Then maybe you can help me out here," Tyson said, "because I don't know what to do. If I go home, they'll find me and either kill me or harm my family. If I don't do this, the Russians will kill me and still help the North Koreans launch a nuclear war."

"We still have a chance to do something if you're willing," Hawk said. "You just need to understand that the odds would be very low."

Tyson chuckled. "You've never been one to care about the odds."

"And look where it's gotten me? I'm sitting on the border of Russia and North Korea with no plan to get out and no way to warn my family that there's danger crouching at the door."

"If you're trying to convince me to join you on one of your damned fool missions, you're failing miserably."

"I had to try," Hawk said.

"Look, I don't know how this is going to go," Tyson said. "According to my assignment, I have to take this package to the North Korean military harbor in Sonbong, which is another half-hour from here."

"You honestly think they're going to let you in with me riding shotgun?"

Tyson shook his head. "Not a chance in hell. But they know I'm coming, so why don't you hide in the back and we'll hope everything works out. Once we get to Sonbong, you do what you feel needs to be done, if the opportunity arises."

"I can live with that," Hawk said.

"And if you can't find a way out of here, you'll be accompanying me back to Yakutsk."

"That's definitely not going to happen, no matter what."

Tyson shrugged. "It's not so bad."

"Your face looks like it's been rearranged several times since you've been here. And I'm pretty sure your nose is still broken."

Hawk reached for Tyson's nose and barely made contact with it before he winced.

"Okay, okay," Tyson said, swatting at Hawk's hand. "You've made your point. There are a million other places I'd rather live than the middle of Siberia, okay? You happy?"

"T-Bone, I'll only be happy when you're back with Sheila and your kids."

"Then you may never be happy. But just take care of them for me, will you?"

Hawk scowled. "You're starting to sound like you don't think you'll survive."

"We're deep in enemy territory, and these people are ruthless. If you think you're going to make it out of here, I suggest you lower your expectations."

"I've faced worse odds. And I *always* think the glass is half full."

"If you want to believe there's even a drop left in the glass, I suggest you climb in the back and pull that blanket over you."

"Roger that," Hawk said and then followed Tyson's suggestion.

HAWK REMAINED STILL as Tyson came to a stop at the North Korean checkpoint. While Hawk was concerned there would be a thorough search of the vehicle, his fears were allayed by the brief conversation between Tyson and the guard. No more than thirty seconds passed—though it felt longer to Hawk—before Tyson was permitted to enter the country.

After a couple of minutes, Hawk, still tucked away in his hiding spot, spoke. "Your Russian accent is very convincing, especially when you use it to speak Korean."

"I've been on several missions here," Tyson said. "It's a necessary skill if you want to live here."

"Well, I'm impressed."

"Don't be. We're not out of the country yet, and I've found that getting out of North Korea is more challenging than getting in."

The half-hour drive to Sonbong passed quickly as Hawk and Tyson reminisced about their time in training as well as how becoming fathers had changed them.

"Did you know being a father would be so difficult?" Hawk asked.

"Difficult?" Tyson asked. "With one kid?"

"You don't know John Daniel."

"Well, if he's anything like his old man, I could see it being a challenge. My boys are wild, but that's nothing compared to having a daughter. Women cry over everything."

Hawk laughed. "I do remember that women crying was your kryptonite. One tear just welling up and you'd give defense secrets to China."

"That's a little bit of a stretch, but an accurate assessment of my disdain for tears."

"That's how Sheila got you to marry her, didn't she? A couple of tears one day when you tried to break up with her and then you ran out and bought a ring."

"Also false, but plausible."

The two men shared a hearty laugh.

"But as emotional as Sheila and Sam are, I still love them to pieces," Tyson said. "I'm hoping that there will come a time when I can return home safely and I'll be able to watch Sam grow up. I really just want to walk her down the aisle."

"Marriage?" Hawk said. "You're already thinking about your

daughter getting married? Samantha's only what? Fourteen now?"

"Yeah, she's a teenager and that time goes by fast," Tyson said. "And when you're living in the middle of nowhere missing your family, you'll think about anything if it's related to your family, anything to stay sane—even if it hurts to do so."

Tyson's tone turned more somber as he slowed the SUV.

"Okay, we're coming up on the drop point at the harbor," Tyson said. "I don't know what's going to happen here, but be ready for anything. And if you can help it, wait until they've notified the Russians that the code has been received. If my family's life is hanging in the balance, I don't want the Russians to think I sabotaged this drop."

"Roger that."

Hawk steadied his breathing as he felt the vehicle come to a stop. He struggled to hear the conversation between a guard and Tyson. After a brief moment of silence, a different man began speaking with Tyson. The man's tone was much more authoritative, leading Hawk to believe Tyson was talking with a higher-ranking officer.

Hawk heard the hum of the automatic windows as the vehicle began to move again.

"So far so good," Tyson said. "I've been directed to drive along the harbor to the military entrance."

"Is that where you're supposed to deliver the codes?" Hawk asked.

"Yes. Now sit tight. We're approaching the next guard station."

Hawk didn't move during the prolonged discussion between Tyson and the new guard. After a few moments, Hawk heard footfalls just outside the rear of the vehicle, followed by a bright light that penetrated the blanket he was under. A tapping sound on the window made Hawk wonder if he was about to be discovered before it stopped. The light also vanished.

As the SUV began to move again, Tyson updated Hawk on

what was happening. There was a warehouse that Tyson needed to visit first.

"Just stay put," Tyson said. "Once we leave this compound, I'll let you out and you can figure out how to deal with this situation. Just be patient a few minutes longer."

When they reached the warehouse, Tyson exited and walked away. Hawk listened as the footsteps faded and then stopped. A man began shouting at Tyson, who attempted to explain himself. Hawk made out something about the codes.

Tyson pleaded with the man before the sound of an intense beating commenced. The scuffle lasted a few seconds before Hawk heard what sounded like a body hitting the pavement.

Hawk shouldn't have been surprised given what he knew about how ruthless the North Koreans were, but Hawk couldn't help but think the situation was a setup from the beginning. The Russians had seen a way to keep their hands clean of the situation, while also giving the North Koreans a gift of a U.S. citizen involved in espionage. North Korea would be able to leverage Tyson for whatever purposes they desired—and they'd also be able to activate the nuclear warheads they'd received from Russia.

Hawk couldn't find anything good about the situation, especially since he was hidden in the back of the vehicle. Without any advance knowledge on what the location was like or even where the codes were now, Hawk was flying blind again.

Moments later, two men walked near the vehicle. One of the men told the other one to take it somewhere and to search it before cleaning it out.

Hawk estimated the soldier drove for about three minutes, making various turns. As he did, Hawk took careful note of each one in hopes that he'd be able to return to the scene. Once the vehicle came to a stop, the man was whistling as he encircled it. After he began cleaning out the interior, Hawk waited for his chance. It'd have to be swift, his aim true. With the element of surprise still on his side, he liked his odds.

When the tailgate swung upward, Hawk dove headlong into the man's midsection, knocking him to the ground. The man grabbed hold of Hawk's shirt, tethering the men as they rolled for a few feet. When they came to a stop, Hawk was on the bottom. He scrambled to regain the upper hand, something he succeeded at after a brief tussle. Sitting on top of the man, Hawk delivered a throat punch. When he gasped for air, he let go of Hawk, who darted behind the man before breaking his neck. The man crumpled to the ground.

As Hawk caught his breath, he looked around the area. He hadn't had any opportunity to analyze the locale before, but now he surmised he was in an impound yard of some sort, probably one belonging to the military or at least controlled by it. Vehicles lined a chain-link fence, some of which had clearly seen better days almost a lifetime ago. Rust covered a portion of most of the cars along with patchy snow and ice.

Hawk dragged the man's body beneath one of the nearby cars before taking his uniform. He also confiscated the man's phone and dialed into a secure line before delivering a code message to Magnum.

"I found the package but misplaced it," he said. "I'm hoping you will send someone over to help me find it. I'll be home tomorrow night at eight o'clock and will send the address later."

He needed help but wouldn't know what to do with it—at least not yet anyway.

Hawk realized he couldn't keep the cell phone. Once the soldier was confirmed missing, they would use his cell phone as a way to find him. And Hawk didn't know when that would be. He switched the phone's language to English and sent a text message to Alex.

code red - orlovsky

They'd developed a quick way to communicate if they believed the other person was in danger. Code Red meant a hostile could be approaching. Hawk knew Alex could hold her own, but that didn't lessen his concern. Under his breath, Hawk said a little prayer for her and John Daniel.

Hawk smashed the phone with his boot before swapping out a license plate on Tyson's car. He needed to determine a safe place to base his operations and then figure out a way to get that message back to headquarters. And he didn't have much time to do it.

The mission had changed and the stakes had been raised.

CHAPTER
TWENTY-NINE

LOS ANGELES

MORGAN STARED at the report a staff member had just handed her detailing Hawk's message. Her team had determined that the package was Eddie Tyson, though they weren't sure if misplaced meant dead or captured. As for the rest of it, he clearly needed a special ops team to help him, which would be challenging given the situation brewing in the Pacific.

Morgan's assistant buzzed in to notify her boss of an incoming call. "Ma'am, Alex is on line two."

"Thanks," Morgan said as she stared at the blinking light on her office phone.

With Hawk in play and presumably armed with intel, she knew there was still a chance at mitigating the situation. But at the moment, Hawk was all alone. And his wife was on the other line, alone and concerned. Morgan didn't want to talk to her, anticipating how unpleasant the conversation would be.

This is why you get the big bucks, Morgan.

"Good afternoon, Alex," she said.

"I need you to start telling me what the hell is going on,"

Alex said, talking hurriedly. "I got this message from Hawk and—"

"Whoa, whoa, whoa. Slow down, Alex. Take a deep breath and start from the top again."

Alex sighed. "Where's Hawk?"

"Right now, we don't know his exact location, just that we believe he's in North Korea."

"And what makes you think that?"

"The phone he called us from was registered to a North Korean number," Morgan said. "It's unlikely that he got the phone while still in Russia."

"And the phone's location?"

"We couldn't get a signal to figure out exactly where, so we're still a little hazy on the details. Now, you said Hawk sent you a message, right?"

"Yeah," Alex said. "And he never would've jeopardized the mission unless he felt like John Daniel and I were in grave danger."

"What did he tell you?"

"That's even more bizarre given that he's in North Korea. Hawk passed along one of our coded messages that I was in imminent danger of being attacked by Andrei Orlovsky."

"Well, I've got two of my best men guarding your property," Morgan said. "You shouldn't have anything to worry about."

"Thanks but that doesn't really put my mind at ease. Orlovsky has an ax to grind with us, and Hawk likely exacerbated the tensions between us and the Russian arms dealer."

"Just relax. I'll send over some more support if you want it."

"I don't think it'll make much of a difference since Orlovsky's men are probably already here. But I want to know when Hawk is coming back and what's going on with him."

"I'm not sure you do."

"Morgan, I'm not playing games. Tell me what's happening with Hawk."

Morgan proceeded to explain Hawk's circumstances to Alex. By the time the conversation ended, Alex was crying.

"We're doing everything we can get to get him home safely to you and John Daniel, believe me," Morgan said.

"But not until the mission is completed, right?"

"Nobody's keeping him there," Morgan said. "The mission we sent him there for is effectively over. But he's staying there of his own volition. And if you trust him like I do, you have to assume that there's a greater threat he's identified. Otherwise, I know he'd be heading straight back to the ranch to be with you and John Daniel. However, the naked truth is that I don't know what he's up to. I'm just trying to trust him and help him in any way I can."

"He never should've left," Alex said. "Everything was fine the way it was. But now what am I supposed to do?"

Morgan drummed her fingers on the desk and closed her eyes, thinking of how to respond, trying to put herself in Alex's shoes. Nothing to say that Morgan thought of could allay Alex's fears.

"When we sign up for jobs like these, we never expect them to go south," Morgan finally said. "But sometimes they do. However, I have faith in Hawk. And I know you do too. His situation may put you more on edge since you're not the only one he might leave behind. But I think he's been in a few scenarios far more dangerous than this, right?"

"Yeah," Alex said with a sigh. "This just wasn't what I had in mind."

"Well, it's not over yet. He's still fighting and we're going to do everything we can to help him succeed."

They said their goodbyes and Morgan hung up. She ordered two more guards to get on the first flight to Billings to go help shore up the security around Alex's property. At the very least, Morgan could give Alex a little peace of mind there.

Morgan asked her assistant to call President Norris. A couple of minutes later, Morgan was discussing the situation in North Korea with him.

"Sir, in light of what's happening in North Korea, I thought I would give you a heads up on something," she said.

"I'm listening."

"We have an operative in Sonbong right now," she said.

"Are you serious?"

"Yes. We don't know much at the moment. He was in Russia trying to retrieve a former Navy SEAL who was supposedly dead, but we found out he was still alive, perhaps still in a Russian prison."

"Then how did your agent end up in North Korea?"

"We intercepted a message that the Russians were strong-arming the Navy SEAL into delivering a code to North Korea. At the time, we didn't know much about it or its significance. But now that we know there's activity in Sonbong, I don't think this is any coincidence."

"But you've lost contact with your asset?"

"Yeah, he had to go dark," Morgan said. "But he's promised to reconnect with us as soon as possible to update us on the situation, as well as get us the coordinates to get a special ops team in there to help him."

"Sneaking a special ops team into North Korea right now? Are you out of your mind? I don't want to know about anything else, unless you succeed."

"We could stop an attack before it starts, sir."

"And what if he gets caught? Then what? He'll be paraded around for the world to see as another reason to distrust the United States"

"Of course, sir," she said. "I just thought I'd let you know that we still have a chance of stopping this thing before it starts, though I'm still not sure how good of a chance it is."

"I'll be looking forward to our next call," Norris said.

Morgan thanked the president for his time and said goodbye.

She shared Norris's apprehension and stared at her phone,

hoping it would hurry up and ring with news of Hawk's whereabouts as well as his state of mind. Meanwhile, hers was becoming more of a mess by the minute.

Uncle J.D. never warned me about this.

She dialed her uncle's number and waited for him to pick up. After a few rings, her face fell as his voicemail message started playing.

CHAPTER
THIRTY

SONBONG, NORTH KOREA

HAWK CROUCHED low in the woods just off the shore and watched for any sign that the Navy SEALs would arrive on time. While they were trained to be punctual, Hawk had learned that flexibility was imperative in situations like this. Aside from fluctuations in the tide or current, any number of problems could arise when navigating foreign seas. Enemy ships, equipment malfunction, an unexpected fog—they were all part of the variables that could change in a second and leave Hawk twisting in the wind.

He checked his watch. The team was fifteen minutes late, which now meant he was officially worried.

Hawk had been able to find another phone and alert Morgan at the Magnum offices about what was going on. He briefed them on his needs as well as giving the exact location where to send the help, all by speaking in code. Then Hawk called Alex to warn her more directly as well as promise her that he'd be back. He hated making those types of promises, but he figured if he broke it, he wouldn't have to worry about being in the doghouse because of it.

He glanced at the time. The SEAL team was now twenty minutes late, which moved him beyond just worried and inching toward outright panic. Without anyone to assist him, Hawk had only a small chance of returning home, much less completing his mission. He'd been in plenty of dire situations before, but this one felt different. There were no safe houses nearby to seek refuge. There were no CIA assets to smuggle him out of the country. He was truly alone—and he felt it.

Another five minutes ticked by and he wondered how much longer he needed to remain there. The wind howled through the trees overhead, the freezing temperatures starting to eat away at the feeling in the tips of his fingers and toes.

With no binoculars to scan the horizon, he began to wonder if he'd missed the team. One wrong number in a string of coordinates could mean the difference in being off by ten miles or more. He thought of Alex and John Daniel and what would become of them if something happened. Alex would likely land on her feet. She was as smart and talented as she was beautiful, lacking in none of those department. But John Daniel needed his father, someone to show him how to be a man in the world. And Hawk cringed at the thought of anyone else taking over that role for him.

Two more minutes elapsed before he noticed a glint on the waves. He looked around to see if there were any fishing vessels entering or exiting the harbor that could've caused the light. But he didn't see any movement on the water. Aside from commercial fishermen or military vessels, no ships were allowed in or out of the Sonbong harbor after sunset.

Hawk looked again as he noticed the light again before it went dark.

That has to be them.

He kept his eyes transfixed on the area, waiting for someone to emerge from the surface. Another minute went by, then two. Still nothing.

Hawk sighed and shook his head in frustration. He decided

to get up and stretch his legs, but when he did, he felt a firm hand on his shoulder.

"Don't move another muscle," the man said in English.

Hawk froze. "It's about time."

The man walked in front of Hawk, a weapon trained on him. "Brady Hawk?"

"Are you cavalry?" Hawk asked with a wry grin.

"It sure seems that way, doesn't it?"

The man dropped his gun and offered his hand. "I'm Commander Wilson, and these are Lieutenants Jackson and Finch. Big Earv also told me to say hello."

Hawk furrowed his brow. "Big Earv brought you guys here?"

"This was a voluntary mission, totally off the books," Wilson said, handing a gun to Hawk. "It was all we could do to scrounge up three of us to go, so Big Earv is running the Russian shrimping boat ten miles off shore. He'll be ready to help extract us when it's time to go."

Hawk thanked Wilson for the weapon and then caught the team up to speed while they buried their scuba gear.

"Just how exactly do you intend to get the codes back?" Wilson asked. "I imagine the North Koreans have made several copies for safe keeping by now."

"Of course they have," Hawk said. "But what good are the codes on nuclear weapons that don't work?"

"So you want to sabotage the missiles?" Finch asked.

Hawk nodded. "At this point, that's our only option. And from what I understand, there were only two codes that the Russians were giving them."

"Those bastard commies," Jackson said. "They just want to start a war and then sit back and watch it all burn."

"Let's just make sure that doesn't happen," Wilson said. "So how do you see this going down?"

"If we're going to get out of here alive, we need to be as discreet as possible," Hawk said. "The harbor is teeming with guards. More arrived this morning, signaling that North Korea must be close to unleashing the weapon on the U.S. I don't think we can delay this operation at all."

"Fine with me," Jackson said. "The quicker we get out of here, the better."

"I think we all feel that way," Finch said.

Hawk offered a thin smile. "I know I am. But before we get back, we've got plenty of work to do. So, here's what I've got. I stole a van earlier tonight and switched out the plates. I doubt anyone will even notice it's gone, so we should have until the morning before that will raise any suspicion. I also have one uniform, which is enough since I'm the only one who'll be entering the area patrolled around the pier."

"So what's your plan of attack?" Wilson asked.

"I'll tell you on the way."

Hawk motioned for the team to follow him to the vehicle. However, just as they arrived at the van, he heard a stick snap in the distance.

"Everybody freeze."

All the men drew their weapons and moved around the side of a large rock, using it for cover. Another minute passed before any of the men said anything. Hawk was starting to question if he'd actually heard anything or if the sleep deprivation—and the events of the last seventy-two hours—had made him paranoid. He had more than his fair share of reasons to be on edge.

"Maybe it was nothing," Jackson said.

Hawk closed his eyes and listened. He was certain someone else was in the woods, though he couldn't be sure if it was a hostile. He shook his head.

"What?" Wilson asked.

"I don't know, but I think someone is out there," Hawk said.

"Could just be a couple of teenagers looking for a place to hook up," Jackson suggested. "This place is isolated enough that it'd make a great spot."

"I doubt it," Hawk said. "I've been here for hours and haven't heard even the slightest engine sound other than a few trawlers trying to beat the dusk curfew. Teenagers aren't that quiet either."

"American teenagers aren't," Finch said. "But maybe they are in North Korea."

"Let's stay here for a few minutes more, just to be sure," Wilson whispered.

Satisfied that no one was there, the team stepped out into the open and headed toward Hawk's van, first Wilson followed by Finch and Jackson. Hawk brought up the rear.

Before they knew what was going on, Wilson crumpled to the forest floor. Finch fell face forward on top of his commander. Jackson almost bowled Hawk over as he scrambled for cover. The two men moved through the darkness and took up a new position.

"Do you have any infrared goggles?" Hawk asked. "Because now would be a great time to use them."

Jackson reached into his ruck sack and pulled out a pair, using them to scan the area.

"Anything?" Hawk asked in a hushed tone.

Jackson shook his head subtly. A bullet pinged off the rock, sending both men diving to the ground for cover.

"Was anyone following you?" Hawk asked, putting out his hand for the binoculars.

"No," Jackson said, handing them to Hawk. "We were miles away from everyone. I don't think anyone would've been able to follow us underwater."

"Well, somebody knew where you were headed and sent a greeting party."

"They're not very friendly," Jackson said.

Another bullet whizzed overhead, taking a few branches with it.

"We need to split up," Hawk said. "Sticking together makes it easy for them to pin us down, whoever they are."

"Roger that."

Hawk stayed low, crouching as he moved around, utilizing

the trees for cover. He snatched Wilson's ruck sack off his back and kept moving. With Hawk's eyes adjusted to the darkness, he could make out a faint silhouette of Jackson darting away in the opposite direction.

When Hawk identified a good spot for a blind, he pulled out the binoculars and surveyed the area. He noticed a group of six seals, huddled together to undoubtedly plot their next move.

Hawk realized he wouldn't have a better chance than this to take them all out. He grabbed a grenade from Wilson's pack and hurled it in the direction of the men. One of the men shouted as the device exploded, sending shrapnel hurling in every direction. Hawk watched everyone scatter, except for two men, who laid facedown and appeared lifeless.

Hawk had reduced the deficit, but he was still in trouble being outnumbered two to one.

At least it isn't three to one anymore.

Hawk had lost track of some of the men. But one man looked very familiar. Hawk gasped as he double-checked the man's face. Despite the darkness, Doug Mitchell's neck tattoo was too distinct.

That's him all right. What the hell is he doing out here trying to kill us?

Hawk couldn't believe Mitchell would betray his country like he was. Throwing all caution to the wind, Hawk shouted into the night air.

"Mitchell, what are you doing?" Hawk asked. "We're on the same side."

Mitchell didn't respond with words, just his weapon. He fired a pair of shots toward Hawk's general vicinity.

Hawk prepared to fire when he heard gunshots coming from the direction of the boulder where the rest of the team had been hiding. For a moment, Hawk thought maybe either Wilson or Finch was still alive. But when he focused in on that direction, he saw Jackson collapse near the other two bodies.

Hawk cursed as he realized the implications of what had just happened.

Now the odds are worse — four to one.

Hawk peered through his binoculars and saw one man still struggling from the aftermath of the grenade. He fired at the man, a bullet striking him in the chest.

Getting better — three to one.

As Hawk was trying to figure out a way to reduce the odds even further, he heard a vehicle engine roaring toward their position. The men began to scatter deeper into the woods as headlights swept across the trees.

Hawk glanced at the three SEALs all lying within a few feet of one another. With the vehicle still rumbling toward their direction but close enough to make visual contact, Hawk sprinted toward the bodies to snag their gear. Without it, he had no chance of survival, let alone sabotaging the weapons.

Hawk dove down and worked frantically to pull the essential items from their ruck sacks and combined them into one pack. However, as he was going through a second bag, he felt a shot rip through his shoulder.

"See ya round, Hawk," a man shouted.

Hawk recognized Mitchell's voice and then blacked out.

CHAPTER
THIRTY-ONE

BRIDGER, MONTANA

VIKTOR KOMAROV HONED in on Alex Hawk's position. He watched as she held her son in her lap and read him a story. She smiled as she turned the pages, her face full of expressions even though the boy was fixated on the pictures inside.

Viktor had readily volunteered for this dangerous mission, though he thought it sounded rather simple. While he specialized in assassinations, he didn't care for them as much as some of Andrei Orlovsky's other men. However, this mission was personal.

Komarov moved quickly across the mountainside, scrambling over boulders and gliding across fallen trees spanning cold water creeks. The most recent snow had been a few days ago, but a recent stretch of sunshine had melted most everything but the places shrouded by heavy shadows. He was careful to avoid muddy or snowy patches so he wouldn't leave behind any trace of his presence there.

Komarov noticed a pair of guards patrolling the perimeter of the home. He'd seen two other men near the gate leading up to the property, but they were easy to slip past in a wide open landscape. However, the two men lurking along the porch, one in the front and the other in the back, created a challenge.

An owl hooted overhead in a pine tree near the edge of the fence where a pair of horses galloped in circles. Viktor remained calm and assessed how he would kill the woman. He hadn't decided if he was going to kill the boy. Letting him grow up without a mother was cruel, something he knew firsthand when he lost his mom during a mafia hit in the marketplace that went south.

Now, Komarov had lost a brother at the hands of a U.S. operative named Brady Hawk. The American had somehow thrown his brother off the side of a cliff. He was the last living relative Komarov had. He'd endured unimaginable pain in his life, but his brother Dima had helped him get through all the suffering, there when nobody else was. But there was nobody to help Viktor get past the death of Dima. Viktor felt abandoned in the world and he couldn't suppress his rage any longer.

Since the death of his mother, Viktor had exacted revenge on every loved one who'd been killed, either violently or senselessly. He was going to make sure Brady Hawk would feel the pain in the deepest of ways.

Viktor focused his binoculars on Alex still sitting with her son. For a moment, Viktor contemplated how traumatic it would be for the little boy to be cuddled up with his mother reading a book only to have her head explode all over him. While Viktor smiled at the thought, he resisted the urge.

No, this has to be more personal.

He smiled again as he moved closer toward the house.

CHAPTER
THIRTY-TWO

SONBONG, NORTH KOREA

HAWK OPENED HIS EYES, trying to focus as his head bounced in rhythm with the bumps in the road. The low hum of tires beneath him clued him in that he was riding in the bed of a military transport truck. As he moved, he winced from the pain in his shoulder, which was still bleeding. He scanned the back and didn't see any soldiers. Instead, there was just a mass of tangled bodies, arms and feet intertwined.

Hawk sucked a breath through his teeth as he freed himself from the weight of the other soldiers. He reached out and closed Wilson's eyes, his blank stare haunting Hawk. The three brave SEALs who'd volunteered for the mission were all dead, and Hawk wanted to know how it had happened. The leak had to happen somewhere between the time the Magnum office received his call for help and the SEALs unit stationed in the Pacific was contacted. And it angered Hawk. Three patriots died needlessly because of a mole. But what made Hawk angrier was the fact that Doug Mitchell, more commonly known as the Reaper, had led such a mission against his own countrymen.

However, Hawk didn't have time to ponder that at the moment. He had a nuclear warhead to sabotage.

Hawk groped around until he found the ruck sack he'd been stuffing before the Reaper took him out with a shoulder shot. Inside, Hawk found all the tools he needed to wreak havoc on Kim Yong-ju's plans to strike America, including a device designed by Dr. Z with his trademarked logo on it. Hawk smiled as he pocketed the gadget, looking forward to talking with Dr. Z more upon returning to the U.S.

Once Hawk strapped the pack onto his back, he crawled near the edge of the bed and waited for the truck to slow down. After a minute, the driver hit the brakes for a sharp curve. When he did, Hawk seized his chance to bail out. He rolled over the side, staggering to avoid falling on his shoulder. He hustled over into the bushes off the side of the road and dressed his wound.

Once he was finished, Hawk used the phone in his pack to let the Magnum office know what had happened. After he left a message filling them in, he stayed in the shadows as he headed back toward the Sonbong docks. He walked for a half-hour before he found the shore line. The rest of the trip back toward the military harbor was uneventful with the exception of a few sweeping headlights that sent him rushing toward the nearest clump of bushes or trees to hide. But the vehicles came and passed without incident.

When Hawk reached the docks, he found a place where he could change into the North Korean uniform he'd stolen earlier. Tugging his hat low across his forehead, Hawk marched down to the docks, nodding at the guard as he confidently strode toward him. The guard acknowledged Hawk with a slight head bob and swung open the gate.

Hawk entered the secure area and began his search for the warheads. As far as he knew, there were only two warheads with nuclear capability. His job was relatively simple—permanently disarm them.

He moved into the interior and found one guard patrolling

the area. Hawk slipped up behind the man and broke his neck. Hawk found a sandbag nearby and attached it to the man's body with a rope before dropping him into the water just off the dock. Then Hawk spied another guard strolling past two missiles, which were still situated on a transport truck.

Affixing a silencer to the end of his weapon, Hawk shot the man at point blank and then stuffed him into a locker in the corner.

With the room clear, Hawk didn't want to waste any time. He scaled the truck and started to disarm the weapon. Following instructions that were in a mission packet on Commander Wilson's phone, Hawk rendered the two missiles toothless in just under fifteen minutes. He fried the motherboard, meaning that the codes wouldn't arm the devices. And as a result, they'd never detonate. Hawk knew North Korea didn't have the expertise in handling the weapons and would see them as useless.

Using Dr. Z's device, Hawk altered the navigational controls on the missile. Then he stripped a handful of wires out, rendering the nuclear capability of the weapon inoperable. If the North Koreans thought that Russia sold them a bill of goods, it'd be even better for the U.S. interests. Putting two of America's biggest enemies at each other's throats was little more than a pipe dream in Washington. But it'd become a reality when Kim Yong-ju ordered the missile strike, and the military would launch a dud. Accusations would fly and Russia would be blamed for the failure.

When Hawk finished, he pulled his cap down low across his brow again and walked toward the gate to exit the facility. His heart was pounding as he approached the guard.

Right as Hawk passed through the exit, a man shouted for him. Hawk stopped and turned around.

"Is your shift up so soon?" the soldier asked in Korean.

Hawk glanced down and saw blood leaking through his uniform. Thinking quickly, he feigned a cough and answered in his best Korean with a gravelly voice. "I don't feel well. I think I have a virus."

The man waved dismissively at Hawk, who put his head down and trudged away.

When he reached a safe distance from the harbor, Hawk found a back alley where he could change. He then hiked in the direction of the most eastern point of the Sonbong harbor. Once he was back in the woods, he pulled out the commander's phone and dialed the number demarcated as Big Earv.

Hawk waited as the phone rang. After the sixth ring, the call went to voicemail. Hawk cursed under his breath before sitting down on a rock. Until Big Earv called him back, Hawk was stranded.

He paced around to pass the time, but that only made him more nervous. Any minute, the woods could be crawling again with North Korean soldiers. If Hawk stayed hidden, it wouldn't be an issue. He couldn't help but think about Alex.

He took a breath and pulled out his phone, checking it again to see if Big Earv had called him.

Still nothing.

The sun started to rise across the water, increasing the difficulty for Hawk's escape across the water. He decided to call Alex and let her know that he'd at least succeeded. And he also wanted to find out how she was doing.

But when he called her, she didn't answer.

CHAPTER
THIRTY-THREE

BRIDGER, MONTANA

ALEX SPLASHED WARM WATER on her face after brushing her teeth. She squinted before taking a moment to study herself more closely, her green eyes unable to mask the redness in them. She'd cried more in the time since Hawk left than she did at any other point in her marriage. The stress of him leaving was heavy. But if she was honest, she was torn.

Raising John Daniel was tough, so much so that on most days she considered tracking terrorists all over the globe with her life on the line to be an easier task. She took a deep breath before tying her hair up in a messy bun. She walked past John Daniel's room before stopping and peeking inside. For a moment, she lingered in the doorway, watching him sleep peacefully.

Maybe it's not so bad.

Alex couldn't help but sense an enormous amount of guilt just for feeling that way.

Surely no other mother feels this way about her own children.

But she wanted to get back in the game. And even though she wasn't playing a pivotal role in Hawk's mission, she craved the action, the intensity, the adrenaline rush that accompanied being within minutes of thousands of innocent people dying before your team stops it. The pros far outweighed the cons, and she wanted back in. But how?

John Daniel required constant attention. He'd be starting school in the upcoming fall, but could she really handle the rigors of hunting terrorists and exposing conspiracies against the U.S. government in between PTA meetings, feeding the horses, and helping John Daniel with his homework every night? She wasn't sure she could, but she was willing to try.

However, she hadn't yet expressed to Hawk her desire to return to the field, who had repeatedly shared how happy he was with their new lifestyle. Yet part of Alex remained empty.

She closed the door to John Daniel's room and walked down the hall, determining to tell him upon his return.

Alex ambled into the kitchen, where she picked up the radio and tried to raise the security team patrolling her property.

"Kyle? Xander? How are things looking out there?" she asked.

A few seconds passed and there was no answer.

"Kyle? Xander? Don't play games with me, gentlemen."

She breathed a sigh of relief when she heard Kyle's smooth voice emanate from the speaker.

"We're both here," Kyle said. "In fact, I'm looking at Xander right now."

"How come he can't answer me himself?" she asked as she heated up a kettle to make some tea.

Kyle chuckled. "He's taking a leak."

She giggled and shook her head. "When I check in and ask for a status update, whether your bladder is full or not or even in the process of being drained isn't something I care to know."

"Sorry, ma'am," Kyle said. "Just trying to remain open and transparent for everyone."

"It's just a bit much," she said.

"Roger that."

"I'm going to bed," she said. "You two have a nice night."

Alex took the kettle off the burner as it started to whistle and poured the water into a mug. She dunked the tea bag inside and turned off the burner. After shuttering all the blinds around the house, she shuffled back to her room.

She grabbed a book to read and then eased into her bed, covering herself with satin sheets. Hawk hated sleeping on them, complaining about how he slipped around all night and one time slid completely off the side. But she loved the sheets. And with him gone, she pulled them out again.

She lit a candle and started reading a book in her favorite Clive Cussler series. She sped through the pages, the tension losing some of its bite for someone who'd been through far more hair-raising adventures than Dirk Pitt. However, she was thankful that she wasn't stuck in the cold like Dirk, mushing across the Arctic.

She stopped and glanced at the gas fireplace in the corner of the room. A faint smile spread across her face as the flames danced behind the glass. Everything was as it should be—except for Hawk. She needed him propped up in the bed next to her while he thumbed through a gun magazine.

A half-hour passed and she started to get sleepy. She finished the rest of her tea before returning the mug to the kitchen sink.

As she did, she heard a creak in the floorboard and darted down the hall to look for John Daniel.

"John Daniel?" she called out in a hushed tone. "John Daniel?"

She was almost at his door and then just went all the way in and peeked in on him.

"Are you awake?" she asked.

"I had to pee-pee, Mommy," he said.

"That's fine, sweetie. You go back to sleep now."

"Okay."

She closed the door, upset at herself for feeling the urge to peek inside. That brief conversation could've awakened him enough that it would be hours before he would go back to sleep.

In five more minutes, she expected to hear more pitter-patters coming down the hallway toward her room.

Alex checked all the doors one final time before heading off to bed. Just as she was about to close the door, she heard the floorboard creak again. She sighed, exasperated that she'd disturbed him so, unsure if she'd get any sleep herself. Not that it'd matter since she hadn't slept well since Hawk left.

She ventured into the hall and made a straight line for John Daniel's room. When she got there, she whispered to him.

"John Daniel, were you in the hall just now?"

He didn't answer. He didn't even stir.

Alex growled as she marched to the kitchen to check in on Kyle and Xander. Using the small device placed on the corner of the counter, she made the outdoor cameras scan around the property where the two guards were supposed to be.

"Kyle? Xander?"

No response. And in the darkness, she couldn't see either of them. She fiddled with the camera for a moment until she switched the image to night mode. A grainy black and white picture appeared. The only things moving were branches swaying with the wind.

"Kyle? Xander? Are either of you there? I hope you're both not taking a leak this time."

She waited a little bit longer, but still nothing.

Her heart began to pound in her chest when she heard another creak, this time coming from the direction of the living room.

CHAPTER
THIRTY-FOUR

SONBONG, NORTH KOREA

HAWK PASSED the time by redressing his wounds. With everything that was at stake, he functioned on adrenaline, almost oblivious to the pain. But now he could feel every little inch of pain spreading throughout his shoulder. He cleaned the blood around the edge of the entry point and used a phone to take a picture of the back of his shoulder.

Hawk studied the image before pondering what had happened earlier with the ambush. The Reaper had an American flag tattoo that spanned his entire back and another one with the first few lines of the Constitution on his right bicep. If he wasn't a dyed-in-the-wool American, he was definitely an American dipped in red, white, and blue ink.

A foolish man would've thought he was lucky, but Hawk knew better. If the Reaper had wanted to kill Hawk, he'd be dead. But he was alive. *Why* was the question haunting Hawk. Was their brief relationship while serving with the SEALs enough to avoid a kill shot? But then why did the Reaper's team kill everyone else?

However, even more perplexing to Hawk was why the

Reaper was even there? Who told him? And why would they want to stop North Korea from obtaining a nuclear weapon?

Hawk's mind was spinning, trying to conceive a hypothesis for everything. The diversion was a welcome one, anything to keep him from worrying about Alex.

With the sun rising higher on the horizon, Hawk gathered his pack and scurried deeper into the woods. He maintained visual with the water but also found a spot where he could remain out of plain view in case any patrols revisited the area.

Hawk picked up a cell phone and dialed Alex's number again. Still no answer. He checked his watch and realized how late it was. If he woke her, he'd feel guilty, but he was desperate to hear that she and John Daniel were still safe. But it didn't matter. He told himself that they were both probably sleeping soundly and not to be concerned about it.

Hawk was lost in thought when he heard a voice that startled him. He turned slowly and looked behind him but didn't see anyone.

"Hawk, it's me," a man said.

Hawk peered through the woods, trying to locate the figure.

"Over here," the voice from Hawk's left.

He turned and saw a familiar face. "Big Earv, boy, am I glad to see you."

"I got your message, and I got here as soon as I could," Big Earv said. "I had to swim to shore, which took quite a bit of time. Did you finish the mission?"

Hawk nodded. "It was easy with this shoulder."

Big Earv scowled as he eyed the area Hawk pointed to. "What happened there?"

"Friendly fire, in a manner of speaking."

Big Earv scanned the area. "Where's the rest of the team I brought?"

"Dead," Hawk said. "We were ambushed."

"The North Koreans knew they were coming?"

Hawk shook his head. "Someone else did. And before you

ask me who, I can only tell you that it was a group of mercenaries—at least that's what I hope it is."

"Americans?"

"Yeah."

Big Earv stroked his chin. "Did you know any of them?"

Hawk held up his index finger. "One guy. A former Navy SEAL buddy."

"There was a Navy SEAL involved?"

"I'm guessing they were all Navy SEALs, but I didn't get a good look at some of the other men. There was only one I recognized."

Big Earv's eyebrows shot upward. "You recognized one?"

"Yeah, a guy named Doug Mitchell, who we all called the Reaper."

"Did he say anything to you?"

Hawk glanced at his shoulder. "He did this to me, which I've been trying to figure out why he didn't aim for my head. Because if he misses, it's only because he wants to."

"What happened exactly?"

"When Wilson got here with the team, we were ambushed almost immediately. Before I knew it, all three members of the team were dead. I probably would've been too had the North Korean military not rolled up on us. As they were coming into the area, the Reaper took one final shot, a clean one through my shoulder."

"You think you can swim out to the boat?" Big Earv asked. "We'll have to lay low until dark to do it, but it's anchored out there."

"Don't have to," Hawk said as he nodded toward a spot of fresh dirt piled up a few meters away. "The SEAL team buried their gear there, including their diver propulsion gear. All I have to do is hold on."

Big Earv squinted as he studied Hawk's shoulder. "From the looks of things, that might be a challenge, too."

"I can make it," Hawk said. "Just help me dig these out and

we'll be out of here before you know it."

The two men uncovered the gear from one of the SEALs before heading down to the water. Hawk squeezed into a wet suit, while Big Earv, who was already wearing one, prepped the rest of the gear.

"Accounting for the current, I think we'll be able to get to the boat in about twenty minutes as long as we don't run into any trouble," Big Earv said.

"Adding that qualifier doesn't make me feel any better," Hawk said as he shook his head slowly. "You know you've just jinxed us, right?"

Hawk and Big Earv hustled into the water and took off for the latter's boat. After arriving at the boat without incident, Big Earv raised the anchor and turned eastward into the Sea of Japan.

Hawk relaxed below deck in the small galley. He used Big Earv's cell phone to try to contact Alex. The phone rang again, but she didn't answer.

It was late, but he knew she'd be waiting for another call from him.

Where is she?

CHAPTER
THIRTY-FIVE

BRIDGER, MONTANA

ALEX JUMPED when she heard the voice coming from the living room.

"Mommy, I'm thirsty," said John Daniel, standing in the living room clutching his stuffed dragon. "Can I have something to drink?"

She put her hand on her chest and exhaled. "Oh, of course, buddy."

He shuffled across the room in his onesie pajama before latching onto her hand. "I miss Daddy."

"Me too," she said. "But he'll be home before you know it."

She pulled a cup out of the cabinet, filled it halfway up with water, and then screwed the lid on tight. "Let's get you back in the bed, okay?"

As Alex led John Daniel down the hall to his bedroom, he gulped down his drink. Then she tucked him in before kissing him on the forehead.

"Sweet dreams, little man," she said.

His eyes were already closed before she left the room, lingering just a while longer at the doorway to enjoy a peaceful moment. She welcomed the distraction from the angst she'd briefly shoved to the back of her mind. The two guards patrolling her property had yet to respond, and she was still concerned.

After she closed the door, she glanced down the hallway and saw one of his rideable metal fire trucks sitting in the entryway. She sighed, aggravated over how John Daniel was a Tasmanian devil, whirling around the house and leaving messes in his wake. However, she stopped short and froze when she heard the floorboards creak again. And this time, she knew it wasn't John Daniel.

She swallowed hard as she turned around, peering through the shadows to try and make out a silhouetted figure. At first, she didn't see anything. She crouched low and moved toward the entryway that gave her multiple exit routes. If she needed to, she could run upstairs or in any direction on the first floor. More than anything, she wanted to make sure whoever was in her house wasn't going to nab John Daniel.

Acting instinctively, she reached for her gun. But she'd put it away after getting ready for bed.

She glanced down the hall leading to John Daniel's room, but didn't see any movement.

Despite being hyperaware of her surroundings, she almost didn't see the man coming until it was too late. Light glinted off the blade in his hand as he lunged toward her.

With her back to the bannister, Alex dropped to the ground and rolled away, ending up at the foot of the stairs. Her options for escape had suddenly shrunk to one. She darted up the stairs, the assailant right on her heels.

On the final step at the top of the stairs, the man grabbed her ankle. Alex tripped on the landing, making her vulnerable for a few seconds. She scrambled to get away, but his arms wrapped around her legs, tackling her face first to the floor again.

Alex kicked and squirmed as the man turned her on her back. She wanted to scream, but if she was going to die like this, she wanted to spare John Daniel the horror of seeing his mother murdered.

"Your husband threw my brother off a cliff," the man said in a clipped Russian accent. "Now, I'm going to return the favor."

He pinned Alex's arms to the floor as he straddled her. She felt the cold steel from the flat side of the blade pressed against her wrist.

I'm not going to die like this.

She appealed to her attacker's ego. "A real man wouldn't need to fight so unfairly."

"You think this is unfair?" he asked. "Fair or not, it's going to end up the same way for you."

"Like hell it will," she said.

As he loosened his grip on her arms to reposition himself, Alex yanked one arm free. As he rushed to pin both her hands down again, she punched him in the throat. He released her other arm as he clutched his neck. Alex hit him in the face with a forearm as he tumbled off of her.

With the knife still firmly in his hand, he jumped to his feet, keeping himself between Alex and the stairs.

Alex's mind whirred as she considered her next move. Her inability to get downstairs without getting stabbed reduced her options to jumping out of a window, though she doubted she had time to get out.

"If you're waiting for your friends outside, they won't be coming," the Russian said. "I took care of them earlier with a bullet to the head."

She scowled, still dancing from one side to the other as the man inched closer to her. "You shot them but you want to stab me? Seems like you're not very good at your job."

"I wanted you to know why you're going to die," he said. "Plus, I have some other plans for us."

Alex decided to keep the man talking, buying her more time to think of a way to escape the situation.

"If you're wanting to go get drinks, you've got a funny way of inviting a woman out," she said.

"You think you're funny," the man said with a growl. "But you're not. I'm going to make you pay with your life."

Alex could tell her goading was starting to irritate the man.

If I just make him mad enough ...

Alex cocked her head to one side and squinted. "What did you say? I couldn't hear that last part. Maybe it's something in your throat?"

She gestured toward her neck and smirked. And that was all she needed to enrage the man.

The Russian rushed toward Alex, who'd danced around so that her back was to the bannister. He held the knife out as he moved toward her. Alex knew she couldn't take the man in a fight, but she could use his size against him.

As he drew nearer, Alex slid aside and grabbed the man's wrist to protect herself from the blade. Then she used his momentum to propel him forward and over the railing. He made contact with it just below his waist, sending him tumbling over the edge. He shouted as he fell.

But he fell quiet when he hit the ground, a sickening crack echoing off the walls. She hustled down the steps as he lay motionless. After retrieving her gun from her bedroom, she returned to the entryway to find the Russian lying in a pool of blood. He tried to say something, but he couldn't get the words out. Alex wasn't sure what had ultimately caused his head wound—the marble floor or John Daniel's fire truck. The Russian struggled to say something while life drained right out of him.

"I'm sorry," Alex said as she pointed to her ear. "I can't hear you nor do I care. You were warned."

The man slowly moved his hand into his jacket pocket.

"That's far enough," Alex said.

He spit at her. "Do you really want to do this in front of your son?"

Alex held his gaze, unsure if he was bluffing. She hadn't noticed if John Daniel had entered the entryway, but she knew better than to even look. With her eyes fixed on the Russian, she moved around the room, blocking any view John Daniel might have if he were to wander out.

"Revenge is rarely satisfying, provided you actually get it," she said. "Farewell, comrade."

She pulled the trigger, hitting him in the head. He collapsed, his eyes staring vacantly into the darkness.

Alex reached into his pocket and took his gun. She felt for a pulse but didn't find one.

The radio crackled from the kitchen, arresting Alex's attention. She rushed over to it, recognizing Kyle's voice.

"Kyle, are you okay?" Alex asked.

"I'm fine, but what about you? I thought I just heard a gunshot."

"I had a visitor," she said. "And I'm gonna need you and Xander to come down here right now and give me a hand getting this mess cleaned up."

"That bad, huh? Was it a raccoon getting into your trash?"

She sighed, realizing that he was completely unaware of what had just happened. "No, just a Russian."

"A what?"

"Just get down here and help me with this."

While waiting for Kyle and Xander, she peeked in on John Daniel again. He was still fast asleep.

"Thank God," she whispered to herself.

She went into her bedroom to grab a housecoat when she saw a notification on her phone. It was from a number she didn't recognize, but she saw there was also a voicemail. Certain the message wasn't someone trying to sell her an extended auto warranty, she listened and immediately dialed the number back.

"I'm okay," Alex said as Hawk answered.

"Thank goodness," he said. "But did you get a visit from one of Orlovsky's men?"

"Yeah," she said. "He eventually came around the property."

"And?"

"He's dead."

Hawk paused. "Did you kill him?"

"In a manner of speaking," she said. "I more or less helped him to his death by tossing him over the upstairs balcony."

"Orlovsky has to think you're dead or he's going to keep coming around."

"I've already been thinking about how I'm going to stage the picture of my death before I send the confirmation image back to Orlovsky."

Hawk chuckled. "I should've known better than to even suggest that to you. Of course you're already on it."

"And based off your voicemail, you're all right too, aren't you?"

"Big Earv and I made it out, but there's still more work to do."

"Like what?"

"We need to hunt down whoever's leaking sensitive information. Three Navy SEALs are dead as a result, and if we hadn't gotten a little lucky, we would've missed our chance to sabotage the nuclear warheads."

"Well, I'm glad I didn't know about everything as it was happening," she said. "I've at least been sleeping some of the night."

Hawk waited a moment before responding. "I need you, Alex."

"What exactly do you mean by that?"

"I mean, if I'm going to do this, I need you helping me."

"So you want to keep working for Magnum?"

"I do, but I know how you feel about it. Can we at least talk about it when I get back?"

"Sure. We can have a conversation," she said. "But right now, I've got a dead body to clean up. And I need to let Morgan know what went down here tonight."

"Of course," Hawk said. "See you soon."

Alex dialed Morgan's number, waking her in the middle of the night.

"What is it?" Morgan asked groggily.

"We've got a mess out here at our ranch, and we're going to need some help covering it up."

CHAPTER
THIRTY-SIX

LOS ANGELES

A WEEK LATER, Hawk and Alex joined the Magnum team in their underground headquarters to discuss the operation as well as the fallout from North Korea's attempted launch of nuclear weapons. Despite the attempt by rogue actors within the U.S. military to provoke North Korea by going beyond what President Norris commanded, the tensions seemed to ease. All U.S. Naval ships had returned to their usual patrolling routes, and Kim Yong-ju was no longer rattling his saber, undoubtedly humbled by his failed attempt to strike at the U.S.

Hawk wore a sling to help with his recovery, though he only used it due to Alex's insistence that he did. He received a raucous ovation when he entered the conference room with Alex.

"Please," Hawk said, holding up his good arm, "this isn't necessary. I was just doing my job, which happened to be something completely different than what I was supposed to do."

As the clapping subsided, Hawk and Alex found a pair of empty seats located next to Morgan, who was seated at the head of the table.

"I can't thank the two of you enough for what you did for this country," Morgan said. "If my uncle knew what you did, he'd be proud of you."

"He's probably chewing on a cigar right now and fishing," Hawk said. "I doubt he even knows how closely we came to war."

"It's just as well that he didn't," Alex added. "If he thought the world was this tenuous, he'd come out of retirement and kick you out of your chair, Morgan."

Morgan offered a thin smile. "He'd have a tough time moving me from here."

Hawk was certain that she meant that too. Magnum was her show, her fingerprints all over it. The thought of J.D. Blunt returning to his post was enough to make Morgan's good-natured self vanish, if only for a moment.

Morgan clasped her fingers together, resting them on the table in front of her. "I'd like to start off by saying that I'm grateful for every single one of you today. This was a total team effort that required us all to be at the top of our games in order to succeed. Dr. Z's inventions, Mia's hacking skills, Big Earv's bravery in piloting a boat into enemy waters with no way out, Alex's help with another semi-related project, and of course Hawk's ability to adapt on the fly and stop an imminent attack on the U.S. that would've undoubtedly killed hundreds of thousands of innocent Americans. Whether you were analyzing data, developing operational tools, or doing the heavy lifting out in the field, you all contributed to Magnum's success."

"Only we didn't get Eddie Tyson home," Hawk said. "That was the primary objective."

"But it doesn't matter," Morgan said. "The fact that we prevented a war should be good enough for you, Hawk."

He sighed. "It is, but I can't stop thinking about Tyson and his young son who needs him. He's stuck in a North Korean prison somewhere, being treated like garbage. We can't just leave him there. If it hadn't been for him, we'd likely already be at war."

"We can't just go into North Korea on a reconnaissance mission," Morgan said. "We have to get word from someone about where he might be before I authorize an extraction team."

Hawk slapped the table with an open palm. "It shouldn't be that way. We can't treat people who've sacrificed everything for their country like this."

Morgan's eyes widened as she cocked her head to one side. "We'll go back for him when we can. In the meantime, we've got plenty of other unresolved issues going on here."

"I'd say everything looks resolved to me," Big Earv said with a chuckle. "North Korea is blaming Russia for sabotaging their warheads, which you have to admit was hilarious when one of them changed course and took out an entire aircraft carrier."

Mia giggled. "That was me."

"And using a device I designed," Dr. Z said with a grin.

The two bumped fists as Big Earv continued.

"Apparently, all those Navy SEALs that Hawk ran into were wearing FSB gear and had fake Russian names and passports."

Mia shifted in her chair as she started typing on her laptop. "Hawk, are you sure they were Navy SEALs?"

Hawk nodded. "Sure as I'm sitting here. The Reaper has too many unique tattoos. And I ought to know since I stared at them half the night during our training. He slept on the bunk next to me and snored louder than a freight train. Now that I think back about it, it's truly amazing I ever got any sleep around that man."

"Well, if you're that sure, would you be willing to visit him?" Mia said.

The Magnum team stared at Mia in disbelief.

"You found him?" Morgan asked.

Mia nodded and smiled. "And he's not that far away either."

"Let's go get him," Hawk said.

Alex glanced at him. "You're not in any condition to go bring the Reaper in."

"I don't have to do it by myself. Besides," he said, shirking off the sling, "this thing's just for show anyway."

"Excellent," Morgan said. "Hawk, Big Earv—I need the two of you to put together an operational plan and have it on my desk by the end of the day."

"Roger that," Hawk said.

"We'll handle it, ma'am," Big Earv said with a wink.

As the team started to file out of the room, Morgan remained in her seat. She grabbed Hawk's arm and told him and Alex to remain behind. She repeated the order to Mia.

When only the four of them remained, Morgan stood. "I think we all know how unnerving it is that someone leaked information about our operation to someone that paid a rogue team of mercenaries to kill their own countrymen. I don't know who's behind this, but I want you guys to figure it out for me. Hawk, you've got an expansive knowledge of potential suspects. Mia, you have the technical skills to trace a digital leak. And Alex, you've got the kind of analyst skills that, quite frankly, are missing at this organization. I think the three of you can figure this out on your own. Agree?"

They all nodded.

"If you decide to loop anyone else in on your investigation, please notify me," Morgan said. "That's all."

"We won't let you down," Hawk said.

"I know you won't," she said, patting Hawk on his wounded arm before leaving the room.

Mia sighed and shook her head. "As if things weren't stressful enough already …"

"Well, why don't you both join the field team? Getting out might do you both some good."

Alex's face lit up. "My aunt and uncle can handle John Daniel for a few extra days."

"That works for me," Mia said. "I'll also send you an idea I have."

"Oh?"

"Yeah," she said, nodding. "I think I know how we can draw him out."

"We?" Hawk asked. "So you think you're fit for field duty again? As I recall, it's been a while."

Mia grinned. "I'll be fine. Besides, I wouldn't miss a trip to the Dominican for the world."

CHAPTER
THIRTY-SEVEN

PUNTA CANA, DOMINICAN REPUBLIC

FROM A SECOND-STORY BALCONY, Hawk peered through a pair of high-tech sunglasses Dr. Z had designed, scanning the poolside at the Zoetry Agua resort on the water. Aside from blocking UV rays and providing a darkened field of vision, Dr. Z's patented Sunglazzes enabled Hawk to run facial recognition searches on anyone in his line of sight. All he had to do was look straight-on at a person. Then the micro-processors embedded in the frames would analyze the person's face and alert Hawk if they were in the database. The technology was especially helpful when trying to identify someone who was good at changing their look to hide in plain sight.

Near the south end of the pool, a man jammed on his guitar joined by the rest of his steel drum band. A group of bikini-clad women swayed to the music, careful not to spill their margaritas. Hawk's glasses didn't identify anyone among the group in the database. He checked a few people relaxing on the steps leading into the water. Still nothing.

"Are you sure he's here?" Hawk asked into the coms.

"I got confirmation a half-hour ago when he showed up on the hotel's security feed," Mia said. "He's here all right."

"Maybe he's in his room," Hawk suggested.

"No, he was just leaving his room when he was spotted on camera. The image was black and white, but he appeared to be in a solid-colored bathing suit, which I would guess is a bright color."

"So, what am I looking for?" Hawk asked. "A neon green or bright orange trunks?"

"Something like that," Mia said.

"You're going to have to walk down there," Mia said. "It's the only way."

"Why don't we give Dr. Gizmo's gadget to Alex?" Hawk asked. "I'm sure she will turn enough heads to get men to look at her straight on."

"I can't blow my cover," Alex chimed in on the coms. "I need to remain out of sight until the operation begins."

"Oh, Alex, I didn't know you were listening in," Hawk said.

Alex chuckled. "Now, you're just trying to score brownie points."

"Either way, you've gotta admit that Hawk's smooth," Mia said.

"Yeah, I guess he's all right," Alex said. "I might keep him."

"Just put your disguise on and go down there," Mia said. "I want full confirmation that he's still on site before we commence."

"Roger that," Hawk said.

He ambled into the closet and put on a faded t-shirt and flip-flops. Hawk tucked a sun hat low across his brow and shuffled downstairs. After wandering around for a few minutes, he bought a drink from the Tiki hut near the water and strolled casually around the pool. He searched for someone wearing a pair of brightly-colored trunks, but none of them even came close to matching the Reaper's physique. His bulging biceps and thick neck would make it almost impossible to hide for very long, but Hawk struggled to identify the man.

After fifteen minutes, Hawk spotted a man sprawled out on a lounge chair near the band. He was lying on his back, his hat strategically positioned over his face and his arms crossed over his midsection. He wore a pair of neon green board shorts.

"I think I see him," Hawk said, his lips moving imperceptibly.

"What do Dr. Z's Sunglazzes say?" Mia asked.

"I can't confirm anything because he won't take that damn hat off his face," Hawk said. "And I have no idea how long he's going to remain in that position."

"Just keep watching him," Mia said.

"Or maybe buy him a drink and have it sent over," Alex suggested.

"See, this is why you need to be down here instead of me," Hawk said.

Hawk asked a woman if she'd buy a drink and have it sent over to the man he suspected was the Reaper. He handed her a fifty-dollar bill, telling her she could keep the change. She readily agreed.

"If you want to impress him, send him a Long Island iced tea," Hawk said. "It's his favorite."

The woman smiled and walked over to the bar to order. A couple of minutes later, the Reaper sat up, curious about why a poolside server was giving him a drink. With his face visible, Hawk's glasses confirmed the Reaper's identity.

"It's a match," Hawk said. "That's him."

"Good," Mia said. "Hawk, fall back so we can prepare for the next phase of the operation."

"Roger that," Hawk said before returning to his hotel room.

———

DOUG MITCHELL CLOSED his eyes, soaking in the warm sunshine. Visiting North Korea and Russia in the winter chilled him to the bone, and he needed to thaw out. He drained the last bit of his Long Island iced tea, resisting his curiosity to find out who sent him the drink. As a mercenary, he didn't have time for distractions like relationships. From the moment he joined the Navy SEALs, he decided that his lifestyle wouldn't be conducive to any long-term relationship, especially since it wouldn't be fair to whoever he was involved with.

He ran his fingers across the tattoo spanning the width of his collarbones. "Freedom cannot be bestowed—it must be achieved" read the tattooed message overlaid on a colorful American eagle. He was drunk and considered himself naive when he entered the tattoo parlor at age 18 to get the artwork inscribed. It served as a reminder to him of his past. Years of battle had jaded him. He no longer believed the words on his chest, nor did he care much for the idea of patriotism. The only person he was loyal to was himself.

Glancing at his forearm, he smiled as he saw the tattoo of the Grim Reaper. He once completed seven successful assassination missions in a three-month span, hitting one target right between the eyes from more than a thousand meters away on a blustery day. In a matter of days, Mitchell's exploits became legendary within the SEALs, which was almost unprecedented. As elite soldiers, rarely were they impressed with anything anyone else did. But Mitchell achieved god-like status, which also earned him the Reaper nickname.

He visited the Zoetry Agua so often that he could get a room whenever he wanted, even if the resort was listed as full. Whenever he completed his latest assignment, he'd retreat to the Caribbean. He felt safe there. And despite his nomadic existence, it felt like home, too.

Mitchell felt free, though he knew that wasn't entirely the case. If he turned down an assignment, there would be questions. And questions were never a good thing, especially from the people he was working for.

His phone buzzed with a text message, alerting him to the arrival of an urgent email.

He recognized the number and navigated on his cell phone to his email.

"On your last mission, you were exposed to a new strand of the Kabalo virus. Please call back for instructions on how to proceed."

Mitchell cursed under his breath as he got up. He'd rather suffer a bullet wound than get the Kabalo virus, though he wasn't fond of needles either. He ordered another drink on his way back to his room, draining it before reached the door. After he collapsed into the chair in the corner, he dialed the number.

IN THE WEEK following Hawk's encounter with Reaper in Sonbong, Mia had hacked into his cell phone and combed through voice messages. She worked with Dr. Z to tweak a voice simulator for Reaper's contact. And she also placed malware on his phone that, when activated, would direct outgoing calls to the number of her choosing.

When Mia's phone rang, she took a deep breath and then initiated the voice simulator.

"This is control," she said after answering. "Please identify yourself."

Reaper recited a string of numbers.

"Thank you," she said. "Now, what can I help you with today?"

"I received an email to contact you about what to do next following my exposure to the Kabalo virus."

"Of course. Thank you for responding so quickly. Based on the length of your exposure, you need to receive treatment immediately."

"And if I don't?"

"You could suffer a severe illness or even death."

"It'd be one helluva way for me to go," Reaper said with a chuckle. "I get pinned down in tight spots all over the world facing enormous amounts of fire power, battling some of the most well-trained soldiers in various militaries, and it's a stupid little bug I can't see that gets me."

"It doesn't have to be that way. We very much value you in our organization, so we've deployed a medical team to your location to administer your treatment. Do you have a pen handy?"

"Give me a second," Reaper said, the line going silent for a brief moment. "All right lay it on me."

Mia read off the address for the clinic before continuing. "Report to that location in one hour to receive your treatment. Use the passcode 'freedom isn't free' to gain entry. Any other questions?"

Reaper sighed. "No, I think that's pretty self-explanatory."

"Excellent," Mia said. "Good luck."

She ended the call and then exhaled.

"Great work," Alex said. "Now we just need to do one final check on our clinic, and we'll be ready to go."

HAWK MAINTAINED A safe distance as he followed Reaper. While everything seemed to be running smoothly, Hawk didn't want to take any chances. They were on the cusp of apprehending Reaper and getting some much needed answers to burning questions.

Reaper hailed a cab and then climbed into the backseat.

Hawk followed suit, waiting a minute to avoid having his cover blown. With the directions mapped out on his phone, Hawk used the GPA navigational app on his phone to see what route the driver of Reaper's cab was likely to take. If the car disappeared too quickly from view, Hawk would know something had gone awry.

The drive would take seventeen minutes, according to the app, most of it occurring on one road leading back to the heart of the city. The first ten minutes were uneventful, but when they reached the city, Reaper's cab driver turned down a different street leading away from the clinic's address.

Hawk covered his mouth with his hand to keep the driver from hearing anything he said.

"Alex, Mia," he said over his coms, "we have a problem."

CHAPTER
THIRTY-EIGHT

WASHINGTON, D.C.

PRESIDENT NORRIS INVITED Robert Besserman into his office before offering him a drink. Besserman glanced at his watch and then declined. Norris poured himself a healthy portion before taking a seat behind his desk.

"Everything all right?" Besserman asked, nodding at Norris's glass.

Norris shook his head. "You tell me. You're the one hunting down the traitors. My answer to your question will depend on what you're about to tell me."

"In that case, you have a reason to smile."

Norris drew in a deep breath and exhaled. "Who was it? Someone on my cabinet?"

"We traced the order back to Admiral Brent Gaston," Besserman said. "Apparently, his unilateral decision to increase our presence off the shores of North Korea only ratcheted up tensions. I suggest you demand his resignation immediately or inform him that he will be subject to a court martial."

"Why not do both?" Norris asked. "I can send a message that

if anyone attempts to usurp my authority as commander in chief, they will be dealt with swiftly and harshly."

Besserman shrugged. "That's totally up to you, but I feel like this might be a scandal you'd rather avoid. If we can usher Admiral Gaston out the backdoor without causing a big stir in the media, everyone wins."

"Justice doesn't win," Norris said. "He'd be getting away with just a slap on the wrist."

"You could have his public position be resignation but technically, you could give him a dishonorable discharge and revoke his pension. That'd be more than a slap on the wrist for an admiral."

"I could go with that. So what else did you find?"

Besserman shifted in his chair. "From all that our investigation gathered, Admiral Gaston acted alone. However, we can't confirm that at the moment. All we know is that he ordered more ships into the area, which stoked the fire. We haven't been able to link anyone else to the action."

"So, in your estimation, is the threat within our military to undermine me eliminated?"

"Like I said, we can't be certain at this point, but removing a high-ranking official like Gaston who was stirring up trouble definitely goes a long way in re-establishing your authority. And while this might not get out to the press for months, this news will definitely circulate among naval officers, serving as a deterrent for anyone who has similar ideas."

"Okay," Norris said. "Good work. Keep me posted if you find any additional links between Gaston and other disgruntled military members."

Besserman chuckled. "All military members are disgruntled, sir. I think it's part of the job description to complain about everything from pay scale to bloated budgets to lack of leadership."

"It's always good to know that the battle isn't winnable."

"That's right, sir. Just keep doing what you're doing and

don't concern yourself with all the added noise. It usually amounts to nothing anyway."

The men stood and shook hands before Besserman exited the office. Norris paced around the room for a few minutes before sitting down again.

Getting rid of a rogue admiral was important for his assertion of authority, but he didn't like Besserman's dodgy answer. Norris had to know who else was involved and how many. And until he did, he wasn't sure he'd get much sleep at night.

CHAPTER
THIRTY-NINE

PUNTA CANA, DOMINICAN REPUBLIC

MITCHELL THREW TWENTY dollars at the cab driver before abruptly exiting the car. The driver thanked him for the generous tip, shouting out the window as he drove off. Mitchell hustled down the street and ducked into an alley. After navigating around the back of a stretch of buildings, he entered the marketplace.

Farmers and craftsmen hawked their wares as an endless parade of tourists snaked their way in front of all the tables set up in the street. On one corner, a mariachi band serenaded ladies as a subtle request for tips. On another, a chef served up niños envueltos, a traditional Dominican dish consisting of rice and ground beef wrapped in cabbage. Everything from wooden carved toys to furniture to colorful clothing and anything else that could be sold as a souvenir was on display.

Mitchell ducked into a tent where an elderly woman was selling scarves. Based on the amount of stock hanging off every rack in her store, her items weren't all that popular in the warm climate.

"*Necesito tomar prestado tu teléfono,*" Mitchell said, asking to borrow her phone.

She scowled at him and shook her head. "*Ladrón!*"

Mitchell wasn't a thief, but if the woman didn't calm down and acquiesce to his request, he considered overpowering her.

"*No soy un ladrón,*" he said, glancing over his shoulder. "*Estoy en problmas. Hay hombres detrás de mí.*"

She glared at him. "*Salir ahora.*"

Mitchell snatched her phone out of her pocket and raced out of the tent. She screeched, begging anyone to help her. But her cries were ignored among the tourists who were unaware of what she was saying and the other store owners who weren't willing to leave their wares unattended.

Mitchell darted down an alley before re-dialing the number. He went through the same process again until he reached his contact.

"I'm sorry to do this to you, but could you tell me the address again for the clinic?" Mitchell asked.

"Clinic?" the man asked. "What are you talking about?"

"Never mind," Mitchell said before hanging up.

Someone almost played me.

He deleted the record of the call before returning the phone to the woman. She smacked him several times with the back of her hand, but he apologized and then thanked her by giving her a hundred-dollar bill. She stopped squawking after that and finally offered a weak smile.

Now, time to disappear again.

He grabbed a scarf and wrapped it around his head.

HAWK TOLD his driver to stop. After the cabbie complied, Hawk paid the fare and hustled toward the marketplace. He wasn't sure where Reaper had gone, but Hawk figured if he was in the same position, that's where he would go. Big crowds were easy for him to disappear into, and he was betting that Reaper was thinking the same thing.

Hawk alerted Alex and Mia to the situation. "I could be completely wrong, so be alert in case he shows up. But if I were him, I'd save my curiosity for another day."

"We'll be ready for whatever happens," Alex said over the coms. "Just keep us posted."

"Roger that."

Hawk wouldn't have been so inclined to play his hunch, knowing that the odds of finding a target in such a crowded place would be infinitesimal. But that's because until today, he'd never worn a pair of Dr. Z's Sunglazzes.

Hawk tugged his cap down low across his face as he mingled with the tourists, going with the flow. He trudged past countless merchants offering everything from traditional food to authentic Dominican clothing. He constantly shook his head as store owners vied for his attention.

As Hawk moved along, he checked every face. An outline encircled every face and flashed red when it didn't find a match in the database. This process continued for ten minutes without any results.

Then Hawk noticed a bulkier woman limping toward him along the edge, dressed in traditional Dominican garb and wearing a scarf. She was hunched over a cane and shuffling slowly. He stared directly at her, but she didn't seem to notice him.

Just as Hawk passed her, his glasses outlined her face and flashed green.

"I've got a visual on him," Hawk said over the coms in a hushed tone. "He's in the market."

"On our way," Alex said.

Hawk waited a moment before turning around and following Reaper. Without the glasses, Hawk would've likely walked right past him. The disguise was good, but not good enough to outwit Dr. Z's facial recognition device.

Hawk maintained a safe distance from Reaper for a couple of minutes. However, when he reached an intersection near the end of the market, he looked around before dashing down a back alley.

"We've got a runner," Hawk said over the coms as he broke into a sprint in pursuit.

Hawk pumped his arms, his lungs feeling as if they were on fire after a couple of minutes. Back and forth through a series of alleys and tight streets, the two men ran. Reaper struggled to find any way to separate himself from Hawk, but Hawk wondered how much longer he could keep up the pace. His target didn't seem to tire, signaling that he was in much better cardio shape than Hawk.

"How you holding up?" Alex asked.

"He's still running," Hawk said.

"Just don't lose him," she said. "We're almost there."

Hawk followed Reaper for two more blocks before he switched directions and raced down a narrow street that took a hard right turn. When Hawk reached the turn, he found himself staring directly at Reaper's gun.

"Over there," Reaper said, motioning for Hawk to move against the wall, which all but hemmed him in.

"Look, we just want to talk," Hawk said.

"I should've finished you off, Hawk," Reaper said. "I didn't want to have to kill you, but I figured you would've received the message."

"All I want to know is who's sending you those messages you're so desperate to pass along."

Reaper huffed a soft laugh through his nose. "You've got a lot of nerve trying to track me down. And I must admit that you almost had me. But I started thinking that maybe I saw you at the pool."

"I'm lousy at disguises," Hawk said before nodding at Reaper. "But your outfit, on the other hand, was pretty damn good."

"Flattery won't get you anywhere," Reaper said. "I'm going to kill you and then make it look like a robbery."

"No one will buy it," Hawk said.

"What makes you so sure?" Reaper said.

"Because it's not going to happen," Hawk said.

Reaper trained his weapon on Hawk. "That's where you're wrong."

CHAPTER FORTY

PUNTA CANA, DOMINICAN REPUBLIC

AS REAPER PULLED THE TRIGGER, Hawk dove to the ground. The bullet ricocheted off the cinder block wall right to the right of Hawk's shoulder. When he glanced at Reaper, Hawk saw the gun lying a few feet away and the muscular soldier collapsed in a heap with Alex standing over him. She held a syringe in one hand, signaling a thumbs up to Hawk with the other.

"Impeccable timing, dear," Hawk said.

She grinned. "It wouldn't have been nearly as close if we didn't need him alive."

Alex sneered at Reaper before kicking him in the ribs. "Mess with my husband again, and next time I won't be so kind."

Reaper's eyes remained closed, the injection already doing its job.

"Let's get this punk into the van," she said.

Hawk scrambled to his feet and then helped Alex and Mia lug Reaper's large body into the back of their van parked along a nearby street. They drove straight to the clinic, preparing the interrogation session.

When Reaper came to a few minutes later, Hawk and Alex had secured the mercenary to a chair. He opened his eyes and scanned the room, groggily muttering something Hawk couldn't quite make out.

"Well, hello there, Sunshine," Hawk said, waving his hand in front of Reaper's face. "Nice of you to join us today."

"What'd you do to me?" Reaper asked as he winced. "My head. My neck."

"You better be thankful that your heart's still beating," Hawk said. "Hell hath no fury like a woman who almost watched her husband being gunned down in a back alley."

"I already told you that it's nothing personal," Reaper said.

"Likewise," Hawk said. "I appreciate you not killing me in Sonbong, though I'm sure you're regretting that decision at the moment."

"When I get out of here, I'll rectify that situation."

Hawk shook his head. "Such bravado up till the very end."

"You're not going to kill me," Reaper said. "If you wanted me dead, I'd be pushing up daises already. So, let's not waste time with any more bullshit. What do you want?"

Hawk paced in front of Reaper for a few seconds and then stopped. "Are you willing to talk? Because I'd rather make this as painless as possible for the both of us."

"Ask something specific," Reaper said. "I can't read your mind."

"Who sent you to North Korea?"

Reaper sighed and shook his head. "I don't know."

"So you want me to believe you just got on a plane and magically appeared in Sonbong at the same time three other Navy SEALs on a black ops mission were there?"

"That's not what I'm saying. I *don't know* who sent me."

"You take orders from anyone, even if you don't know them?"

"I take orders from anyone who pays me. That's the definition of a mercenary. I'm just a soldier for hire."

"Even against your own country?"

Reaper shrugged. "I'm a man without a country these days, so my loyalty stretches only as far as my bank account."

"I have to admit that I admire your bravado."

Reaper narrowed his eyes as he stared at Hawk. "Am I on trial here or something?"

"In a manner of speaking, you are. I need some information from you, and if you can't give it to me, I'm going to pronounce you guilty."

"Again, be specific."

"Okay," Hawk said as he set his jaw, "what is the name of the person who told you about the mission in North Korea?"

"I don't know."

"You don't know or you won't tell me?"

Reaper closed his eyes and grunted. "I don't know it. I just get jobs and I do them. I don't ask questions and I don't know who's responsible for originating them."

"You want me to believe that you saw an assignment for taking out a Navy SEAL team and didn't question where it was coming from?"

"That's correct."

"What happened to the Doug Mitchell I knew in Navy SEAL training?"

"He's long gone," Reaper said, "battered by the realities of black ops life. If you think you can shame me into telling me something—something I don't even know—please continue. I'll warn you that it's not going to work, but you can still try."

"I've answered everything you've asked me as truthfully as possible," Reaper said as he started to struggle against the bindings keeping him seated in his chair. "I have a guy who offers me jobs. I take almost all of them and perform as well as possible. Then, I get a lump sum deposited into my account. I don't ask questions. I don't dig deeper. I just do the job. And your team in Sonbong was the job."

"But you didn't kill me?"

"I thought serving with you earned you at least the decency to have a fighting chance against the North Koreans. I see now that decision was wrong."

"I knew you'd come around," Hawk said.

"I'm not agreeing with you. I'm just telling you what's what. It's not always the best decision to kill your enemies when you can extract information from them."

"That's the smartest thing you've said all day," Hawk said. "It's also why you're not going to die right now."

"How kind of you," Reaper said. "Do you want me to bow down and kiss your feet?"

"I want you to tell us everything."

"I am," Reaper said. "You know everything I did."

Hawk knocked on the door leading to the interior. "Somehow, I just don't believe that."

A handful of CIA agents poured into the room, cuffing Reaper and toting toward him to a van waiting outside the back of the building.

"I don't know anything, Hawk," Reaper said. "You've got to believe me."

"I wish I could," Hawk said as he watched Reaper forcefully constrained by a trio of CIA agents.

"You're going to regret this," Reaper said.

Hawk shrugged. "Maybe. But I can promise you that you're going to regret not helping me more than I'll regret anything about this conversation."

The man holding Reaper froze and looked at Hawk.

"This is your last chance," Hawk said.

"If you don't believe me, you can go to hell," Reaper said with a sneer.

Hawk nodded at the men, who resumed wrestling with Reaper. After a brief struggle, they subdued him and placed him in the van.

Hawk looked at Alex. "At least we tried."

Mia, who'd been quiet while taking in the scene, shook her head and grinned wryly. She held up Reaper's phone. "We're not done trying yet."

CHAPTER
FORTY-ONE

BRIDGER, MONTANA

HAWK PLACED JOHN DANIEL on a hay bale and gestured for him to jump. The boy crouched low, wrapping his arms around his legs and refused to move. Hawk held his hands out wide and coaxed his son to take the leap.

"You jump off everything else, son," Hawk said. "Why are you afraid all of a sudden?"

"You promise you'll catch me?"

Hawk nodded. "Of course. When have I ever not caught you?"

John Daniel stood, took a couple of steps back, and leaped into his father's arms. Hawk spun his son around a few times before placing him on the barn floor.

"I need your help feeding Tucker and Dusty," Hawk said. "Think you can help me carry this hay bale over to their trough?"

John Daniel nodded as he rushed around to the other side of the bale. He placed his hands in the air and did his best just to maintain contact with the hay. Once they reached the fence, Hawk cut the bale and filled the trough. He whistled at the two horses, who quickly galloped over and began eating. Hawk tousled John Daniel's hair as they watched the animals munch on their food.

After a few moments of silence, John Daniel looked at Hawk. "Dad, did you get the bad guys when you were gone?"

"I guess you could say that."

"Good," John Daniel said. "I don't want any more of them coming around here."

"Well, if they do, they'll have to deal with me and your mom. She's tough, too."

"And pretty," John Daniel said with a grin.

Alex called for them, causing the pair to turn their heads in the direction of her voice.

"Better go see what she wants," Hawk said.

When they reached the house, Hawk ushered John Daniel to his room and warned him not to come out.

"No more bad guys are coming here, are they?" he asked.

Hawk knelt so he was at eye level with John Daniel. "Now, why would you ask a question like that?"

"I don't like bad guys."

"Me either, son. I'll come get you when it's time to come out of your room."

Hawk shut the door and returned to the kitchen where Alex was fiddling with her laptop on the table.

"You ready?" she asked.

Hawk nodded and hesitated. "Did John Daniel see anything when Orlovsky's goon attacked you?"

"I don't think so," she said. "I checked on him after everything, and he was fast asleep. Why do you ask?"

"He just said something to me that made me wonder if he'd witnessed any of your fight. He's worried about the bad guys."

"Like father, like son," she said before typing a password on her computer.

Seconds later, they were connected with the Magnum team for a video meeting.

"How's Montana?" Morgan asked.

"Still cold, but beautiful as ever," Alex said.

"Well, in that case, I won't tell you about the seventy-two degree weather here in Los Angeles today," Morgan said with a wink.

"And don't tell me about the commute either," Hawk said.

"Touche," Morgan said. "Now, let's get down to business. We wanted to loop you in on this because we've had a breakthrough in our investigation. Well, to be more exact, Mia's had a breakthrough."

The camera shifted over to Mia, who was holding up a cell phone. "Reaper wouldn't talk, but he didn't need to. This little guy did all the talking for him."

"What'd you find out?" Hawk asked.

"I went through all his recent calls and was able to identify the phone number of a call he received right before the ambush on Sonbong."

"And?" Alex said.

"I tracked it back to a cell phone located at the Pentagon," Mia said.

"Great," Hawk said with a sigh. "That only narrows it down to one of several thousand people."

Mia shook her head and smiled. "Don't underestimate me, Hawk."

"You narrowed it down to several hundred?"

"Guess again."

"Several dozen?"

"Try one," Mia said. "I created a list of officials who would've had access to the information as well as all their aides. I then cross-referenced their phone locations with the location of the burner to see if they coincided out of the office. And I was able to trace it back to one person."

"Was it Admiral Gaston?" Alex asked.

"Good guess," Mia said. "But he wasn't the one."

"Out with it," Hawk said.

"One of President Norris's most trusted members of the Joint Chiefs of Staff," she said. "None other than vice chairman James Miller."

"He was working to create a pretext for war," Hawk said. "That's a sick man."

"He's a man I want you to visit," Morgan said. "Can you do me the favor of closing this case by bringing in Miller?"

Hawk looked at Alex. "Go," she said. "I'll be fine here with John Daniel."

"Looks like the boss is okay with it," Hawk said. "Let's finish this."

"Fantastic," Morgan said. "I'll send the plane to pick you up in the morning."

Alex ended the call. She patted Hawk on the hand.

"Are you sure you're okay with me going?" he asked.

"Absolutely. You need some closure with this case."

"What I need are answers."

Alex nodded. "Let's hope you get some from Miller."

CHAPTER
FORTY-TWO

WYNN'S ISLAND, VIRGINIA

HAWK STEPPED OUT of the SUV and zipped up his jacket. The wind whipping off Chesapeake Bay chilled him, and he was grateful Alex had told him to prepare for colder weather. He glanced at Big Earv, who was sporting short sleeves, apparently unbothered by the temperature.

Hawk gawked at the Victorian-style home surrounded by thick pine trees. However, he could still see the water in the distance behind the house.

"Nice place," Hawk said.

"A place fit for a history buff," Big Earv said.

Hawk nodded. "And for a Navy man, too."

Their feet crunched beneath the pebble rocks comprising the walkway up to the house. Hawk continued to scan the area, noticing a dock stretching out into the water.

Seconds later, the front door swung open and a pair of black Newfoundlands bounded onto the porch and raced toward Hawk and Big Earv. Hawk held his hand out for the dogs to smell him before kneeling and petting them. Big Earv stood back, not quite as enthusiastic about the two canines.

"It's okay, Big Earv," Hawk said. "You're bigger than they are."

Big Earv mustered a chuckle before the two continued up to the porch where Admiral James Miller was standing with a bemused look on his face.

"Lewis! Marion! Get back here," Miller said.

"Sorry, sir. We didn't realize we'd create such a ruckus just by showing up."

Miller stared intently at his guests. "Now, that's certainly unusual."

"What's so unusual, Admiral?" Hawk asked as he glanced down at the hundred-and-fifty-pound animals. "Are your dogs not normally that friendly?"

"Always," Miller said, "Those dogs would nuzzle up next to Hitler while he was shoveling dirt on a mass grave. I'm talking about you two visiting my property. I don't recall having a scheduled meeting with anyone from the administration."

"Don't worry," Big Earv said. "We're not from the administration."

Miller scowled. "Now that really worries me because nobody else even knows I have a place out here."

"Sorry," Hawk said, offering his hand. "Where's our manners? I'm Brady Hawk, the bastard son of Thomas Colton of Colton Industries. And this is Malik Earvin. We have a few questions for you."

"I'm not sure I like the looks of this," Miller said.

"We just want to have a conversation," Hawk said, "about some recent events overseas."

"Who are you guys with?" Miller asked, eyeing them closely.

Hawk put his right hand behind his back and wrapped his palm around the grip of his gun, keeping it there in case Miller made any sudden moves.

"Like I said, we're just here to ask a few questions," Hawk said.

"You still haven't answered any of mine," Miller said with a growl.

"You asked who we are, and I gave you our names," Hawk said. "This doesn't have to be that difficult."

"Actually, you're making this incredibly difficult," Miller said as he put his hands on his hips. "Now, if you're with the media and you want to do an interview out here, contact my office and we'll arrange a time to talk. But this is my time off and my private property, and I'd appreciate it if you'd respect my wishes and leave."

Big Earv cocked his head to one side. "Sir, is there a reason why you were recently in contact with a former Navy SEAL named Doug Mitchell?"

"Damnit," Miller said. "I knew something wasn't right. Who are you? NSA? Spooks? I'm not gonna warn you again. Unless you have a warrant to be here, leave or face the consequences."

Hawk put his hands in the air in a gesture of surrender. "All right, Admiral. Just calm down. We don't want any trouble."

"That's right," Miller said. "Now get the hell outta here."

Not wanting to take his eyes off Miller, Hawk walked backward as did Big Earv. The dogs had returned to the porch and were lapping up water from their bowls. But Miller hadn't acknowledged their presence, his steely gaze fixated on his two visitors.

Hawk and Big Earv eased back into their car.

"Now, scram," Miller shouted, waving his hand at them.

Miller remained on his porch, refusing to move until they left. But Hawk wasn't going anywhere.

"Stubborn *sonofabitch*," Hawk said after two minutes had passed and Miller hadn't moved.

"Well, we can't stay here all day," Big Earv said. "We need Miller to talk, but I'm not sure that's going to happen how we envisioned it."

"How we *hoped* it would happen," Hawk said, wagging his index finger. "We wished he would just sit down and tell us everything, but this is exactly how I envisioned it."

"He's a dyed-in-the-wool patriot," Big Earv said. "If he thinks that his way is what's best for the country, he's going to stick with it until the bitter end, like a soldier dying on a hill actually worth dying on."

Hawk ignited the engine and then goosed the gas pedal a few times.

"What's that going to accomplish?" Big Earv asked.

Hawk shrugged. "Put a little fear in him. Desperate people do desperate things. If I make him realize this is a desperate situation, he might make a mistake and play right into our hands."

"You mean, like that?" Big Earv asked, pointing at the house.

Miller darted into the house and slammed the door behind him.

"You think he's going to get a gun?" Big Earv asked.

"Maybe."

"And that doesn't concern you?"

"I'm betting that he doesn't want to get into a shootout with us. It'd be a short one. He's probably calling the cops, thinking his status as an admiral is going to coax the police to escort us off his property."

"He's not wrong about that, you know," Big Earv said.

"Trying to win a trespassing conviction against us will be the least of his worries when the whole country finds out that he's a traitor."

Still no sign of Miller.

"Where *did* he go?" Hawk asked after another minute.

In the distance, Hawk heard the whine of a boat engine, the sound muffled to some degree.

"He went for the boat in the back," Hawk said as he hustled out of the SUV, Big Earv right behind him. "Let's grab the neighbor's."

Hawk raced across the back lawn toward a neighboring house. A man was working on the railing as the two agents approached. Hawk didn't request permission, instead just holding out his hands and demanding the keys.

"Who are you?" the man asked as he dug into his pocket.

"That's what the admiral wanted to know," Hawk said.

They fired up the engine and tore out across the water behind Miller. Hawk turned on the coms to see if he could reach Alex.

"Are you there, Alex?" he asked.

"Loud and clear," she said. "How are things going with the admiral?"

"At the moment, not too well," Hawk said. "He took off in a boat and headed up the Chesapeake."

"So how can I help?" she asked.

"Can you get satellite over our position?"

"Already on it."

"Good," Hawk said. "Do you see a boat headed north near us on the Chesapeake?"

"Tracking him right now," she said.

"Whatever you do, don't lose him," he said. "We're in the boat trailing him now, maybe a half-mile behind. For the moment, I can see him. But if he goes up the Potomac, I need you to track him, especially if he gets on land."

"Roger that."

Big Earv joined Hawk near the steering wheel, their conversation consisting of shouting over the wind roaring past them.

"Where do you think he's taking us?" Hawk asked.

"I told you, the man is a Revolutionary War buff," Big Earv said. "One of his dogs is named after the man who led patriots' charge against the British on Wynn's Island. The other one is named after Francis Marion, also known as the Swamp Fox."

"I was looking for something a little more specific."

"I have no idea where exactly he wants to go, but I can tell you it'll be somewhere swampy."

"In that case, we're probably headed all the way back to Washington."

Big Earv chuckled and slapped Hawk on the shoulder. "Your level of cynicism is another stratosphere."

Hawk smiled wryly. "When you've been around Washington

as long as we have, it's not cynicism any more. It's just reality."

The two men settled in as Miller skimmed across the water, his boat outpacing Hawk and Big Earv but not by much. Over the next hour, Hawk kept a visual on Miller but could tell the admiral was consistently faster. Hawk contacted Alex to let her know they were relying more heavily on her once Miller turned west into the Potomac's brackish waters.

For the next half-hour, Miller hugged the eastern shoreline of the river before taking a hard left and heading straight toward the mouth of the Yeocomico River.

"Alex, I need you to be my eyes and ears here," Hawk said.

"He's holding steady," she said. "He won't be going much farther because the river gets shallow quickly."

Hawk estimated he was about two minutes behind Miller, which was ample time for the admiral to disappear in the swamp if he was familiar with the area. But Alex was Hawk's ace in the hole.

"He's beaching his craft," Alex reported over the coms. "You should see his boat up ahead on the northern shore of the river."

"Roger that," Hawk said.

The Yeocomico snaked its way through a mix of cleared farmland and swampy forest. Hawk sped past docks, creating a much bigger wake than was permitted in the area.

"I see you," Alex said. "You'll see his boat around the next bend."

"Do you still have visual on the admiral?" Big Earv asked.

"Roger that. He's heading west, running up a rise at the moment."

As Alex described, Hawk found Miller's boat in short order. Hawk and Big Earv beached their boat and followed Alex's directions.

Hawk palmed his weapon and as they trudged through the muddy terrain, Big Earv right behind him. They reached a rise and looked down into a small valley. With trees densely packed and daylight fading, they struggled to see the admiral.

"Alex, you gotta help us out now," Hawk said. "We can't see a damn thing out here."

She sighed. "Look, the last location I had for him was about a hundred meters from where you're at. But there's a hollow down there and the vegetation is too thick. Even without the leaves, I can't see anything."

"So, we're on our own?" Hawk asked.

"At least for now. When the sun goes down all the way, I'll be able to pick up heat signatures more effectively."

Hawk and Big Earv moved stealthily toward Miller's last known position. They slogged along a small trail for a few minutes. Hawk couldn't tell if it was a creek or a footpath, but it didn't matter as long as it allowed them to travel quietly and efficiently.

In the pine tree directly over Hawk, a raven cawed. Then another and another. The woods were soon filled with a cacophony of cries from ravens and a plethora of other birds.

"Anything new, Alex?" Hawk asked over the coms.

"No," she said.

Hawk looked at Big Earv and spoke in a hushed tone. "Let's keep moving."

When they reached firmer ground, Hawk looked for the most logical route out. For all they knew, Miller might have been leading them in a giant circle so he could make it back to the boats, maybe even sabotage theirs. If he'd done that, he'd be able to return home for the evening and shore up his security in case Hawk and Big Earv returned. But they knew this was their only shot. If he got away, he could smear them, frame them, murder them—whatever he wanted to do—and get away with it. Even with the president on Hawk's side, he wasn't sure it'd be enough to overcome a man as powerful at Miller. That's why they had sprung a visit on him in the first place. If he didn't have cover, maybe they could catch him.

But that was proving to be more difficult by the minute.

Hawk scanned the area and turned to Big Earv. "Which way do you think we should go?"

He shrugged. "I've just spent my last few years training to dive in front of bullets. I'll leave the tracking to you."

Hawk shook his head as he shot Big Earv a sideways glance. "Let's go right."

They ripped through briars and brambles, pressing deeper into a thicket before they reached a clearing. "There's got to be something around here somewhere."

Spotting a clearing with a few fallen logs, Hawk slapped Big Earv on the chest and pointed toward the tree. "I think we found a spot to rest for a few minutes."

As they drew nearer to the trees, Hawk lost his footing.

What is this?

Hawk and Big Earv both slipped and started to fall into a large pit, covered over by sticks and leaves and pine needles.

MILLER LAUGHED and rubbed his hands together before scurrying out of his position up in the nearby trees. Once his feet were planted firmly on the ground, he rushed toward the pit.

If necessary, Miller was prepared to wait out the two men, who were undoubtedly government agents. He was unaware that Thomas Colton even had a son, a comment Brady Hawk had likely made just to get Miller to let his guard down and think they were friends. But the pair had followed him all the way up the Chesapeake and into the Potomac—and now here.

A half-hour earlier, Miller wasn't sure he wanted to win. He deeply cared about his country, but he was tired of taking orders. He'd grown weary of being a pawn in the game. He'd just as soon make it all stop as he would continue to follow commands. He wanted to give them—and give them with authority. North Korea would've already been a sheet of glass if he'd been able to convince President Norris to go along with his idea.

But here he was, scrambling though the forest with his hands becoming more numb by the second, hoping to kill a pair of agents who were surely on the cusp of exposing him. Miller wanted to go out on his terms. Even though he knew what he was doing was patriotic, he didn't want to be branded a traitor and tossed into a prison. Benedict Arnold was forever reviled for turning his back on George Washington, but at least Arnold had a life.

That's all Miller wanted at this point—his old way of life back. But he was afraid those days had long set sail on a ship never to return. And he wasn't sure what was left for him. His position of power and prestige had been reduced to the latter, all his power being usurped by someone else.

Whatever happened, Miller smiled over using his Revolutionary War tactics to outsmart a pair of trained agents. Until a few months ago, the war re-enactment group he'd been a part of for more than a decade regularly trained at this site in the woods of Kinsale, a small Virginia farming community.

Miller paused to catch his breath before peering over the edge into the pit.

"Mr. Hawk? Mr. Earvin?" he called out.

That was the last thing he said before uttering a string of expletives as someone pushed him from behind and into the pit.

WHEN HAWK HAD started to slip, he instinctively reached up and grabbed a vine dragging the forest floor. Big Earv almost suffered a less noble fate, but wrapped his arms around Hawk's feet. Hawk was able to hold on just long enough for Big Earv to get on solid ground and avoid tumbling down.

Their shouting had alerted Miller that his ruse had likely worked, sending him sprinting toward their position.

As soon as the admiral reached the edge, Hawk eased up behind Miller and pushed him in.

Miller fell to the ground, cursing all the way down.

Hawk used a flashlight from his ruck sack to illuminate Miller's face. The admiral shielded his eyes as he looked at Hawk.

"Why'd you run, Admiral?" Hawk asked. "Because in my experience, the only people who run are guilty ones or those who are afraid someone is out to get them. So, which is it for you?"

"Isn't it obvious?" Miller asked.

"Not to me, it isn't," Hawk said. "We just wanted to talk."

"Sure you did," Miller said. "That's why you have weapons right now."

"You led us up here to kill us," Hawk said. "It's a good thing we brought our weapons."

Miller sighed and shook his head. "You don't even know what you're doing here, do you?"

"We're here because you tried to sabotage us," Hawk said. "And I think we all know that you ran because we mentioned the name Doug Mitchell."

Miller shook his head. "You've got it all wrong. I've never even heard of that man."

"Is that why you called him and told him about a special operation by Navy SEALs that occurred recently on the coast of North Korea where their nuclear missiles were housed? There were only a handful of people privy to what was happening there."

"You don't understand," Miller said. "I didn't have a choice."

Big Earv jumped into the fray. "Who made you do this, Admiral Miller? Was it the president?"

"Of course not. I've been trying to do everything I could to get him to get rid of the North Koreans once and for all. If he had, I might be free too."

Hawk kept his beam steady on Miller. "You keep acting like you're a slave to someone else's whims. If that's the case, you must know who?"

"Have you ever heard of The Alliance?"

Hawk shook his head. "Who are they?"

"They're going to come for you one day," Miller said. "And when they do, you're going to wish you'd listened to me. You do what they say, or they take everything you hold dear in life, mark my words."

Then Miller started to raise his gun.

"Don't, Admiral," Hawk said, placing his hand out and gesturing for Miller to lower his weapon.

"Then stop me," Miller said.

Hawk didn't hesitate, putting two bullets in Miller's chest. The weapon fell out of his hand as he collapsed to the ground clutching his chest.

Hawk and Big Earv jumped into the pit. After collecting the gun, Hawk knelt next to the admiral.

"We only wanted to talk, sir," Hawk said.

"Thank you," Miller said. "Now, I'm free."

Miller's body went limp, leaving Hawk and Big Earv sitting there in disbelief, not at what had just transpired but what they'd heard.

"Have you ever heard of The Alliance?" Hawk asked.

Big Earv shrugged. "Maybe as a myth, but nothing that ever sounded serious."

"What Miller just said sounded serious to me."

"I'm with you," Big Earv said. "And this isn't a mystery I'm excited to explore."

Hawk drew in a deep breath and exhaled. He contacted Alex over the coms.

"We're safe, honey," he said.

"I know. I was watching."

"Then you know we're going to need a cleanup out here—and a cover story."

"Already on it," she said. "Now, when are you coming home?"

"Soon," Hawk said. "But I've got one more stop to make."

CHAPTER
FORTY-THREE

CHARLOTTE, NORTH CAROLINA

HAWK CONVINCED BIG EARV TO head back to Los Angeles in order to attend to some personal business. While Big Earv put up a fight, he eventually acquiesced, leaving Hawk with some solitude for a long drive to Charlotte. During that time, he had plenty of time to think about his past—and his future.

Hawk reflected on his time with Eddie Tyson, wondering if he was still alive in North Korea. If the opportunity arose as intel became available, Hawk would go back and get him. But he wanted to talk with Sheila, at least give her some closure in a way that only he could. And if one day Tyson walked back into her life, they could sort things out then. On the long car ride from Siberia to Sonbong, Tyson had expressed how he wanted her to move on, even though it'd hurt to see her with another man. And he'd asked Hawk to convey that to her in as delicate of a way as possible.

Hawk parked by the curb of the Tyson family home and closed his eyes, plotting how he could tell her. He'd picked up a couple of pizzas and brought gifts for all the kids. When he found the nerve, he rang the doorbell, instigating instant chaos.

Sheila, Tyson's wife, barely had time to hug Hawk before Joey and Sam swarmed over the pizza and carried it off.

"Make sure Caleb gets a piece," she shouted as they darted off toward the kitchen with their food and gifts.

"Uncle Brady" hadn't stopped by to visit in several years, and Hawk was sure that none of the kids remembered him.

Sheila offered a thin smile and tucked her hair behind her ears. "They're a motley crew, aren't they?"

"They take after their dad," Hawk said with a grin.

"Thank you," she said. "I'm glad someone else sees that. I was always trying to convince Eddie that I had nothing to do with these children."

Hawk chuckled and then paused. "How have you been?"

She gestured for Hawk to come in and led him into the living room where they both sat down. "Oh, I have my good days and bad days. More than anything, I miss our talks. I miss the way he could calm me down from my hysterical moments. And let me tell you, those seem to have increased substantially since he's been gone."

Hawk nodded. "I miss him, too. He loved you guys so much."

She shrugged. "I guess he loved his country more."

"I—I don't think that's true."

"It's why he's dead, isn't it?" she said, her eyes narrowing, tears welling up. "He just had to do one more mission. I begged him not to go, but he did it anyway. It wasn't like him to defy me, but maybe he knew what was going on and just wanted an easy way out."

"I know it's rough right now, but it will get easier," Hawk said. "I've endured some unimaginable pain in my life, and the only soothing balm that exists is time."

"Well, I just wish I had one more day with him. There's so

many things I'd want to tell him, even as angry as I've been at him."

"I understand," Hawk said. "And while I can't divulge the details of his last mission, I want you to know that he had to go. It was for your benefit, as difficult as that might be for you to believe. He wasn't going for his country at all, to be honest."

Her eyes widened. "What are you trying to say?"

Hawk looked down. "Like I said, I can't tell you any details. But just know that what he did was for you. And he wants you to be happy."

Her eyebrows arched upward. "Wants?"

"Wanted," Hawk said, correcting himself.

She cocked her head to one side. "How do you know this?"

Hawk shifted in his seat. "One day we were hanging out and the conversation drifted toward more morbid topics. We all talked about what we'd want for our families if we died. Most of us couldn't conceive of the idea that our wives would marry someone else and start new lives. But not Eddie. He was insistent that he'd want you to move on so you could be happy."

"He said that?"

Hawk nodded. "He said the only thing he wanted for you was to be happy and fulfilled with your life."

Tears streaked down Sheila's face. "He never told me that."

"It's not something we like to talk about, but it's something we all think about."

She got up and hugged Hawk, thanking him profusely. "The gifts, the meal, the comfort—I appreciate it. Alex doesn't know how good she has it."

Hawk chuckled and shook his head. "I'm not sure she thinks that all the time, but thanks. I'll take that as a compliment."

"As you should," Sheila said.

Hawk said goodbye and called Alex as he drove to the airport.

"How'd it go?" she asked.

"Lots of tears," Hawk said, "but I'm hoping maybe that was the closure Sheila needed."

"I'm sure it was."

"Alex?"

"Yes?"

"I love you. I can't wait to see you and John Daniel soon enough."

"Me either," Alex said. "Because there's something we need to talk about."

CHAPTER
FORTY-FOUR

BRIDGER, MONTANA

HAWK TUGGED ON THE ROPE, ensuring that the line was taut. Strung between a pair of trees, he invited John Daniel to climb up so he could try out the latest addition to the homestead. For most four-year-olds, the height would've seemed daunting, but John Daniel wasn't like most. He didn't need his father to ask him a second time as the preschooler bounded up the ladder, two rungs at a time.

Hawk fastened a harness to John Daniel and then secured him to the pulley.

"Ready?" Hawk asked.

John Daniel's face lit up as he nodded vigorously.

"Just remember to hold on," Hawk reminded.

Seconds later, John Daniel leaped off the platform and zipped toward the other tree, which was padded with a mound of loose hay about six feet thick. Hawk watched as John Daniel disappeared into the hay only to emerge seconds later with a grin plastered across his face.

"This is the best, Dad," John Daniel said as he sprinted back to Hawk to try again.

Hawk showed John Daniel how to operate the apparatus so he could entertain himself. Then Hawk returned to the house where Alex was waiting on the porch, sitting in a chair while sipping a cup of steaming tea.

"If only I had that zip line for John Daniel when you were gone," she said.

Hawk chuckled and shook his head. "Give me enough time and I'll have this place converted into a quasi-amusement park."

"And he'd probably be bored with it after a week," she said.

"Probably."

They both laughed as they watched John Daniel crash into the hay again and then squeal with delight.

"This is the life, isn't it?" Hawk said as he looked at Alex.

"Actually, that's what I wanted to talk with you about."

Hawk settled into a chair next to her. "I'm listening."

"While you were in Virginia, I was thinking about the future, specifically our future," she said as she looked down. "And I'm not sure I can do this much longer."

Hawk furrowed his brow. "Do what much longer?"

"This," she said, "waving her hand in front of her. Living on a ranch in isolation while so many other people need us."

"You want to move back to Washington?"

She shook her head and scoffed. "Of course not. I *want* to live here. I know it's what's best for John Daniel. But I don't think *our* time is done out there."

"I thought we agreed that this would just be a one-time assignment," Hawk said.

"We did, but I reserve the right to change my mind," she said before taking another sip of her tea. "Tell me you didn't enjoy this last mission, the hunt, the exhilaration of stopping a man who was intent on sabotaging good Americans for some misguided agenda."

"I loved it," Hawk said. "But what about you and John Daniel? What if something happens to me?"

"We'll be fine. In case you forgot, a Russian mafia assassin tried to kill me in our home—and I took care of him without you."

Hawk smiled faintly. "Yes, you did."

"The fact is there are other people just like us, families with kids who have wonderful lives right now but could have it all stripped away if the wrong people take control of this country and the world. Freedoms could be eroded. Innocent lives could be lost. Dreams for a generation could be snuffed out. And I don't want to get to the end of our lives and think that we just put in our time. I want to help. We've had enough time out of the game, but it's time to get back in it."

She paused, letting the words sink in before continuing.

"At least, that's how I feel. Maybe you feel differently, but I needed to let you know that in case you're feeling the same way, too."

Hawk nodded. "This last mission lit a fire in me again. And while I know there are significant risks, what I realized is that there are dozens of Eddie and Sheila Tysons out there, families who could be torn apart by the actions of a few evil men. And if I can stop them, then I feel like I must."

"So, what you're saying is that you want back in, too?"

"Only if you're okay with it."

Alex put her tea down and jumped in Hawk's lap, wrapping her arms around him. She kissed him and then drew back before glancing at her watch.

"Speaking of getting back in the game, we have a conference call in five minutes with the Magnum team," she said.

In the distance, John Daniel laughed as he careened into the haystack.

―――

HAWK AND ALEX sat at their kitchen table as they joined the video conference headed by Morgan. She was joined by several members of the team, including Big Earv and Mia.

"I thought I would wrap up with you two about what we were able to learn from Admiral Miller's private communications as well as Reaper's," she said. "But before I do any of that, I want to thank you for helping us on this mission. I know it wasn't what we set out to do, but it ended up being the mission our entire country needed. President Norris wanted me to make sure that I conveyed his gratitude to the both of you."

"We're a team," Hawk said. "We all had a role to play in this."

"But you were the one out there risking everything," Morgan said. "And, Alex, you were too. We're grateful."

"Happy to serve," Alex said.

"On that note," Morgan said, "let's move on to the purpose of this meeting. I'm going to turn things over to Mia, who's going to tell us about what she found."

Mia nodded. "Thank you. Now after hours of work and some help from Dr. Z, we were able to crack the password for Admiral Miller's burner phone. And what we found was that he was receiving messages instructing him what to do. We tried to trace the number to someone, but were unable to do so, which means it was a burner phone paid for in cash. Making things even more impossible was the fact that the phone was never used in the same place twice. But based on what we gathered from his computer, he was receiving handsome payments deposited into an offshore account he owned. The source of those payments proved even more difficult to pinpoint."

"So where does that leave us?" Hawk asked.

"As I was searching through his computer, I found one document outlining his protocol for contact. The name of the group listed was one called The Alliance. Up until now, The Alliance was little more than a myth, concocted to explain the unexplainable. But we don't think that's the case now."

Hawk leaned closer toward the screen. "And what about Reaper? Did he know who he was working for?"

Mia shrugged. "I'm not sure about that yet, but we do know

that he had contact with another person before Miller started handling him."

"That's good," Alex said. "Apply a little pressure on Reaper, and he should help connect the dots for us."

"There's only one problem with that," Morgan said. "Last night, Reaper escaped CIA custody."

"How?" Hawk asked.

"He was preparing to be flown from the Dominican where he'd been since you caught him to another foreign black ops site on an agency jet. But in the middle of the flight while going to the restroom, he overpowered one of the agents, grabbed a parachute, and dove out of the plane. The CIA is searching for him, but they haven't been able to locate where he went down."

"Sounds like we have our work cut out for us," Hawk said.

"We?" Morgan asked. "I thought you were only going to help us with this one mission. Hunting down Reaper would be an entirely new one."

"I know," Hawk said. "But Alex and I have been talking about it, and we'd like back in—that is, if you'd have us."

A grin spread across Morgan's face. "Absolutely."

"As long as we can continue living out here," Alex added.

"Of course," Morgan said. "Welcome back."

THE END

THE PHOENIX CHRONICLES

The Shadow Hunter
The Reaper
Covert Invasion
The Cobbler
The Widowmaker
A Bridge Too Far

ABOUT THE AUTHOR

R.J. PATTERSON is an award-winning writer living in southeastern Idaho. He first began his illustrious writing career as a sports journalist, recording his exploits on the soccer fields in England as a young boy. Then when his father told him that people would pay him to watch sports if he would write about what he saw, he went all in. He landed his first writing job at age 15 as a sports writer for a daily newspaper in Orangeburg, S.C. He later attended earned a degree in newspaper journalism from the University of Georgia, where he took a job covering high school sports for the award-winning *Athens Banner-Herald* and *Daily News*.

He later became the sports editor of *The Valdosta Daily Times* before working in the magazine world as an editor and freelance journalist. He has won numerous writing awards, including a national award for his investigative reporting on a sordid tale surrounding an NCAA investigation over the University of Georgia football program.

R.J. enjoys the great outdoors of the Northwest while living there with his wife and four children. He still follows sports closely.

He also loves connecting with readers and would love to hear from you. To stay updated about future projects, connect with him over Facebook or on the interwebs at www.RJPbooks.com.

Printed in Great Britain
by Amazon